A
Curve
in the
Road

ALSO BY JULIANNE MACLEAN

The Pembroke Palace Series

In My Wildest Fantasies
The Mistress Diaries
When a Stranger Loves Me
Married by Midnight
A Kiss Before the Wedding: A Pembroke Palace Short Story
Seduced at Sunset

The Highlander Series

Captured by the Highlander
Claimed by the Highlander
Seduced by the Highlander
Return of the Highlander
Taken by the Highlander
The Rebel: A Highland Short Story

The Royal Trilogy

Be My Prince
Princess in Love
The Prince's Bride

Dodge City Brides Trilogy

Mail Order Prairie Bride
Tempting the Marshal
Taken by the Cowboy

STAND-ALONE HISTORICAL ROMANCE

Adam's Promise

A
Curve
in the
Road

JULIANNE
MACLEAN

LAKE UNION
PUBLISHING

Published by Lake Union Publishing, Seattle

www.apub.com

Amazon, the Amazon logo, and Lake Union Publishing are trademarks of Amazon.com, Inc., or its affiliates.

ISBN-13: 9781503904453
ISBN-10: 1503904458

Cover design by Caroline Teagle Johnson Design

Printed in the United States of America

For Stephen and Laura

CHAPTER ONE

Intuition is a funny thing. Sometimes it's a gut feeling, and you look around and just know something bad is about to happen. Other times, it's elusive, and later you find yourself looking back on certain events and wondering how in the world you missed all the signals.

Tonight, I'm on my way home after Sunday dinner with my mother. It's a one-hour drive on a dark two-lane highway.

As I turn the key in the ignition and shift into reverse, my mother comes running out her front door, waving her hands. "Wait! Abbie! Wait!"

I see a look of panic in her eyes and wish she wouldn't rush down the concrete steps as if the house were up in flames behind her.

Careful, Mom . . .

I shift into park and lower the car window.

My golden retriever, Winston, rises in the back seat and wags his tail. Mom reaches toward us and passes an enormous Tupperware container through the open window. It's full of chicken leftovers from the dinner she just cooked for me.

"You forgot this," she says, out of breath.

I take it from her and set it on the passenger seat beside me. Winston sniffs and paws at my shoulder, wanting to know what's under the blue plastic lid. I give him a pat on his big, silky head.

"Settle down, mister. This isn't for you." Then I turn to smile at my mom, who is shivering in the late-November chill.

"Thanks, Mom," I say. "The guys would never forgive me if I came back empty-handed."

By *guys*, I am referring to my husband, Alan, a cardiologist I've been married to for twenty years, and my seventeen-year-old son, Zack, who didn't come with me today because he had a hockey game this evening.

"Are you sure you don't want to take some of that pie with you?" Mom asks, speaking to me through the open window as she wraps her sweater around herself to keep warm.

I know it's not a conscious thing, but it's obvious that she wants me to stay a little longer. She's never enjoyed being home alone in that big, empty house—especially on cold, dark nights like this. You would think that after more than twenty years of widowhood, she'd be ready to downsize, but I can't fault her for anything. I love her too much. It's why I drive over an hour from the city every Sunday afternoon to spend time with her in the house I grew up in.

"No, thanks," I reply. "Alan's trying to cut calories again."

Truthfully, he isn't, but I don't have time to wait because I'm hoping to make it back to the city in time for Zack's game. Then I have an early-morning case in the OR—a gallbladder surgery scheduled for seven o'clock.

Mom gives my hand a squeeze. "Okay, dear. Wish our boy luck on the ice tonight, and say hi to Alan for me. Tell them I missed them today. And please drive safely."

"I will. Now get back inside, Mom. It's freezing out here."

She nods and hurries back up the stairs, while I feel a familiar twinge of guilt over leaving her alone. I can't help it. I always feel like I should do more for her or call her more often than I do. But I tell myself not to worry. She's independent, and I know she'll be fine as soon as she turns on the TV.

Winston turns in circles on the back seat, then finally settles down to sleep for the next hour. I shift into reverse and back out of the driveway.

Despite the heavy fog, the roads are dry as I make my way out of my beloved hometown. Lunenburg is a picturesque fishing and ship-building community and a burgeoning center for the arts, and the Old Town area is designated as a UNESCO World Heritage site to preserve its historic architecture. As might be expected, it has a robust tourism trade in the summer.

As I pass by the brightly lit restaurants along the waterfront, I can't help but glance wistfully at the sparkling reflection of the moon on the harbor and the undulating shadows cast from a tall ship's masts over the dockyard. The image is beautiful and serene, yet I feel a pang of sadness, and I'm not sure why. Something just feels off today. Maybe it's because Mom has seemed so much older these past few months. She never used to refer to herself as a senior citizen, not even when she turned sixty-five, but lately she's been making jokes about it, saying things like "Old age ain't for sissies!" and "If only I could remember what it is I'm forgetting to remember!"

Today, when she couldn't figure out how to get the messages off her phone, she said, "Look out, nursing home. Here I come."

While I love that she has a sense of humor about growing old, it reminds me that she won't be around forever and eventually our Sunday dinners will be a thing of the past.

I find it rather unsettling how time has been flying by so quickly lately. What is it about growing older that makes the clock hands start to spin like a whirligig? I suppose it doesn't matter, as long as I'm happy with my life.

Am I happy?

Surprisingly, I have to think about that for a few seconds.

Then I wonder . . . am I nuts? Of course I'm happy. Why wouldn't I be? My life is perfect. I have a job that I love, a beautiful home, a brilliant husband, and a son I'm incredibly proud of. In his final year of high school, Zack is captain of the hockey team and president of the student council, and his grades are top-notch. Most importantly, he's a decent human being—sensible and kindhearted.

But Zack will head off to university next year, and then it will just be Alan and me. I can't imagine what our lives will be like without Zack living at home. There are always activities to work into our busy schedules. There's noise, music, and laughter when Zack's friends come over. The house is going to be shockingly quiet.

Boy, oh boy. These solitary drives home from Lunenburg make me think too much. I remind myself that college is a whole year away.

Winston's heavy sigh in the back seat pulls me out of my reverie. I glance over my shoulder to see him curled up on his woolly blanket with his eyes closed, which makes me feel sleepy because I worked late in the OR again last night.

I turn on the radio to help me stay awake, crack a window to let in the chilly air, and shake my head as if to clear it. I check the dashboard clock. It's only seven, so I have just enough time to make it home, drop Winston off, and reach the hockey rink before the game starts at eight fifteen.

I flick my blinker on and merge onto the main highway, switching to cruise control and tuning in to a classic rock station.

It all happens in an instant, so fast I don't have time to think.

An oncoming vehicle crosses the center line, and I'm blinded by headlights. Adrenaline sizzles through my veins. Instinctively, I wrench the steering wheel to the right to swerve around the oncoming car, but it's too late. It clips my back end with a thunderous crash of steel against steel and sends my SUV spinning like a top, as if I'm on a sheet of ice.

My head snaps to the left. I shut my eyes and hang on for dear life as my car whirls around in dizzying circles. Winston yelps as he's tossed about in the back seat. Suddenly, we catapult into the air. The vehicle flips over the edge of the highway, and then we bounce like a ball—crashing and smashing—as we tumble down the embankment.

Something strikes me in the side of the head, and I feel multiple slashes cutting the flesh on my cheeks. I realize it's Winston, who yelps as he's thrown back toward the rear.

I want to hold on to him, to keep him safe in my arms, but there's nothing I can do. It's all happening so fast. All I can do is grip the steering wheel with both hands while the world spins in circles in front of my eyes and glass shatters all around me.

We crash hard against something—the bottom of a ravine?—and then everything goes quiet, except for the pounding of my heart as it hammers against my rib cage.

Panic overtakes me. My eyes fly open. It's pitch-dark outside, but my headlights are shining two steady beams into the shifting mist, and the dashboard is brightly lit. I blink repeatedly and realize blood has pooled on my eyelashes. I wipe it away with the back of my hand.

Think, Abbie. What do you need to do?

An alarm has been beeping since we came to a halt, as if it's confused and wants me to fasten my seat belt. Or is there some other urgent problem? Is the engine about to explode? I quickly shut off the ignition. I am enveloped by darkness.

With another rush of anxiety, I fumble for the red button on my seat belt, desperate to escape, but my hands are shaking so violently I can't release it. I shut my eyes and pause, take a few deep breaths, then try a second time.

Click.

The seat belt comes loose, and I think—for one precious second—that I am free to move, but I'm not. My legs are stuck. I'm trapped.

I fight to break loose, but I'm pinned under the dash. The roof is pressing painfully on the top of my head, and I can't free myself. I try to open the door, but it's dented and won't budge.

My heart pounds faster. I feel light-headed, and I'm certain I'm about to pass out from shock and fear.

I shut my eyes again and fight to remain calm. *Breathe. One thousand one, one thousand two . . .*

"Help . . . ," I whisper in a trembling voice.

I realize I don't hear Winston and turn my head to the side. "Winston? Are you okay?"

No response. I twist uncomfortably, struggling to see into the back seat. There's no sign of my dog anywhere, and the rear window is completely blown out.

"Winston!" I shout. *"Winston!"*

I can't make out anything in the darkness, and I worry that he's injured or dead, lying somewhere outside the vehicle. I fight wildly to free myself, but it's hopeless.

I reach frantically to find my purse on the seat beside me to locate my cell phone and call for help, but the seat is empty. Everything's flown out the windows.

Then I hear sirens in the distance, and I exhale sharply with relief. *Thank heavens. Help is on the way.*

I let my head fall back on the headrest and try to calm my racing heart.

If only I had my phone to call Alan. It's all I can think about as I wipe blood from my forehead. *Alan, I just want to hear your voice . . . to hear you tell me that everything's going to be okay . . .*

CHAPTER TWO

"Try and stay calm," a young firefighter says as he removes a glove and takes hold of my hand through the driver's-side window. It has no glass left in it. "We're gonna get you out of here. What's your name?"

"Abbie. Abbie MacIntyre."

"Hi, Abbie," he says. "I'm Troy. Everything's going to be fine now."

"Have you seen my dog?" I ask. "He was with me in the car, but he must have been thrown out the back window."

"What kind of dog is he?"

"A golden retriever. His name is Winston."

"As in Churchill?"

"Yes."

Troy directs one of the other first responders to use his walkie-talkie to report my missing dog and search the area.

I hear the wail of more sirens and vehicles arriving—fire trucks and cop cars and ambulances. Colored lights flash up on the highway, but they're swallowed by the fog.

I shake my head, fearing I might be sick. "I don't feel so good."

"No wonder. You just took a nasty tumble, but don't worry. You have a whole team coming to help you."

Two other firefighters do a 360 around the vehicle, shining flashlights everywhere. I watch the beams sweep across the dark ravine. One of them speaks on a walkie-talkie to someone above us. I can make out his words that the patient appears to be stable.

It takes me a few seconds to realize that he's talking about me. I'm the patient.

"If I could just get my legs free," I say with a grunt, fighting to move them, but it's hopeless, and any movement makes my head hurt.

Troy pats my forearm. "Don't strain yourself. Just relax, and leave it to us to get you out. We have all the right tools. It'll just take a few minutes to get the equipment down here."

I nod my head. "Can someone please call my husband? I don't know where my phone is."

"Sure thing. What's his name?"

"Alan."

Troy whistles and waves to the police officer who is skidding down the steep embankment. "Can you call Abbie's husband?"

The cop arrives and peers in at me. "How are you doing in there, ma'am?"

"I'm okay. Just pretty shaken up, and I can't move my legs." I don't know why I'm telling him I'm okay when I'm nothing of the sort. "Can you please call my husband?"

"Absolutely." He pulls out a cell phone and dials the number as I recite it. I watch as he waits for a reply, then shakes his head. "There's no answer. Should I leave a message?"

"Yes," I say without hesitation, frustrated that Alan isn't answering his phone when I need him most.

The officer reports that I've been in an accident and will be taken to the Fishermen's Memorial Hospital in Lunenburg, only five minutes away.

"I'll try again in a few minutes," the cop reassures me.

I thank him, then realize I'm shivering uncontrollably. I focus hard and try to relax my body, but not even my most determined force of will can stop the shaking.

"Just try and stay calm," Troy says. "You're in good hands, and we'll have you out of there before you know it. Here come the firefighters now."

I nod and try to be patient, wishing this nightmare would hurry up and end.

A team of five firefighters arrives with heavy equipment, which they set down around my SUV. This includes a noisy generator, a giant steel cutter, and a powerful spreader.

I turn to Troy, who is still at my side. He looks so young—not much older than my son.

"Any sign of my dog yet?" I ask.

Troy turns toward the cluster of flashing lights and emergency vehicles on the road above. "I don't think so."

"Can you please find out?" One of the other firefighters is letting the air out of my tires and placing blocks under the wheels to stabilize the car. "I'm worried about him, and I don't want to leave him behind."

Still holding my hand, Troy calls out to the cop who stands at the base of the embankment, talking on his phone. "Hey, Bob! Can you check on Abbie's dog? He's a golden retriever, and he was thrown from the vehicle. His name is Winston, and he probably hasn't gone far."

With every passing second, I grow increasingly worried, because Winston is very attached to me and extremely protective. If he ran off, he must have been terrified or in shock.

The cop trudges up the hill, and I try to be brave while Troy tells me he's going to cover me with a tarp.

"They're going to use the Jaws of Life to cut the car apart and lift the dash upward to free your legs," he explains. "This tarp will shield you from bits of flying glass and metal."

I agree because I want more than anything to remain calm, but I'm terrified, and he knows it.

"I'll be right here the whole time," Troy says as he covers me, then moves out of the team's way.

The noise of the cutter is deafening. All I hear is the roar of machines, the crunching of metal, the shattering of glass. I'm afraid it's all going to collapse on top of me, but the feel of Troy's hand squeezing my shoulder and the sound of his voice in my ear, explaining everything along the way, helps me stay grounded.

"They're making a series of relief cuts in the frame," he explains. "I know it's loud . . ."

My stomach turns over as I recall the horror of the crash and the rapid, tumbling descent.

This was my second brush with death. The first occurred seventeen years ago when I gave birth to Zack and nearly bled out in the delivery room. Since then, I'd always considered myself fortunate to be alive. Now I'm starting to wonder if the grim reaper has a mark out on me.

"Okay . . . ," Troy says when the cutter shuts off, "you're doing great, Abbie. Now they're going to use a spreader to lift the dash, which should ease the pressure on your legs. Just hang in there. We're almost done."

I try not to think about the potential damage to my legs. It's not easy to assume everything will be fine. I'm a surgeon. I know there are certain things that simply can't be fixed.

Instead, I focus my thoughts on Alan and pray that he's gotten the message by now, and I think of Zack at the rink. He has no idea that his mother is trapped in a car at the bottom of a ravine.

The spreader begins to slowly lift the dash, and I feel a weight come off my legs. Suddenly, my thighs ache with a bone-deep pain, but at least I can wiggle my toes. A good sign.

As soon as there's an opportunity, I reach down to run my hands over my knees and calves. My jeans are ripped, and there are a few surface abrasions, but I'm able to unbend my legs at the knee joints.

Another good sign.

Troy removes the tarp, but I barely have time to look down and get a visual on my legs before a brace is fastened around my neck and I'm being lifted out of the vehicle and onto a backboard laid on a gurney. All of this is carried out by two paramedics, one male and one female, who must have scrambled down the slope with their equipment while the firefighters were cutting my vehicle apart.

"I'm a doctor," I tell them. "What are your names?"

"I'm Carrie, and this is Bubba."

I can't move my neck, but I can shift my gaze to Bubba, who looks like a bouncer with a brush cut. The name suits him.

Carrie, on the other hand, is a pretty, petite blonde who appears extremely focused and capable as she wraps a blood pressure cuff around my arm. I give her a few seconds to read the dial and release the air in the cuff.

"What's my BP?" I ask.

"It's excellent. One twenty-six over eighty-five."

"That's a bit high for me, but given the situation, I'll take it."

Others gather around to transport me up the hill.

"How's your pain?" she asks.

"Manageable. My legs are sore, and these abrasions on my face are stinging a bit, but it's nothing I can't handle."

I'm aware of Troy still at my side, helping the paramedics carry me up the steep slope, which is no easy task because the rocks and debris are unsteady.

As luck would have it, it begins to rain. Soon enough, I'm feeling ice pellets on my cheeks, and I'm forced to close my eyes.

A moment later, we are cresting the top of the embankment and are back up on the road. The gurney wheels touch down.

Again, I ask, "Has anyone reached my husband yet?"

"I'm not sure. We'll check on that," Carrie says.

"And has anyone seen my dog?"

Carrie is busy pushing my gurney toward the ambulance. She slips and slides on the ice. "You had a dog with you?"

"Yes."

Troy helps me out. "He's a golden retriever. His name is Winston." Troy leans over me. "Don't worry, Abbie. We're looking for him. I promise we'll find him."

"I really need to know that he's okay."

Troy nods and leaves my side to see if there's been an update.

I wish I could sit up and look around, but I'm strapped tightly to the gurney, and the neck brace is restricting. There's even a strap across my forehead, and two red foam blocks press against my ears, so I can't turn left or right. All I can see is the cloudy night sky over the paramedics' heads and the glistening freezing rain coming down in curtains as Carrie and Bubba prepare to slide me into the back of the ambulance.

I hear a lot of commotion from the rescue vehicles on the road, and the cops are directing traffic.

I say to Carrie, "Was anyone else hurt? Please tell me no one was killed."

"The other driver is on his way to the hospital right now," she answers. "Still alive."

"That's good news, at least."

Bubba grips the front leg-release levers, and they slide me in.

"But I don't understand how this even happened," I say. "He just crossed the center line for no reason. It wasn't even raining then."

"Yeah, well . . . ," Bubba replies. "It may not have been raining at the time, but the other guy smells like he's been swimming in a sea of booze all day."

"What?" I feel an explosion of rage in my belly. The other driver was drinking? My hands clench into fists, but I don't have time for anger, because they're about to close the ambulance doors.

"Wait. Please . . . I don't want to leave without my dog. *Winston!"* I shout, hoping he'll hear me and come running.

My heart rate accelerates.

Carrie speaks reassuringly while she secures the gurney inside the vehicle. "Don't worry, Abbie. Troy's a dog lover. He'll do everything he can to find Winston. But we really have to get you to the hospital."

Bubba closes the ambulance doors, and I feel a lump form in my throat. I want to cry because I can't bear for Winston to think for one second that I've abandoned him.

And what about Alan? Does he even know about my accident yet? I ask Carrie to try calling him again, but there's still no answer. I ask her to call Zack, but he must be on the ice by now. He doesn't answer either.

Please . . . I need my family.

At last, I ask Carrie to call my mother, and she gets through. She holds the phone to my ear so that I can speak to Mom and reassure her that I'm okay.

Mom begins to cry, but I tell her not to worry.

She pulls herself together and says she'll meet me at the hospital. Carrie ends the call, and we speed toward Lunenburg, sirens blaring.

It's hard not to think about the drunk driver and how badly I want to shake him and shout at him for being so stupid and irresponsible, but my anger won't change anything. At least not now. He was injured in this accident too.

And what about Winston? It's killing me to imagine where he might be. What if he's lost and alone in the woods? Traumatized by what happened? Fearful of the noisy rescue vehicles? He's terrified of fireworks. He always darts into a corner and shakes.

Please, Troy . . . please find him.

CHAPTER THREE

"I have half a mind to march over there and tie a knot in his oxygen tube," my mother says under her breath as she sits by my side in the ER.

My x-ray shows no broken bones, but I have a gash on my head, which explains my headache and why they want to keep me for overnight observation. Otherwise, I'm remarkably unscathed, with just minor cuts and bruises. My neck brace has been removed, but I have to wait for further treatments because it's a small rural hospital with limited resources, and the drunk driver in the trauma room is the priority at the moment.

"Mom . . . ," I say with a hint of scolding in my tone, but of course I know she would never actually do such a thing. Besides, I can't blame her for being angry. If something like this happened to Zack, I'd probably want to murder the drunk driver too. Metaphorically speaking.

Another part of me wants to go to the trauma room and lend a hand, because I'm a qualified medical professional and I understand how stressful this must be for the team, with so few doctors and nurses on duty.

If it had been up to me, I would have rushed the guy to a larger trauma center in Halifax, but it wasn't my judgment call. Maybe the paramedics were worried about making the longer trip in the freezing rain.

"Has the pain medication kicked in yet?" my mother asks.

I nod and try to relax on the pillow.

They've given me a shot of Toradol, a nondrowsy anti-inflammatory, and while part of me wishes it were something stronger, I know it's important to keep me coherent to monitor my head injury. They've already asked me all the usual questions: Do I know what day it is? Do I know where I am? Do I know who this woman sitting beside me is?

The blood on my face came from a deeper laceration on the top of my head, most likely caused by Winston's claws as he was thrown around inside the vehicle.

Thinking of him again, I turn to Mom. "Would you mind asking Carrie to come in? I want to find out if they've found Winston yet. And could you try Alan again?"

Mom digs her cell phone out of her purse and dials Alan's number.

"Still no answer," she says as she rises from her chair to look for Carrie.

I glance at the clock. It's just after nine. Zack is still on the ice, and since I'm more or less okay, I see no reason to pull him out in the middle of the game. It's an important one. But maybe that's crazy. I don't know. I can't think straight.

While I'm waiting for news from Carrie, I take the opportunity to call the hospital where I work and let them know I won't be able to perform the surgery I have scheduled in the morning. The head nurse tells me not to worry. They'll reschedule things and get one of the other surgeons to cover for me for a few days. She tells me to take care of myself. "That's the most important thing," she says.

I end the call and try to be patient while I wait for the ER doc to return and stitch me up.

Carrie walks into the private examination area behind the blue curtain. "Everything okay?" she asks.

I lift my head off the pillow. "Yes, but we still haven't been able to reach my husband. I don't know where he is and why he's not answering. I wish we could get ahold of him." I shut my eyes and shake my head. "I'm sorry . . . I know there's nothing you can do about that. Is there any word about my dog?"

Her compassionate eyes meet mine, and I already know the answer before she tells me.

"I called Troy five minutes ago. He's off duty now, and he called a few friends to help him search the woods. They've also put out an informal APB on Winston. The cops are keeping an eye out."

"My word. Your dog is a fugitive," Mom says to me as if scandalized, hoping to cheer me up with a joke.

I appreciate the attempt, but nothing will cheer me more than news that they've found him alive and well. Or that Alan has finally received all the messages we've left and is on his way.

"Thanks, Carrie," I say. "Let me know if you hear anything."

"I will."

She turns to go, and I wonder how the other driver is doing. Despite the fact that he brought this on himself and almost killed me in the process, I can't help but feel sorry for him and his family. I wonder how old he is. Is he a teenager with his whole life ahead of him, like Zack, with parents who love him and are beside themselves with worry? Or is he a parent? Does he have children who need him?

Ten minutes later, Carrie sweeps the blue privacy curtain aside and appears with a cardboard Bankers Box. "Good news. They found your purse and a bunch of stuff from your car." She carries the box closer to the bed. "Lieutenant Smith said it was like a debris field on the road and down the slope of the ravine. They tried to collect as much as they could, but it was dark. If anything is missing, you might find it tomorrow in the daylight."

I blush with embarrassment because I have no idea what's inside this box. The previous night, Zack borrowed my car to go to a basketball game with some friends. This morning, there were empty water bottles, his stinky sneakers, and a few McDonald's bags with wrappers on the floor of the back seat. I anticipate that's what I'll find inside.

Carrie sets the box on the edge of the bed so that I can rummage through it.

Right away, I find my brown leather purse with my wallet, still miraculously containing all my credit cards and personal identification.

"Thank goodness." I pull my purse out of the box. "It would have been a major pain to have to replace all of this."

Immediately, I feel a stab of regret for caring about such trivial inconveniences when I could have died in that accident tonight. I should be grateful.

A little less greedily, I hunt for my cell phone in the usual zippered pocket where I keep it in my purse, but it's not there. Then I remember that I set it on the passenger seat before pulling out of my mother's driveway, so I may have to search the accident site in the morning. Who knows where it might have ended up.

I continue to rummage through the box and find Winston's leash but only one of Zack's sneakers. At least it's part of an old, worn-out pair, so he probably won't care.

Again, what am I thinking? He'll be overjoyed just to hear I'm alive. He won't care about sneakers, old or otherwise. And I don't care about the mess he left in my car. Not today.

In the bottom left corner of the box, I find my cell phone.

Okay, I can be happy about this. It's my connection to Alan and Zack. I check my text messages, but there are none.

Facebook Messenger. Nothing there either.

Wrestling with my frustration, I pick up the blue plastic lid that belonged to the Tupperware container. There's no sign of the chicken and vegetables.

In that moment, my mother pulls out her own cell phone and begins to make a call. "I'm trying Alan again," she says.

"Thank you."

I continue rifling through the box and find my phone charger, a bunch of junk from the back seat, and the green canvas case from the glove box that contains my vehicle permit and insurance documents. I'm definitely going to need those.

Suddenly I hear music. It's the familiar, dramatic theme from *Star Wars*, and I feel an instinctive thrill of joy and relief because I recognize it as Alan's ringtone.

He must be here at last!

Then I realize that the music is coming from inside the cardboard box on my lap. With a pounding heart, I dig through the rest of the contents, searching for the phone that's playing his song. I find it at the bottom, under some tattered papers. I pick it up and stare at it in confusion. Did he leave his phone in my car? Is that why he hasn't been answering?

But no, he didn't. We spoke earlier in the day, and he hasn't been in my car since. Everything in this box was picked up from the accident site. They found things on the road.

As I hold it aloft, a wave of panic washes over me, because if Alan's phone didn't come from my car, it must have come from the other one involved in the accident.

I turn to look at my mother. She's distracted, sitting in the chair beside me, waiting for my husband to answer his phone—the very phone that is ringing in my hand. Here and now.

CHAPTER FOUR

In a flash of movement, without a word to my mother, I leap off the bed and onto the hard floor. Nearly collapsing on buckling knees, I hobble toward the trauma room. I reach the open door and stare.

The driver who nearly killed me tonight is lying intubated and comatose on a bed, fighting to stay alive. He is scarred, bloody, and almost unrecognizable. There is only one nurse at his side—the one who took me for my x-ray. Her name is June.

With a sickening pool of dread forming in my belly, I limp into the room. The smell of alcohol halts me on the spot.

Nurse June sees me approach. She hurries toward me to usher me out. "I'm sorry. You can't be in here."

"But . . . I think that's my husband." I point at the man on the bed.

Nurse June frowns at me. I can see in her eyes that she's very concerned as she begins to lead me out of the room. "No, Dr. MacIntyre. This is the driver who collided with you on the highway. Do you remember what happened? Do you know where you are right now?"

I understand that she thinks I'm confused, possibly delusional, and I wish more than anything that I was. But I recognize Alan's shoes and his plaid shirt in a heap on the table. They must have cut them off him when the paramedics brought him in.

My eyes flood with tears, and my heart squeezes in agony as I fight to slip from her grasp. As I approach the bed, I can't believe what I'm seeing. This isn't real. It feels like a nightmare, but I know it isn't, because I'm awake.

Nurse June tries to take hold of my arm, but I pull away from her. "No. This is my husband. I'm telling you . . . his name is Alan Sedgewick. He's forty-six years old, and his birthday is August tenth. He's a doctor."

June's eyebrows pull together in a frown as she realizes I may not be suffering from a psychotic episode after all—that what I'm saying is the truth.

"I kept my own name when we got married," I explain, feeling dazed and nauseated as I lay my hand on Alan's bare arm.

"We've been trying to call his home number," Nurse June explains.

"But there was no answer," I finish for her. "Because no one's home. I'm here, and my son is at a hockey game."

I'm in such shock over what is happening that my muscles shake.

I glance at the clock. It's nine fifteen. Zack will answer his phone soon. I can't imagine how I'm going to explain this to him.

I look down at Alan again—at his bruised and bloody face, the tube snaking down his throat, the IV in his arm. I glance at his legs. His jeans have been cut away to reveal multiple lacerations and bruises.

"There must be some mistake," I try to rationalize. "One of the paramedics said the other driver was probably DUI, but my husband's not a drinker. He sometimes has a glass of wine with dinner, but he's very responsible. He's a family man. He would never get behind the wheel if he was intoxicated."

She regards me with compassion and squeezes my shoulder. "I'm so sorry, Dr. MacIntyre. This must be a terrible shock for you."

I shut my eyes and tip my head back. Tears spill onto my cheeks.

I didn't see the damage to his car, but I can only imagine what it must have been like if he is this badly injured.

The terror. The shock of losing control at such a high speed. Crashing.

Half of me is devastated and grief-stricken—I can't bear the thought of my husband suffering in that way, nor the idea of losing him—but the other half is boiling with anger.

How could Alan have done something so stupid as to get behind the wheel of a car if he had been drinking?

And what was he doing on the road to Lunenburg in the first place, when he knew I was on my way back to Halifax? He told me he had to work all day. We were supposed to meet at the hockey rink in time for Zack's game.

I look at him on the trauma table and want to shake him awake, to demand answers.

Was he trying to find me for some reason? Was there an emergency? But then why wouldn't he have just called?

I remember the two police officers sipping coffee in the waiting room, hovering . . . and I know how this works. There are rules and protocols. I know why they're here.

"Do you know what his blood alcohol level was?" I ask the nurse.

She hesitates and speaks tentatively. "Um, we took a level . . . yes."

"And what was it?"

Nurse June's eyes grow wide as saucers. She wets her lips and looks away. "I'm sorry, but I'm not sure I'm authorized to reveal that." She pauses. "You should probably ask the doctor."

"I'm the patient's wife," I tell her firmly. "His next of kin. If there are decisions to be made here—which clearly there are—I need to know the facts."

Nurse June stares at me uncertainly for a moment, then says, "I'll get the doctor." She turns and bolts from the room.

My heart races as I move around the bed on unsteady legs, barely aware of my own physical pain as I check the readings on the monitors and try to determine what I'm dealing with.

Dr. Sanders, who has been a fixture in this hospital for more than thirty years—he put a cast on my broken arm when I was thirteen— walks in and sees me reading the tape from the heart monitor. His cheeks flush red.

"Abbie."

I hate that I'm forced to limp toward him and that I have no medical privileges here when all I want to do is to take charge of my husband's care.

"Why wasn't this patient sent to the QEII?" I demand to know. "He needs a CAT scan and a full trauma team . . . a neurologist and . . ." I feel sick and dizzy and lose my train of thought, but I quickly fight to regain it. "And what was his blood alcohol level? I heard he was DUI, but I just can't believe that—"

"We've already called for a chopper," Dr. Sanders cuts in, "but it's freezing rain out there, and we've had some delays. The pilot is doing his best to get here, and we're doing everything we can to keep your husband stable."

I swallow hard and struggle to remain calm—which isn't easy under the circumstances—because this is my husband and I love him desperately, and I still can't accept that he was driving under the influence.

Information is what I need. "Tell me everything, Dr. Sanders."

From the other side of the bed, the doctor reveals what he knows. "Your husband was awake when they pulled him out of the wreck, but he lost consciousness just before he arrived at the hospital. His pulse is a bit high, but his blood pressure is okay. As you can see, he's intubated and has good oxygen levels, but the fact that he hasn't woken up yet leads me to believe he might have a brain bleed. He needs a CAT scan and to see a neurologist, but we don't have that level of care here. On the upside, his chest x-ray looks good. C-spine and pelvic x-rays are good too, but he's got a fractured humerus. Even so, that's the least of his problems. We haven't given him anything for pain or sedation . . ."

He pauses. "But there might be other things in his bloodstream keeping him sedated."

Other things . . .

I ask the pertinent question again: "You have to tell me . . . what was his blood alcohol level?"

Dr. Sanders hesitates, and then he bows his head and shakes it. "Honestly, Abbie, this is new territory for me, from a legal perspective. I'm not sure how to handle this." His gaze lifts. "You're a victim from the other car in the crash, but you're also his next of kin, and he's incapacitated, so I'm going to give you this information. His blood alcohol level was 0.33."

My head draws back as if Dr. Sanders has just swung a punch at me. "No. That can't be right."

"I'm sorry, but there's no mistaking it."

I cup my forehead in a hand. "I can't believe this is happening. Alan never drinks. At least not heavily. He was supposed to be at work all day, and then we were going to watch Zack's hockey game." I glance up with a new realization. "I still haven't gotten in touch with Zack. He doesn't know anything about this. I need to call him."

Dr. Sanders nods, circles around the bed, and rests his hand on my shoulder. "I'm so sorry, Abbie. Please know that we're doing everything we can."

I nod and swallow hard over the giant lump rising in my throat, because I don't want to cry. I need to keep it together and stay strong. There's so much I'll need to deal with in the next few hours.

But first, I need to call Zack and break the news to him. Then I'll need to be on that chopper with my husband when it takes off. I want to be with him every step of the way to make sure he gets the best possible care and that we do everything we can to bring him back to us.

I thank Dr. Sanders, then limp out of the room to tell my mother what is happening and pick up my phone to call Zack.

CHAPTER FIVE

At last, Zack answers his phone. "Mom. Where are you? You didn't make it to the game. We won."

I pace beside my bed in the ER and can't keep my voice from quavering. "That's great, honey. I'm so sorry I didn't make it, but . . . something happened on the highway." I wait a few seconds for him to absorb that much. "I was on my way home, but I only made it a few minutes outside of Lunenburg when I got into a . . ." I pause and clear my throat. "There was an accident."

There's a brief silence on the other end. "Are you okay?"

"I'm fine," I quickly reply. "I have a few cuts and bruises but nothing serious. Nothing that won't heal in a week or two. Gram's here with me."

"Where are you?"

"I'm at the Lunenburg hospital. The car's totaled."

I don't know why I tell him that. I suppose I'm stalling, avoiding what must come next.

"Jeez," he says. "What happened?"

I swallow uncomfortably because I don't know how to explain all of this, but I do my best.

"An oncoming car crossed the center lane and clipped me in the back end," I say. "It was enough to send me into a spin, and then I hit the shoulder and flipped and rolled into a ravine."

"A ravine? Oh my God, Mom! Are you sure you're okay?"

"Yes. Thank goodness for seat belts. But they had to use the Jaws of Life to get me out. It took a while."

I feel totally incoherent as I try to describe it.

I hear Zack breathing hard. "I need to get there. I want to be with you. Where's Dad?"

My heart pounds like a jackhammer, and I can't find the right words. All I can think about is what if both Alan and I had been killed. Zack's an only child. He would have been left all alone.

I swallow and take a breath.

"It's complicated. I don't know how to tell you this, so I'm just going to say it flat out. Dad was the driver who crossed the center line, and after he hit me, he crashed as well. He survived, but he's unconscious, and we're waiting for a helicopter to take him to the QEII."

Zack shouts into the phone. "What? How could that happen? You guys collided with each *other*?"

I sit down on the bed, wishing there was a way for me to help my son cope with this. "I don't know how it happened—I'm just as confused as you are—but . . . it was foggy, and there was freezing rain."

I feel like a coward for blaming the accident on the weather when there's no doubt that the icing didn't begin until at least twenty minutes after the crash.

"But why was Dad driving to Lunenburg when he was supposed to come to the game?"

I have no answer to give because Alan didn't call me, and I have no idea why he didn't stick to the plan. I feel helpless and muddled.

"I don't know, Zack. I'm not sure what he was doing. I'm trying to make sense of it, but I can't worry about the why right now. I just need to stay with him and pray that the helicopter arrives soon and that he's going to be okay. That's what you need to do too. Say a prayer, because he's in bad shape."

"How bad?"

I hesitate, not knowing how much to reveal because this is my baby and I want to protect him. Then I remind myself that's he's seventeen years old, practically a man. I have to be honest.

"He hasn't regained consciousness since he arrived at the hospital, so he might have a brain injury. Right now, they have him on life support—"

"No . . ."

I hold up a hand. "Please, we can't lose hope. It could just be some swelling, and when the swelling goes down, he could come out of it. Brain injuries are difficult to predict."

"But . . ." Zack is quiet for a moment. "Could he end up as a vegetable?"

"Let's not use that word," I gently say. "We need to stay positive. Let's just take it one day at a time."

I hear Zack crying softly, and I give him a moment.

"Are you still at the rink?" I carefully ask.

"Yes," he replies in a low, broken voice.

"Can you get a ride home with someone?"

"Jeremy can take me."

"Good. And keep your cell phone on. I'll let you know when we're getting on the helicopter."

"Okay, Mom."

"I love you." I'm about to end the call when he asks one more thing.

"Wait, Mom. Where's Winston? Wasn't he with you?"

I close my eyes and exhale heavily. "Yes, he was in the back seat, but he got thrown, and . . . well, we're not sure where he is right now. He must have run off."

"He's lost? On the highway?"

"Yes, but some men from the fire department are searching for him, and the local cops have been informed as well. They'll find him, Zack. I promise."

Knock on wood.

26

"I hope so," Zack replies. "What if he gets hit by a car?"

I squeeze my eyes shut and shake my head. "Let's not think those kinds of thoughts. Just say more prayers, and I'll let you know more as soon as I hear something."

We say goodbye, and I look up at my mother, who has just swept past the privacy curtain with two cups of coffee, one in each hand. She looks pale from all the stress. "I thought you might like one."

"Thank you. But you should sit down, Mom."

She moves closer and hands me the cup. I peel back the plastic lid and take a sip. The warmth feels good between my palms—a welcome comfort after so many ordeals.

Mom sits down. "How did he take it?"

I shrug with resignation. "As good as can be expected, but he's upset and worried. I told him to go home and wait until I call." I cup my forehead in a hand. "Where is that damn helicopter?"

Just then, the *Star Wars* theme begins to play at the foot of the bed, and I see Alan's cell phone flashing. "Someone's calling him. What am I supposed to say?"

Neither of us makes a move to reach for the phone. "You don't have to answer it," Mom says. "You could just let it go to voice mail."

I consider that briefly because I've been through so much and I don't feel ready to talk to anyone—especially about what happened to Alan—but what if it's about work? I can't just let it ring. "Could you pass it to me?"

She quickly hands me the phone, and I check the call display. "It's a local number."

Mom inclines her head.

"Hello?"

There's a long pause at the other end, and then a woman asks, "Is Alan there?"

I wet my lips and take a breath. "No, I'm sorry—he's not. Would you like to leave a message?"

I perceive another conspicuous pause. "Um . . . I'm calling from Handy Hardware in Lunenburg. I don't suppose this is . . . is this Abbie?"

I slowly sit up on the edge of the bed. "Yes. Who is this?"

"It's Paula Sheridan. We went to high school together."

I remember Paula Sheridan, though we haven't spoken to each other since I graduated. We didn't know each other that well because she was a year behind me, but we sometimes moved in the same circles and went to the same parties. I remember bonding with her one night at a summer campfire when her boyfriend dumped her. She cried her eyes out, and I held her hair back when she threw up in the bushes. But that was it. I went off to college in Ontario. I don't know what she did after high school, and I have no idea why she's calling Alan's phone. Yet more questions to add to the growing list.

"Why are you calling?" I ask.

"Oh . . ." She seems lost for words. "I'm just looking for Alan because he ordered something from the store. He was supposed to pick it up today."

"The hardware store . . . ?"

"Yes. My husband and I own Handy Hardware in Lunenburg. Your husband comes in sometimes to get things, usually on Sundays."

Ah. Now I understand. He's always helping my mother with handiwork around the house. I glance up at Mom, and she's watching me curiously.

"He was supposed to pick up a . . ." Paula hesitates. "Let me see . . . a power washer."

My stomach turns over as I struggle to figure out how to respond. "I'm sorry—he won't be coming in." Does she not realize there's an ice storm out there? "Are you even open?" I ask, checking my watch.

"Oh, we closed at six. I'm just here taking care of a few courtesy calls."

Neither of us says anything for a few seconds.

"Could you let him know that I'll hold the power washer here for him?" Paula finally asks. "He can come by anytime."

I sense that she's ready to say "Thank you and goodbye," but I don't want to end the call just yet.

"Wait a second, Paula. Did he say specifically that he was going to pick it up today?"

"Yes."

"When did he say that?"

She pauses again. "Earlier today, when he called."

"I see." I don't know why I suddenly want to divulge something personal to a woman I haven't spoken to in years, but I can't help myself. She's someone I used to know, someone from my hometown, and I really need a friend right now. The words come spilling out.

"Actually, Paula . . . something terrible happened. He had a car accident. We both did. We crashed into each other, believe it or not. I'm at the hospital in Lunenburg, and we're waiting for Alan to be airlifted to Halifax."

Paula is silent before speaking in a halting, disbelieving voice. "My God. I heard there was an accident on the 103. It was Alan? Is he okay?"

I begin to pick at a loose thread on my hospital gown while I struggle to keep my emotions in check. "I don't know. He's in a coma."

Suddenly I'm forced to press my fingertips to my mouth to keep from weeping into the phone. I hold the phone away while I fight to pull myself together. Then I bring it back against my cheek. "We're very worried."

"Of course you are. My goodness." She pauses again. "Is there anything I can do? Are you by yourself in the hospital? I could come down there if you need help."

I sniffle and wipe the back of my hand under my nose. "No, you don't have to do that. My mom's here, but thanks for asking." Then I think of something. "Actually, if you could keep your ear to the ground about our dog? He was in my car when we had the accident, but he ran off at the scene, and we haven't seen him since. The fire department is looking for him, but if you could spread the word in town . . . he's a golden retriever, and his name is Winston. He might be injured."

"I'll do that."

"Thank you."

I'm about to end the call when Nurse June sweeps the curtain aside. "The chopper is five minutes away. We're getting your husband prepped for the flight. I assume you'll want to go along?"

I nod and say to Paula, "I have to go now. The chopper's almost here."

I end the call without saying goodbye.

"Mom," I say as I slide off the bed onto throbbing, unsteady legs. "Can you tell Carrie, the paramedic, that I have to go to Halifax? And can you take care of Winston if . . ." I stop myself. "*When* they find him?"

"Of course I will," she replies. "I'll stay on top of it. Don't worry about a thing. Just stay focused on Alan."

I reach for my jacket but freeze when someone shouts from the trauma room.

"Code blue! We need some help in here!"

I drop my jacket and immediately start running.

CHAPTER SIX

I hear alarms going off in the trauma room. Dr. Sanders is standing over my husband, listening to his chest with a stethoscope. There are two nurses present, and a third enters behind me.

"What's happening?" I ask, hobbling into the room, wanting to help.

Dr. Sanders speaks as he scrambles for defibrillator pads. "He just had some short runs of VT, and then he went into V-fib."

Nurse June has her finger on Alan's carotid artery. She shakes her head. "No pulse."

"Start chest compressions."

My stomach explodes with heat, which isn't the usual adrenaline I feel in a medical emergency. This isn't the same, because it's Alan and I'm terrified that he's going to die.

I want to step in, but my heart is racing, I'm petrified, and I can't move. All I can do is watch Dr. Sanders place the pads on Alan's bare chest, then plug the cord into the crash cart.

"Stop chest compressions," he says. "It's still V-fib. Set to two hundred kilojoules."

Nurse June says, "Charging."

The machine makes a whirring sound.

Dr. Sanders glances around the table. "I'm clear. You're clear. Everyone's clear!"

Shock! We all watch in focused silence as my husband's body lurches, then settles.

"Resume compressions," Dr. Sanders says. He designates one of the other nurses as timer and notetaker. "Let me know when two minutes are up. We'll do a pulse check. Get epinephrine ready, and have amiodarone on standby. Keep up with chest compressions."

I snap out of my trance and move to help out, but I don't have hospital privileges here. Besides, I'm the patient's wife, and I know I should be standing back and letting the others do their jobs.

Dr. Sanders begins to think out loud. "Why is he arresting? Trauma patient . . . most likely cause is blood loss and hypovolemia . . ."

He looks at me sharply, and I know he wants help. I immediately step forward. "Other possibilities—he could have tension pneumothorax. Could be cardiac tamponade."

"Yes." Dr. Sanders addresses the younger nurse. "Give him a liter bolus of Ringer's lactate." Then he picks up the stethoscope and listens to Alan's lungs. Next he checks his neck veins, looking for jugular venous distention. "Veins are flat. He's dry, losing blood somewhere."

"Bruising on left lower ribs," I offer.

"Could be a ruptured spleen. He's losing blood. Abdomen is distended. He needs to get to an OR. Is the helicopter here yet?"

"It just landed," the younger nurse says.

June is still doing chest compressions, and I see that she's perspiring. The other nurse speaks loudly. "Two minutes almost up."

I circle around the bed. "Move aside, June. I'll take over."

June steps back, and I lean over the table and begin chest compressions. I'm counting in my head, but I'm also praying at the same time. *Come on, baby, come on . . .*

I feel an almost manic energy as I push on my husband's heart with the heels of my hands—*one, two, three*—willing it to start beating properly on its own. My own heart is racing, and I, too, begin to perspire.

Dr. Sanders says, "Stop compressions." He checks for a rhythm. "Let's shock again. Still in V-fib. Three hundred kilojoules."

We go through the process again, and I watch vigilantly, impatiently. I'm distressed and frightened, but I'm focused.

Come on. Come on!

Nothing.

I resume chest compressions.

It goes on and on. Everyone is stressed, but no one gives up.

The chopper paramedics come running in, and my eyes connect with one of them. He understands the look on my face. He sees the exhaustion, and without a word, he takes over for me.

I step back in a daze, weak and dizzy. My emotions explode and shoot to the surface, and my knees buckle beneath me. It's as if my legs have turned to Jell-O. I collapse like a house of cards and hit the floor hard but quickly scramble to my feet before anyone can see that I've fallen, because there can be no distractions. I need this team to save my husband's life, not to be concerned with me.

They continue to make every effort. They do everything possible to bring him back, but the internal bleeding is extensive. I recognize what is happening. All his organs are shutting down.

I recognize it, but I can't accept it. He's my husband.

Surely there's still hope . . .

Dr. Sanders prepares to shock Alan again. He places the pads on his chest and shouts, "All clear!"

Alan's body heaves, but the results are the same, and the adrenaline in my veins becomes a thick, oppressive dread that pours through me slowly and agonizingly. I can barely move. I feel like I'm going to pass out.

The second paramedic takes over chest compressions.

Feeling nauseated with despair, I back into a corner, hold my forearm up to my eyes, and cover them while I weep. Then I turn my back on the table, unable to watch any more of this unbearable scene, because I know where it's heading. I see it on everyone's face, even though they're still trying.

I've been in this situation many times but never with a loved one of my own. I don't know what to do. I'm choking.

In the end, it doesn't matter what I do. Nothing can change the fact that my husband is not going to make it to the QEII for surgery tonight. He's not even going to make it out of this ER.

The thought of losing him is excruciating. I don't want to face this. I continue to turn away.

Eventually, all the sounds of rapid activity slow to a halt. Total silence descends upon the room.

Dr. Sanders begins to speak in a somber voice, and I double over in agony as he finally calls the time of death.

CHAPTER SEVEN

My husband is gone.

Tears roll down my cheeks as I watch the medical team shut off the machines. Slowly, with an air of defeat, they roll them away from the bed.

A nurse quietly removes the tube from Alan's throat while another peels the defibrillator pads from his chest and respectfully covers him with a blanket. No one speaks a word.

I can't think or breathe or move, and my body is numb. How can I accept that it's my beloved husband lying on the table, dead?

And Zack . . . oh God, Zack . . . he just lost his father. I can't bear to think about what this will do to him. Our happy family has been decimated. It can't be real.

This morning started out perfectly normal. Alan was fine when he ate breakfast and left for the clinic.

Please, let this be a nightmare . . . I'll go home soon, and everything will be okay. Alan will be there, sitting on the sofa, waiting for me, and our lives will be just as they were before.

I realize Dr. Sanders is standing beside me. He lays a hand on my shoulder. "I'm so sorry, Abbie."

I wipe the tears from my cheeks and nod my head to acknowledge his kind words of sympathy, but still, I can't seem to move from my spot on the floor.

The other members of the medical team express their sympathies as well, and one by one, they walk out. Nurse June is the last to leave.

"Take as much time as you need," she says as she passes by.

I thank her. Then I am left alone in the quiet room, besieged by death and unfathomable misery.

I take a moment to prepare myself for what must be done, because I can't stand here forever. I have to take this time to say goodbye to my husband before breaking the news to my son.

More tears pool in my eyes and stream down my cheeks. I wipe them roughly from my neck and taste their salty wetness on my lips. My body shudders with each breath.

Swallowing hard over the jagged lump in my throat, I force myself to take a few steps forward and look down at Alan's bruised and bloodied face. I run my fingers along his bare arm and stand at his side for ten minutes, maybe more. I have no idea. Then the sobs come like a tidal wave, and I bend over him, lay my cheek on his chest, and cry inconsolably for what feels like hours, pleading for him to wake up because I can't bear the thought of living without him.

Eventually, I draw back and look down at his face again. His flesh is pallid, and his lips are blue. There is no life left in him. He can't speak or explain why this god-awful thing happened, which causes yet another emotional upheaval in me. My heart hammers in my chest, and piping hot anger ripples down my spine. Right now, we should be at home in our pajamas, settling down to watch television after cheering for Zack at his hockey game.

I imagine us there, and my breathing becomes ragged, because future happiness like that has been stolen from me. It'll never happen again, but I want it so badly—to be curling up on the sofa with Alan beside me, each of us relaxed and content. It feels impossible that I'll ever be relaxed or content again. Alan is dead. I'm a widow. My son is fatherless. The grief is overpowering.

I hear a sound and turn to see my mother standing in the doorway, staring at me with a look of anguish. She walks toward me, and I step into her arms.

"He's gone," I say.

"I know, sweetheart. I'm so sorry."

She holds me tight and rubs my back and strokes my hair. We sob and cry together.

Eventually, we step apart, and I look down at Alan again and wonder how in the world I'm going to explain this to Zack. He was so close to his father. They did everything together. How will I find the words to tell him that his life will never be the same?

This quadruples my agony.

Meanwhile, Alan's own father is on the other side of the country. I'll have to call him as well. And Alan's colleagues at the hospital. They'll be shocked. He probably has patients to see in the morning whose appointments will need to be canceled.

Oh God, why am I thinking about such stupid practicalities? What is wrong with me?

"I feel overwhelmed," I say to my mom, "like I'm suffocating. I don't know what to do. He can't be dead. Mom, what do I do?"

"I'll help you," she says, trying to calm me. She takes hold of my shoulders and looks me in the eye. "I've been through this before. I know what you're feeling."

I reach for her hand and squeeze it.

"I need to call Zack," I add, "but he's home alone. Do I tell him over the phone? I can't do that, Mom. I should go there. I need to tell him in person." I feel rattled, confused, and flustered. My eyes dart around wildly. "But my car is totaled. Can I take yours? Or I could call a cab."

"No, Abbie," she firmly says. "It's freezing rain out there. The roads are like skating rinks. You can't risk getting in another accident. Zack can't lose both parents tonight."

I cover my face with my hands. "This isn't happening."

"Do you want *me* to call him?"

"No," I reply. "I need to do it. He needs to hear it from me, but I can't do it over the phone. I want to be there with him when he finds out. Maybe I could call and tell him we need to stay here overnight because of the storm. Then I can go home in the morning and tell him in person." I consider that for a few frenzied, chaotic seconds. Then I shake my head. "No. I can't lie to him—especially because there were news vans at the accident site. I can't let him find out that way. I have to tell him tonight."

"Is there anyone you can call to go over there and be with him?"

I consider that as well. "I can call Jeremy's parents. They live a block away, and they're like a second set of parents to him."

I look back down at Alan and feel another stab of grief in my heart. My husband . . . how will I survive without him? And how is Zack going to cope with this loss?

Swallowing heavily over the painful emotions lodged in my throat, I bend forward and lay a soft kiss on Alan's cheek, then gently unclasp his watch, which was a gift from me on our tenth wedding anniversary. He had worn it every day since. I slip it into my pocket and force myself to step back.

"We need to go," I say to my mother, because I have no other choice. As much as I want to stay here and never leave Alan's side, Zack needs me. "I have to call Jeremy's parents . . . and Zack. And then Alan's father."

We walk out together and back to my bed in the ER, but I feel suddenly nauseated. "I need some air. Just give me a minute."

I turn away from her and head to the main entrance, where the sliding glass doors open in front of me. The bitter-cold air strikes me in the face, but I welcome the shock of it because I need to wake up from this daze I'm in. Standing under the overhang in the glare of the bright spotlights, I listen to the crackling sound of the freezing rain as it batters the ground. The whole world is cloaked in ice—the pavement, the naked tree branches, and all the parked cars in the lot. It hardly seems real. None of this does.

I begin to shiver, so I hurry back inside the hospital.

As I limp back to my bed in the ER, I realize that Winston still hasn't been found, I haven't gotten the stitches I've been waiting for, and my head is pounding. The nausea hasn't passed, and my stomach turns, so I dash to the nearest washroom, where I expel the contents of my stomach and grimace at the pain in my head and heart.

I'm probably concussed. Or maybe it's just the emotional effects of this horrendous ordeal.

A few minutes later, after I rinse out my mouth and splash water on my face, I look at myself in the mirror and recoil at my ghastly reflection. I haven't seen myself since the accident. My eyes are puffy from crying, and my face is bruised, bloody, and swollen. My hair is caked in blood. But I don't care what I look like—my husband is dead.

I want to cry again, to sob like a baby, but I smother the urge because I need to stay strong for Zack and make it through my phone call to him, and then I'll have to somehow endure the next few days. Somehow, I'll have to endure the rest of my life without Alan.

My skull throbs as I open the washroom door and return to my bed. I push back the privacy curtain and find my mother sitting in the chair, wringing her hands together in her lap. She takes one look at me and frowns, then quickly rises and comes over to me.

"Abbie. You need to get off your feet before you collapse."

I allow her to help me onto the bed, where I lay my head on the pillows and close my eyes for a moment or two. I still feel nauseated. My body trembles.

"You've been through so much," Mom says, stroking my hair away from my face.

All I can do is nod my head. Then I do something I don't want to do but that must be done. I pick up my phone and dial Jeremy's parents' number to deliver the worst news possible and ask for their help.

CHAPTER EIGHT

Jeremy's parents, David and Maureen, are devastated to learn what happened to Alan. Maureen cries on the phone and tells me repeatedly how sorry she is. She wants to help in any way she can.

I ask her to go over to my house and get Zack. "I have to tell him tonight because it's probably going to be on the news and I don't want him to find out that way. And I don't want him to spend the night alone either. He needs to be with people who care about him."

"Of course," Maureen replies. "I'll take Jeremy with me. We'll go over there right now and ring the doorbell."

"Thank you so much, Maureen," I reply. "I'm about to call him, so he's going to be upset when you get there. Please do what you can. Give him a hug, stay by his side."

"You know I will. He's like a son to me, Abbie. We'll take good care of him, I promise. And whatever else you need, just say the word. We're here for you."

I think about that for a moment. "There is something, actually. Maybe in the morning, as soon as the weather clears, could you drive him down here? I think it would be best if we stayed in Lunenburg with my mom for a few days while we come to grips with all of this. And there are so many arrangements that need to be taken care of."

I can't bear to think of what I'll have to face in the coming days, like deciding where to hold the funeral and where to bury Alan. He and I have wills, and we always knew we wanted to be buried together, but we never reached a final decision about where that would be. We thought we had lots of time to figure that out. And what about the obituary? I'll have to call our friends and family and think about a headstone. I have no idea how I'm going to get through it all.

Maureen tells me to take care and to call if I need anything.

We hang up, and I breathe deeply to summon the courage to dial Zack's number. He picks up right away.

"Mom. I've been waiting. What's happening? Are you in Halifax yet?"

I shut my eyes and try to speak in a steady voice. "No, honey. I'm still in Lunenburg, and I have some news. I'm afraid it's not good." I take a shaky breath. "Your father had a lot of internal bleeding, and he was in really bad shape. The helicopter arrived to pick him up, but we couldn't get him there in time. The doctors and nurses did everything they could, but . . . but he didn't make it, honey."

The silence is ominous.

"What do you mean he didn't make it?" Zack finally asks.

My throat clenches so tight I can barely get air into my lungs. "He didn't make it," I say again in a shaking voice. "He *died*, sweetheart."

There's another long pause. "What do you mean? He can't be dead."

"I'm so sorry, honey. It was a very bad accident. Worse than we thought."

"No!" Zack sobs. "It's not true. It can't be!"

I cover my mouth with my hand, smothering a sob of my own because it breaks my heart to know that my son is suffering and I'm not there to hold him and comfort him.

"We did everything we could," I explain, "but he was badly hurt."

Zack's voice quavers. "You were there?"

"Yes. I helped as much as I could, and I tried my best. We all did. There was nothing anyone could do."

I listen to the sound of my son crying, and soon we are crying together. I can't stop the tears. They pour down my cheeks in a terrible flood of despair.

"Did he say anything to you?" Zack asks when we collect ourselves. "Did he know he was dying?"

I pull myself together and try to answer honestly. "No. He was unconscious by the time the ambulance arrived at the hospital. He never woke up after that."

I hear the doorbell ring in the background.

"Someone's here," Zack says.

"It's Maureen," I tell him. "I asked her to stop by. Go and let her in."

"No, Mom. I can't move. I can't breathe."

"Try to calm down, Zack. Take a slow, deep breath in. Good. Now another."

"Okay. I'm going to go let her in."

I listen as he gets up and answers the door. I hear Maureen's loving voice, and I know that she is hugging my son. Jeremy's there too. I listen to them talking, and I'm so thankful they're all together.

Zack returns to the phone. "Mom? I don't know what to do."

"I don't know what to do either, honey. I'm stuck here because they want to keep me overnight for observation, and the weather is too risky to venture out anyway. But Gram's here, and she's taking good care of me. I've asked Maureen to drive you here first thing in the morning when the roads are clear. You'll have to miss some school."

He sniffles, and his voice shakes. "I still can't believe this. How can he be gone? I'm never going to see him again?"

The question squeezes at my heart. "You'll see him . . . at the wake. We'll have an open casket, and you'll be able to say goodbye."

Zack breaks down completely. *"Oh God . . . Mom . . . !"*

"I'm so sorry, Zack. I shouldn't have said that. I can't believe any of this either, but we'll get through it together. It's going to be rough for a while, but at least we have each other. Don't forget that. You know how much I love you."

"I do, Mom." He's quiet for a moment. "But are *you* okay? You were in the accident too."

I sniff and rub under my nose. "I'm totally fine. Please don't worry."

"Did they at least find Winston?" Zack asks.

I shut my eyes. "Not yet, but they're still looking. I'm sure they'll find him soon."

But how can I say that when I don't know for sure? After everything that's happened tonight, I can't help but fear the worst.

Dr. Sanders walks in and sees me on the phone. He points to his own head, indicating that he wants to examine the gash above my hairline.

I nod at him and say to Zack, "Listen, I have to hang up now. The doctor's here. I'd like you to sleep at Jeremy's tonight, and I'll call you a little later, okay?"

"Okay, Mom," he says. "I love you. Please call back soon."

"I will, and I love you too, honey. More than anything."

We hang up, and Dr. Sanders approaches to ask me some questions about my head. He grows concerned when he learns I was just sick in the bathroom, and he makes sure I understand that I need to stay for overnight observation.

"No one should be going anywhere in this storm anyway," he adds, as if he knows how badly I want to go home and be with my son.

I have no choice but to agree, and the nurses are kind enough to offer my mother a bed to sleep on.

They are in the process of wheeling me out of the ER to a private room when I see my paramedic, Carrie, walking toward me with a look of concern. She's talking on her cell phone, nodding her head, and somehow I know that she's speaking to the first responder, Troy, and there's news about Winston. My belly turns over with panic. For yet the hundredth time on this cursed night.

CHAPTER NINE

Carrie approaches. "I'm so sorry about your husband, Abbie. I really am." She walks beside my wheelchair and gives my shoulder a gentle rub.

"Thank you."

"But I thought you might like to know that I have Troy on the phone. He found Winston."

I lay a hand over my heart. "Oh, thank goodness."

Then I realize that Carrie isn't smiling, and I'm not sure how much more heartbreak I can handle. "Please tell me he's okay."

The porter angles the wheelchair in front of the elevator door and pushes the button.

"He's alive," Carrie tells me. "But you should talk to Troy."

She hands me the phone.

"Hello?"

"Hi, Abbie?" Troy asks.

"Yes."

"I heard about your husband. I'm so sorry."

I fight another onslaught of tears and reply shakily, "Thank you."

Troy pauses a few seconds. "I have good news and bad news. The good news is that we found Winston."

"Where?" I ask, needing to know all the details but not wanting to hear the bad news just yet. I pray it's not what I fear. I don't know if I can take another hard blow at the moment.

"Near the off-ramp on the way back to town. We think he might have tried to follow the ambulance, but he gave up and collapsed by the side of the road."

"Oh God." I break down again. More tears stream down my cheeks because I can't bear to think about how distraught and frightened Winston must have been as he chased after the ambulance. Did he think I'd abandoned him? Or that I was in trouble and needed him?

"It's lucky we found him," Troy says. "We'd just about given up the search because the weather was getting worse. We were on our way back to town when we spotted him. He was lying under a streetlight."

I imagine my loyal dog, alone in the darkness and freezing rain, wanting only to protect me and thinking he'd failed.

"Where is he now?" I ask desperately. "Is he with you? Is he okay?"

The elevator bell dings, and the doors slide open. The porter pushes my chair forward, and my mother and Carrie both get on the elevator with us.

"He's in the truck with me," Troy replies. "I have his head on my lap. His eyes are open, but he's cold, and he's weak."

"Put the phone next to his ear." I want Winston to hear my voice. I wait a few seconds, and then I speak to him in a soothing, melodic tone. "Hey, Winston. What a good boy you are. They're going to take good care of you, and I'll come for you soon. I love you. Stay strong, okay?"

My voice breaks on the last words, and Troy takes the phone back.

"I just called one of the vets in town," he says. "He has a clinic in his house, so he's going to open up for us."

"Which clinic?" I ask.

"It's called Oceanview Animal Hospital. The vet's name is Dr. Nathan Payne."

"Okay."

"Don't worry—he's good. And I'm off duty now, so I can stay at the clinic until I know more. I'll keep you posted. Just keep your phone on, and tell Carrie to text me your number."

My heart aches, and I'm filled with regret for leaving Winston behind. I wish things were different and that I could be with him now.

"I'll call you as soon as I know anything," Troy says, "and I promise I won't leave his side. Not for a second."

"Thank you so much, Troy." My eyes fill with tears again, because I'm grateful for Troy's help—and for everyone else who has come to my rescue in so many ways tonight. The police officers . . . the firefighters and paramedics . . . and the medical team that worked so hard to try and save Alan. I feel as if this town is full of heroes.

The elevator doors slide open, and the porter pushes my chair onto the floor.

Then I think of Zack.

My son just lost his father. He can't lose his dog too—a dog that's more than just a pet to him. Alan brought Winston home for Zack one day as a surprise when Zack was being bullied in the sixth grade. Winston was only a puppy then—nine weeks old—and he became Zack's best friend, and mine too, in so many ways.

Winston has to survive. Not just for me but also for Zack.

I end the call and hand the phone to Carrie, who texts my number to Troy.

"Shouldn't you be off duty by now?" I ask Carrie, who is helping the porter get me settled. "I've been seen by the doctor, and I'm admitted. I'm pretty sure that means your work is done."

"Yes, but I'm waiting for Troy anyway," she replies. "He's supposed to give me a ride back to our place."

"Your place." I give her a questioning look. "Are you and Troy together or something?"

She holds her hand out to show me an engagement ring. "Yes. We're getting married next July."

I'm happy for her. Truly I am, but her love story makes me think of Alan and the day he proposed. He took me to Cape Split, where we hiked up the mountain and picnicked on a grassy meadow overlooking the beautiful Bay of Fundy. It was a clear day, and we could see for miles across the blue, while the hiss and roar of the powerful tidal currents below us made it feel dangerous and exciting.

"You're my best friend," he said, "and I want to spend the rest of my life with you. I want to have children with you and grow old together and never be apart. You're the love of my life, Abbie. Will you marry me?"

My grief returns with a vengeance, and I wonder if I'll ever feel happiness again. Tonight, it seems impossible. It feels like this dark cloud of loss will hang over my head forever.

"Congratulations," I say to Carrie, fingering my own wedding and engagement rings.

"Thanks." She covers me with the blue sheet, and I can tell by her modest reply that she understands my pain and feels guilty for showing off her bling.

"I'm happy for you," I manage to say. "He seems like an amazing guy. Very caring."

There are two beds in the room, and my mother sets her purse down on the other one.

"I'll get some sheets for that," Carrie says. "And I'll make sure they bring two breakfast trays in the morning. You've both been through so much."

Again, I'm moved to tears by yet another act of kindness.

My phone rings, and I scramble to pick it up. When I see that it's Troy, my heart races.

"Hello?"

"Hi, Abbie?" He sounds out of breath.

"Yes, it's me. Is everything okay?"

"Yes. I just want to let you know that I'm at the vet clinic now, and Dr. Payne just took Winston into the examination room."

"That's great. But why are you so out of breath?"

He takes a minute to answer. "The truck couldn't make it up the hill. It was too icy. We kept sliding back down, so I had to get out and walk."

"You walked? What about Winston? Tell me you didn't have to carry him up that icy hill."

"I did."

I struggle to comprehend this. "But he weighs over sixty pounds! I can't believe you did that. I can't thank you enough, Troy. You've earned a spot in heaven tonight."

He chuckles as if it were nothing, but it's not nothing. Not to me. It's everything.

"Will you ask Dr. Payne to call me when he knows something?"

"Of course."

We end the conversation, and I decide to call Zack right away. He's lost so much tonight that he deserves to have some hope to hold on to.

After that, I will finally contact Alan's father, Lester, on the West Coast.

Only then do I realize how much I've been dreading that phone call. It means that an already excruciating day is about to get worse.

CHAPTER TEN

As I pick up my phone to call Lester and deliver the news of his son's death, I find myself thinking about how he handled a similar situation many years ago, when Alan's mother passed away.

Alan and his brother, Bruce, were both at school when it happened, and for some reason I'll never understand, Lester didn't pull them out of class. He simply left them to finish out the day while their mother was removed from her private room in the hospital and taken to the morgue.

Hours later, Alan and Bruce rode the bus home from school and played street hockey with some of the neighborhood kids until the sun went down. Then they cooked Kraft Dinner for themselves because Lester didn't come home for supper. According to Alan, this wasn't unusual. Whenever their mother was in the hospital for treatments, they looked after themselves and didn't bother to ask their dad when he was coming home. He worked odd hours, and there were no expectations that he would be there for them as a father.

That night, Lester came home very late, completely bombed, and Alan never forgot that pivotal moment in his life. His father burst into his room without knocking, thrusting the door open with such force that a picture fell off the wall. Alan, who had just fallen asleep, nearly jumped out of his skin.

"Your mother's gone," Lester said. "She died early this morning. Funeral's on Friday. She's gettin' cremated. Tell your brother."

Lester left the room, shut Alan's door, and that was that. Alan was never given the opportunity to say goodbye to his mother, and from that day forward, he and Bruce weren't permitted to talk about her or feel sorry for themselves. Neither of them dared to cry in front of Lester for fear of getting smacked or ridiculed. There was no love left in their house after she was gone, and Alan said that every day felt like a black hole. At least until he met me.

And now I have to call this heartless man to tell him that his son has died. I hope that he responds differently this time.

With a deep breath to prepare myself, I dial Lester's number and wait for him to answer. His voice is deep and gruff when he picks up the phone. "Hello?"

"Hi, Lester. It's Abbie."

"Abbie?" he barks. "Alan's wife?"

I'm not surprised that he doesn't recognize my voice. We haven't spoken in years. "Yes, it's me. I'm afraid I have some bad news. Is anyone with you?"

"No, I'm here on my own," he replies. "Verna's gone to the store. But whatever it is, just spit it out."

My heart pounds heavily, and I draw in a deep breath. "Okay. Well . . . Alan was in a car accident tonight, and . . ." I pause and clear my throat. "I'm very sorry to tell you this, but it was serious, and he . . . he didn't survive."

Lester says nothing for a moment. All I can hear is the thunderous pounding of my heart in my ears. "Are you still there?" I ask him.

"Yeah, I'm here."

The conversation grinds to a painful halt, and I close my eyes. "Are you all right?"

"Of course I'm all right," he replies testily. "I'm not the one who died in a car accident. So what happened?"

I gather my thoughts and try to explain as clearly and gently as possible. "Alan was on his way to Lunenburg, and it was foggy and dark, and the roads were starting to freeze. He drifted across the center line."

Lester scoffs. "That little idiot. Was he drinking?"

The question, combined with his hateful tone, catches me off guard. "Actually, he was . . . but why would you ask that?"

"Because Alan never could hold his liquor. He was always a lightweight."

I take another deep breath and try to remain calm when all I want to do is tell my father-in-law to stick it where the sun doesn't shine.

"So when's the funeral?" Lester asks pointedly. "I suppose you'll expect us to be there. Flights aren't cheap, you know."

"I don't expect anything from you, Lester. It's up to you if you want to come. I'm not sure when the service will be, but I'll certainly let you know."

"Fine. I'll tell Verna and Bruce."

"Good. I have to go now. Goodbye."

Fighting against the rising tide of my anger, I end the call and slam my phone down on the bed. Then I stare at the ceiling and listen to the tinny sound of ice pellets striking the windowpane.

"How did he take it?" Mom asks.

"Sickeningly well," I reply. "Didn't shed a single tear. You'd think I was calling to tell him that his roof needs replacing."

This comes as no surprise to my mother. She knew all about Alan's difficult relationship with his father, who had always been mean-spirited and abusive.

She pats my hand.

"That's Lester for you," I add. "I don't even know if he's going to come to the funeral. I hate to say it, but I hope he stays away, because I don't want to see him. Honestly, I don't know if Alan would have even wanted him there."

I continue to lie on the bed, quietly seething over Lester's emotionless response to his son's death. I think about Alan and how he turned out to be such a good man despite having been raised by a terrible father.

All I want is for Alan to walk into the room so I can pull him into my arms and hold him tight.

Then Lester's words hit me full force, and I remember that Alan was driving drunk and nearly killed the both of us. The husband I loved—since the first moment we met—suddenly feels like a stranger to me, and I don't like the feeling. I don't like it at all.

For the next hour, Mom and I watch television in silence. Maybe it's the pain medication or mere exhaustion, but I'm barely aware of what I'm looking at—a sitcom I've never seen before, with a laugh track that is strangely hypnotic. A nurse comes to check on us, then leaves again. Another nurse comes later. Ice pellets continue to beat against the window, relentlessly. Time passes slowly.

I wish I could shut down my brain, but I can't stop thinking about the trauma room and how I was forced to perform CPR on my husband and then watch Dr. Sanders call the time of death. I see Alan lying there, dead on the table, and I feel as if I'm awake in a nightmare that simply won't end, as it carries me lightly into a memory of how we met.

It was just the third day of medical school, when we were introduced to the dead body that would serve as our group's cadaver for the year. The class had been warned in advance about the importance of behaving in a respectful manner, and the mood was solemn as we entered the lab, which smelled strongly of formaldehyde. I was nervous to begin with. We were also told that some of us might become nauseated or experience some other unexpected emotional response.

For me, the timing was unfortunate. I had buried my beloved father a month earlier. As soon as I saw the dead man, I became distraught and had to leave the lab.

Alan followed. He asked if I was okay. I said no and told him about my dad. Alan let me cry on his shoulder. He rubbed my back and said he understood because he had lost his mother to cancer when he was thirteen.

Alan and I formed an unbreakable bond that day, surrounded by death. The friendship carried us through the highs and lows of medical school, and when graduation loomed, I didn't know how I would ever live without Alan if our professional lives separated us. He felt the same way, but fate was kind and placed us together in Halifax to complete our residencies. We tied the knot three months later.

Now here I am in another hospital, two decades later, wishing he were here so I could cry on his shoulder again.

Never in a million years could I have imagined I would lose him like this. Nothing about it is right.

My cell phone starts ringing and pulls me from my thoughts. I glance at the screen and pick it up. "Hello?"

"Hello, is this Abbie MacIntyre?"

"Yes," I reply.

"This is Dr. Payne." He pauses. "I'm very sorry to hear about your husband. Troy told me."

I feel like I might start to cry again, but somehow I manage to keep it together. "Thank you."

There's a long silence before the vet clears his throat. "Please know that I'm doing everything I can, but your dog is in pretty bad shape. You're lucky that Troy found him when he did."

I sit forward on the bed. "Is he going to be okay?"

"I hope so, but as I said, it's serious."

My stomach burns. "What's wrong with him? And please be clear, Doctor. I'm a physician myself."

"I see. Well . . . he's had some internal bleeding, which I believe is coming from a ruptured spleen, he has serious bruising everywhere, and his skull is fractured."

"What?" All of this knocks me off-balance emotionally, and I fight to keep it together. "But he ran such a long distance after the accident. He did that with a ruptured spleen and a fractured skull?"

"Yes," Dr. Payne replies. "Clearly, he's a very faithful dog, but I need your permission to open him up. I suspect I'll have to remove his spleen and see what else we're dealing with internally."

I squeeze my eyes shut and pray Winston will come through. "Yes, you have my permission. Do whatever's necessary to save him, whatever the cost. I don't care. I'll pay anything. But no matter what happens . . . please don't let him suffer." I take a deep, shaky breath. "And, Doctor, you should know that after losing my husband tonight, I'd prefer not to lose my dog too. Not to put extra pressure on you, but my son would be devastated. We love Winston so much."

"I understand," he says matter-of-factly, without missing a beat. "I'll do everything I can. You have my word. I'll call you the minute he's out of surgery, which should be in a few hours. Maybe more. It's hard to say."

I speak firmly. "It doesn't matter what time it is, because I doubt I'll sleep much tonight anyway. Call as soon as you have news."

I end the conversation and tell my mother what's happening. Then I call Zack to fill him in as well. My son cries softly with relief over Winston but also grief over his father. He wants to come and be with me and to be with Winston too. To be reassured. But I tell him he has to wait until the morning, when it will be safe to travel and the light of day will help us see everything more clearly.

I try to sleep, but I can't. My emotions and stress levels are like a dark abyss from which I can't escape. So when my phone buzzes at two in the morning, I'm already wide-awake. I sit up instantly and swipe the screen.

Mom continues to snore softly from the bed beside mine, and I try to answer quietly so that I don't wake her, but it's no use. She hears me talking, sits up, and switches on the light.

"Hi, Abbie. It's Dr. Payne."

"Yes. Hello." My stomach lurches. "How did the surgery go?"

"Well, we had a few tense moments, but Winston is a fighter. He made it through, and he's in recovery now."

I bow my head and press the heel of my hand to my forehead. "Thank goodness." I turn to my mother. "He survived the surgery."

Dr. Payne responds immediately. "But he's not out of the woods yet. There was a lot of bleeding, and we nearly lost him. I had to remove his spleen, and that skull fracture has me worried. I'm going to stay with him tonight and watch him closely."

Suddenly I'm hit with a spell of déjà vu because everything reminds me of what just happened to Alan—the head injury and the internal bleeding and the damage to the spleen. It's all too similar, and it brings back the same feelings of panic I had in the ER only hours before. I want to get out of this bed and go straight to the clinic, but I know I can't. It's the middle of the night, and I've been given pain medication. Besides all that, Winston is still anesthetized.

"When will he wake up?" I ask.

"It's hard to say. He's been through a lot. I'll certainly call you if there's any change, but in the meantime, I suggest you get some sleep. If he makes it through the night—and I have faith that he will, Abbie; he's very strong—he'll want to see you in the morning. He's going to need a reason to wag that tail."

Dr. Payne's encouraging words fill me with emotion. My eyes tear up, and I find myself marveling at the fact that I'm still capable of feeling some form of joy, even if it's tearful. It's a tremendous gift on this night.

"Thank you," I say. "I'll call first thing in the morning."

"Good," he replies. "And get some rest, Abbie. It sounds like you need it."

"I will. And thank you again. You have no idea what you've done for me and my son tonight. We'll never forget it."

CHAPTER ELEVEN

I wake with a start and sit bolt upright in bed. The morning sun is beaming through ice crystals on the window glass. They shimmer like diamonds, and I'm momentarily blinded because my pupils are dilated from sleep. Only then do I remember where I am and why I'm here.

Last night I was in a car accident, and my husband died.

I feel as if I've lost a limb or an internal organ. I wish someone would walk in and tell me it was all a bad dream, but I know it wasn't. Today I must rise and come to grips with Alan's passing and start to think about practical details I don't want to face—like coffins and obituaries, hymns and flower arrangements.

If only I could go back in time and relive yesterday. If that were possible, I would get up in the morning and insist that Alan forget about work and come with me to my mother's house. Then none of this would be happening. I wouldn't be waking up in this hospital, drowning in grief, unable to hear my husband's laugh or smell his musky aftershave or find comfort in his arms.

Then I think about Winston, and I want both Zack and me to be at the vet hospital when he wakes up. I want to stroke my dog's soft golden head and tell him everything is going to be okay.

I need to say those words out loud, to hear them myself, to try and believe them—for Zack's sake as well as my own.

Tossing the covers aside, I slip out of bed and look out the window. It's still early, but salt trucks and snowplows have done their job through the night, and the street appears to be clear.

I wipe the tears from my cheeks, collect myself, and turn to my mother, who is still sleeping.

"Mom, wake up," I say, gently shaking her.

She opens her eyes. "What's happening?"

"It's morning, and the roads are salted," I say. "I'm going to call Zack now and get Maureen to bring him directly to the vet hospital so that we can see Winston together. Can you drive me there?"

She sits up and glances around. "Yes, of course, but are you allowed to leave?"

"They can't hold me against my will," I reply, sitting down on a chair to pull on my sneakers and tie the laces. "Besides, I'm fine. Just a little stiff and sore in the legs, that's all."

It's my heart that hurts the most, but I don't need to tell my mother that—she knows.

I call my son, and we take a few moments to comfort each other on the phone. Then I tell him where he and Maureen should meet me.

I also ask him to pack a bag for me at our house and bring it with him. I give him specific instructions about what I'll need—my toothbrush, socks and underwear, jeans and sweatshirts. A black dress.

The sound of a meal cart rolling down the hall on squeaky wheels causes my mother to rise from her bed. "You should eat something."

"Yes. We both should, but let's try to be quick because Maureen and Zack are leaving Halifax now and should be at the vet hospital in just over an hour. God, I can't wait to see him."

The porter brings in two trays, and I thank him. Even though I have no appetite, I force down a few bites of oatmeal before I go to the nurses' station to let them know I can't wait around for the doctor to discharge me. I need to leave immediately. I explain why—because of

Winston—and the duty nurse understands because she's a dog owner too. I promise to return for a follow-up with Dr. Sanders very soon.

Fifteen minutes later, Mom and I are pulling out of the hospital parking lot, and I feel a sudden pang in my gut to be leaving the place where Alan died less than twelve hours ago—where his body is still being held. I turn in my seat to look out the rear window and watch the building grow distant.

I hate leaving him behind. A jagged lump forms in my throat. *Stop!* I want to say. *Take me back.* But I know we can't stop. We have to keep going. I need to stay in the car and keep moving toward something that could potentially be fixed.

My mother turns a corner at the end of the street, and the hospital disappears from view. I face forward again, finding it difficult to breathe through a thick haze of sorrow.

As we pull into the driveway of a blue Victorian mansion with white trim, the warmth of the sun is melting the icicles that hang on trees and power lines. The whole world is shiny and dripping.

We find the clinic accessible from a side entrance leading in from the yard, which has been converted to a small paved parking lot with space for about five cars. There's a charming painted sign over the door that says OCEANVIEW ANIMAL HOSPITAL, with paw prints at all four corners.

"This is it," I say to Mom, who pulls into a spot next to the only other vehicle in the yard—a white van with the Oceanview logo printed on the side. As I get out of the car, I realize it's a fully equipped ambulance for furry creatures.

"I'll meet you inside," I say to Mom, not wasting a second as I shut the car door and maneuver through slushy puddles toward the entrance.

An old-fashioned bell jingles over the door as I cross the threshold into a cozy reception area that matches the Victorian exterior. A gigantic aquarium full of colorful tropical fish fills the space to the right, and there are several amusing plaques on the walls with phrases like Children left unattended will be given an espresso and a free puppy and Love is a four-legged word.

Directly in front of me, a red-haired receptionist with a bouncy bob and red plastic-rimmed glasses sits behind a high counter. Her name tag says Ruby. She immediately glances up from her computer and smiles.

"You must be Winston's mom."

"Yes." I feel winded and anxious but also comforted to hear my mother enter the clinic behind me.

Rising from her chair, Ruby moves out from behind the counter and waves both of us forward. "Come with me. He's out back, and he's doing great."

My entire body floods with relief. I'm grateful for this precious, sorely needed moment of good news.

Ruby pushes open a glass door to a back hallway. She leads us past two small examination rooms and finally to an expansive, ultramodern, and brightly lit treatment area with floor-to-ceiling windows at the back. The walls are white, and the surfaces are stainless steel.

A female technician in blue scrubs sits at one of three computer workstations in the center of the space, and to my right, there's a high-tech surgical suite with a glass door and glass walls for easy viewing.

The whole world disappears, however, as Ruby escorts us into the recovery unit located behind sliding glass doors. There's my Winston, lying on his side in a large cage.

As soon as our eyes meet, a smile spreads across my face, and I say in a quiet, loving voice, "There's my boy."

He's too weak and medicated to move, but his tail begins to thump on the floor of the crate. Soon he's trembling with happiness, and I burst into tears.

Ruby opens the cage door so that I can stroke him and kiss him, and I weep openly. "My sweet boy. I'm here now, and everything's going to be okay. We're going to take care of you and get you home soon. You're so good. Yes, you were so brave."

Though he can barely lift his head, his tongue sneaks out to lick away my tears. Soon, I'm laughing and crying at the same time, feeling unexpectedly jubilant, considering all that's happened over the past twelve hours.

Ruby pulls up two rolling chairs so that we can sit next to Winston's crate. I lay my hand in front of his nose, because I know it comforts him to smell me. He's quieted down since my arrival and is content to simply lie there, blinking slowly and reveling in my presence as much as I revel in his.

After a short while, the sliding glass doors open, and I turn to see a man in a white lab coat, who I assume is Dr. Payne. His voice on the phone led me to picture an older gentleman, perhaps in his sixties, with white hair and wire-rimmed glasses, but the Dr. Payne who stands before me now appears to be in his late thirties, with brown hair and blue eyes.

"You must be Abbie," he says.

I rise from the chair. "Yes. Thank you so much for everything you've done. I'm so grateful. You have no idea."

"It was my pleasure," he replies, and I notice that his jaw is unshaven and his eyes are bloodshot. It's obvious that he's been up all night. Just like me.

"Your dog's a real fighter," he says.

For some reason, Dr. Payne's words hit me hard, and I can't help it—I start to cry again. My feelings are so intense my knees buckle, and I reach for the back of the chair to keep from hitting the floor like I did in the ER last night. It's embarrassing because I'm not usually an emotional woman, but so much has happened, and I can't seem to stop crying.

"I'm sorry," Dr. Payne says, gripping my elbow to help steady me. "I didn't mean to upset you."

My cheeks are on fire, and I struggle to collect myself. "You didn't. It's just been a really rough night, as I'm sure you can imagine."

He regards me with a mixture of concern and compassion. "I understand. I'm sorry about your husband. If there's anything I can do . . ."

"You've already done everything I could ever ask for. You saved my dog last night. My son is on his way here now, and I'm so glad I won't have to deliver more bad news."

Appearing confident that I'm not going to collapse again, Dr. Payne lets go of my arm and steps back. "How old is your son?"

"Seventeen. My neighbor is driving him from Halifax right now. I told them to come straight here. I hope that's okay."

"Of course it is. You can stay as long as you like."

"Thank you." I squat down and reach a hand through the open door of the crate to stroke Winston again. "How long before we can take him home?"

Dr. Payne kneels beside me to look in on him. "He's doing well, but I'd still like to keep him until tomorrow. He'll probably sleep most of the day anyway because of the pain medication, but we'll aim to get him on his feet and walking by this evening."

"This evening. That's great."

Dr. Payne rises and turns to leave. "If you'll excuse me, I have a few other patients to see. Don't be shy about asking Ruby if you need anything."

"I won't. And thanks again . . . for everything."

He looks at me intently for a moment before he turns away and disappears into one of the private examination rooms.

"He's an excellent doctor," my mother says. "He's kindhearted. You can just tell."

"I agree." It feels good to know that Winston is in such good hands.

CHAPTER TWELVE

Mom and I sit in mournful silence as we wait for Zack to arrive, until she asks a pertinent question.

"Have you given any thought to where you'd like to bury Alan?"

I'm so tired right now. The compulsion to close my eyes and fall asleep is overpowering. Still, I do my best to stay awake and face this. "Not really. We had our wills drawn up, so at least we took care of that, but we never decided on a cemetery. At our age, we figured it wasn't a terribly urgent question."

"Well . . ." She gazes wistfully through the glass doors to the central treatment area, where the technicians are busy at their workstations. "Death comes to us all eventually. I'm just sad that it came to Alan so soon. I loved him like my own son, you know."

I reach for her hand and squeeze it. "I know you did, Mom. He loved you too."

After Alan lost his own mother to cancer, he was never close to his father or brother. We were the only family he had.

"He couldn't do enough for me," Mom adds with a tear in her eye, and I see that she's remembering all the times Alan raked the leaves in her yard, cleaned out the gutters, or fixed a leaky faucet in the kitchen. He even replaced the roof on her shed, and whenever she had car troubles, he was the first person she called.

I gently scratch behind Winston's ears. "I do know one thing for sure. Alan would have wanted to be close to us, and Lunenburg is our hometown. It's where Dad is buried, in the cemetery overlooking the Back Harbour, and that's where you'll want to be buried someday—right next to him. That's where I want to be buried too. So maybe we should lay him to rest there, in our family plot."

Mom nods with approval. "I think that's a wonderful idea. It's the right thing. So it's decided then?"

I let out a breath. "Yes. That means we can have the funeral here in town."

She squeezes my hand. "I'm glad you want to do it here, Abbie, because I know all the right people to call. I'll help you take care of the arrangements. You're not alone, dear."

Her words comfort me momentarily, until I realize that for the first time since I walked down the aisle to marry Alan, I *am* alone again. There's no escaping it.

After about a half hour, I hear the bell over the door jangle, and I know that Zack and Maureen have arrived. I leave my mother with Winston and step outside to the reception area.

As soon as Zack sees me, all the color drains from his face. He moves toward me, straight into my arms, and we both cry over Alan.

"I can't believe this is real," Zack says. "I can't believe he's gone."

"I can't believe it either." We continue to hold and comfort each other.

Maureen enters and hugs me too.

"I brought you a casserole and a homemade pie from my freezer," she says gently, stepping back.

"Thank you so much. You're a good friend." I wipe a hand under my runny nose.

"Mom, you look awful," Zack says. "Are you sure you're okay?"

Only then do I realize how shocked he must be to see my black-and-blue face, though Dr. Payne didn't even flinch or mention it when he saw me.

"I'm fine," I assure him. "This is nothing, really. Why don't you come back and visit with Winston? He'll be so happy to see you. But you should prepare yourself. He's sedated and weak. Let's not get him too excited. It's important to speak in quiet tones."

Ruby waves at us to go on back. Soon we are crowded around Winston's cage, and his tail is thumping again. When he sniffs Zack's hands, Winston's eyes grow wet, and I'm convinced that he's weeping with happiness and we are seeing tears of love.

At the same time, I sense that the excitement is too much for him, and I suggest that we leave him alone to rest.

Besides, we have a lot to talk about. There's going to be much to do over the next few days. I'm not sure how I'm going to get through it all, and I feel tired again, as if my body weighs a ton.

After Maureen returns to Halifax, Zack, Mom, and I get through the day together, leaning on one another through all the decisions and painful tasks that must be dealt with—visiting the funeral home and choosing a casket, speaking to the minister at our church, and setting a date and time for the service and burial.

We then return home and are content to eat the casserole and pie Maureen cooked. I'm so grateful for it. After a brief rest, I begin to make phone calls to family and friends to let them know about Alan's funeral. I call Alan's father first, and he informs me that he already bought his plane ticket. I try not to get worked up about it because he's not my favorite person in the world, but it's his son's funeral, and he has a right to be there.

The rest of the phone calls to friends and colleagues are equally difficult, especially when I'm forced to listen to expressions of shock and dismay over what they had seen on television the night before. Apparently, video footage of Alan's car wreck was broadcast on all the local news programs and the internet, and it was revealed that Alan—a prominent, respected Halifax cardiologist—had been driving under the influence. It's a dark and dirty scandal I can't bear to stomach.

Though everyone I speak to is sympathetic, I'm deeply ashamed of what occurred. I want to shield Zack from what's being said about his father in the news, but it's not possible unless I take his phone away from him, and I don't want to do that. I need to let him face this and do my best to talk him through it. But that's not easy, because I have no idea why Alan did what he did or what he was doing on the road that night. The question eats away at me, on top of everything else.

Later that night, my sister, Carla; her husband, Braden; and their two young daughters arrive from New Brunswick.

Carla and I have always been close, and as soon as our eyes meet in my mother's foyer, we step into each other's arms.

"I'm so glad you're finally here," I say.

"Me too."

A short while later, we manage to steal a moment alone together in my bedroom, away from the children. I tell her everything about the accident and the excruciating and impossible pain of watching Alan die and being helpless to stop it.

"I don't understand how it happened," I say, bowing my head and slowly shaking it. "How could he have gotten behind the wheel if he was drinking? I never imagined he would ever do something like that."

Carla rubs my knee. "I know. It's a shock. But there's got to be some sort of explanation."

My eyes lift. "But how will I ever know? He was alone at the time, and no one expected him to be on the road to Lunenburg. I've searched through all my messages, and I've checked his phone. I've talked to his colleagues. No one knows why he was coming here, let alone why he was drunk on a Sunday."

I lean toward the bedside table to pull a tissue from the box and blow my nose. "I'm so angry with him right now. Part of me hates him for what he did to us. For what he did to our family."

Carla says nothing. She simply nods and provides the sympathetic ear I so desperately need.

"At the same time, I don't want to think about him that way—as the drunk driver who ran me off the road. I want to remember him as the wonderful father and devoted husband that he was. That's how I want Zack to remember him too."

"He will, and you will too, when the shock of this wears off."

After we're finished talking, Carla and I prepare the spare bedroom for her and Braden while Mom opens the sofa bed in the den for Zack and makes beds for the children on the floor in the family room. Carla chooses a movie for them to watch, and I make a pot of coffee so that she, Mom, and I can sit down at the table and take care of some practical details about the funeral.

Later, despite having drunk two cups of brew, I fall into a deep slumber as soon as my head hits the pillow. Still, I wake often during the night, with fretful dreams about the accident. I dream that I can't get out from under the dash and no one comes to rescue me. I scream for help and thrash about. I pound my fists against the steering wheel. Then all the dashboard lights go out, and I'm alone in the dark ravine. Winston is gone. He doesn't come back. But I don't want to give up. I tell myself that the sun will come up in the morning and then it won't be so scary. I pray that someone will find me. My heart pummels my rib cage, but I try to hold on and make it through the night.

When I pull myself out of the dream, though, and reach across the bed in search of Alan's warm, sturdy body, I can't help but think that my present reality seems just as dark and hopeless as the dream, and I wish there were a way to wake from it too.

The next day begins with a task far more pleasant than planning funerals. Zack and I head over to the veterinary hospital to pick up Winston.

Ruby brings him out into the reception area, and the moment I see him up on his feet, walking and swishing his tail, I feel a ray of hope. Zack and I drop to our knees and greet him with hugs and kisses. He sniffs and licks our hands and faces and whimpers with emotion.

"Is Dr. Payne here?" I ask Ruby as I rise uncomfortably to my feet on legs that still ache from the accident. "I'd like to thank him."

"I'm sorry—he left to pick up his daughter from school. The poor little thing's sick. I shifted a few of his morning appointments around, so I don't expect to see him until this afternoon."

"I see," I reply. "Will you thank him for me when you see him?"

"I most certainly will."

Ruby hands me a sheet of paper with instructions about Winston's care over the next few days. Then she fastens a large plastic cone around his neck to prevent him from licking his incision. She also gives me pain pills for him and schedules a follow-up appointment for us to return in a week.

"Don't hesitate to call if you have any concerns or questions," Ruby says. "And I wrote Dr. Payne's personal cell phone number on that sheet of paper as well, just in case you need to call after hours. He explicitly asked me to do that."

"Thanks so much, Ruby. I can't tell you how grateful we are."

I reach under the cone, hook Winston's leash on to his collar, and hand it to Zack. A few minutes later, we are buckled into my mother's car with Winston in the back seat, heading home to her place for what I assume will be a quiet, somber day before the wake.

But I should know by now that life doesn't always go the way one expects.

CHAPTER THIRTEEN

My father-in-law, Lester Sedgewick, surprises all of us by arriving at my mother's house unannounced at lunchtime, when he said on the phone that he would see us at the wake. With him is Alan's older brother, Bruce, a car mechanic I've met a handful of times, and their stepmother, Verna, who is Lester's second wife. Lester married Verna ten months after Alan's mother passed away. According to Alan, she showed very little affection or compassion toward him or Bruce—two teenage boys who had just lost their mother and were in dire need of loving arms. To Verna, they were nothing but a couple of inconvenient add-ons she was forced to tolerate until they were old enough to move out on their own. As soon as Alan left home, that was it. She made no effort to keep in touch. He reciprocated in kind.

"My goodness. Hello." I invite them in and hug each of them in turn, because it's the proper thing to do. "It's good to see you. Thank you so much for coming."

While I say all the words one is expected to say in circumstances such as these, I try to hide the fact that I am sickened by the stench of stale cigarette smoke on their clothing.

Mom—who only met Lester and Verna once, at my wedding—walks out of the kitchen and greets them. "Hello. Welcome. I'm so sorry about Alan. We're all just devastated."

She hugs them as well, and we take everyone's coats.

"When did you arrive?" Mom asks as she opens the closet door and reaches for a hanger.

"We flew from Victoria yesterday," Lester replies in a deep, guttural voice as he glances around the foyer and peers into the living room. Without covering his mouth, he hacks out a phlegmy cough. "Lost four hours with the time difference. Now we're all jet-lagged."

"It's a long trip," I politely agree.

He didn't call to let us know where they will be staying, so I feel a twinge of unease about their expectations. We certainly don't have room here in my mother's house.

"Did you book into a hotel last night?" I ask as I hang up Verna's coat. Bruce insists on keeping his on.

"Yes, we did," Verna replies triumphantly. "Thought we'd make a vacation out of it, so we rented a car at the airport and drove straight to the casino hotel in Halifax. What a glitzy place! They had a minibar in the room, and Bruce won a hundred and sixty dollars at the slot machines. I'm telling you, we had a ball!"

"Lucky bastard," Lester adds with a chuckle under his breath, elbowing Bruce in the ribs and knocking him into the wall.

Bruce shoves him back. "Frig off."

I clear my throat and try to suppress my annoyance, because everyone seems to be missing the main point, which is that Alan is dead. And yet, here is his family, celebrating Bruce's winnings and their extravagant night in the hotel. It all feels terribly disrespectful.

"That's wonderful," I reply with sarcasm, which goes right over their heads. Part of me would like to hand their coats back to them and send them on their merry way, but they're Alan's family, and I don't want to cause a scene or stir up conflict, which is exactly what happened the last time we visited them in BC, ten years ago.

We had flown across the country so that Zack could meet his grandfather for the first time. Unfortunately—but not surprisingly—Lester was his usual bigoted self. He said some horrendous, insensitive things about a neighbor across the street, and since Alan was tired of letting things slide, he stood up to his father for the first time.

It was a loud, ugly argument that nearly became violent, but I was proud of my husband. We had originally planned to stay a full week. We returned home after three days.

Over the years, part of me always entertained the hope that Lester might reflect upon his behavior that day and turn over a new leaf or gain some wisdom with age. I also secretly dreamed that he and Alan might bury the hatchet, but it's too late for that now.

Nevertheless, Alan's wake is tomorrow night, and they flew thousands of miles to be here. I can't be inhospitable.

Suddenly, Verna seems to realize that one of them should say something about Alan. "We're so happy we could be here for the service," she mentions in a sober voice. "I can't imagine what you must be going through."

"Thank you. It's been a difficult few days." I invite them into the living room to sit down.

My mother joins us as well. "We're about to have lunch. Have you eaten yet?"

"Just breakfast at the hotel," Verna replies demurely as she squeezes her purse on her lap. "But we don't want to put you out."

"It's no trouble," Mom says. "The neighbors have been very generous, stopping by to deliver casseroles and all sorts of things. I have a pot of soup on the stove."

"What kind of soup is it?" Lester asks.

Mom blinks a few times. "It's beef and barley."

"All right then," Lester says with authority. "We'll take you up on your offer."

Mom manages a smile and returns to the kitchen, leaving me to sit with my in-laws.

Suddenly, I feel very tired. Normally, I would be quick to fill the silence with small talk, but at this moment, I don't care about making them feel welcome. Their tactless comments about their luck at the slot machines killed any chance of that. All I want to do is take a nap.

"So the wake is happening tomorrow night?" Verna prods.

"Yes, that's right," I reply. "Seven o'clock. I'll get you the address of the funeral home before you leave. Where are you staying?"

I hope that makes it clear that I don't intend to offer them accommodations here.

Verna smiles sweetly. "We just booked rooms at a charming B and B in town. This whole trip is turning out to be quite a treat! I feel like we're staying with the queen of England."

"A treat indeed," I reply flatly.

Verna inclines her head. "If only it could be under better circumstances." She points at my face. "Is that painful?"

"Not really," I say, touching a finger to my cheek. "My legs are a bit sore, though. I was trapped under the dash."

Lester slaps his knee, and I jump. I wonder if he's about to ask about Alan's accident, which I am fully prepared to discuss to the best of my knowledge, but he changes the subject. "Where's that grandson of mine? He must have grown at least a foot since I last saw him. What is he . . . fifteen, sixteen?"

"He's seventeen," I tell him. "He's a senior in high school now, and we're very proud of him." It hits me that I just said *we* when Alan is no longer here, and I have to force myself to push past that thought. "He's captain of the hockey team and president of the student council."

I'm not usually a mother who brags about her child, but I can't control myself. I want Lester to know what he's missed out on over the past decade—and what a wonderful father Alan was.

"Is that a fact?" Lester says. "Well? Where is he then? Too busy with hockey and school to greet his grandfather?"

I clear my throat and squeeze my hands together until my knuckles turn white. "He's in the basement," I say. "He wasn't expecting you to arrive until tomorrow. I'll go get him."

I rise from my chair and go downstairs, where I find Zack lying on the carpet in front of the television, reading on his phone, while Winston is stretched out beside him with the big plastic cone around his neck. At the sound of my approach, Winston sits up and thumps his tail.

"Hey there." I pick up the remote control to turn down the volume on the TV. "We have company. It's your grandpa Lester."

Zack lowers his phone and regards me with bafflement. "He's here now?"

"Yes. With his wife, Verna, and your uncle Bruce."

Zack's forehead crinkles. "Have I met Bruce before?"

"Once, briefly," I say, "when we visited them. You were only seven, so you probably don't remember. But you should come up and say hello. They're going to stay for lunch."

"Okay."

Zack moves to get up, and I wait until he is on his feet and facing me before I fill him in on the situation. "Listen . . . you know that your father wasn't close to his family, right?"

Zack nods at me.

"This is the first time you're going to meet them in person since you were little, and I just want to warn you—they can be a bit . . ." I struggle to find the right words. "They can be a bit insensitive sometimes, and I want you to be prepared. Don't take it personally if your grandfather says something rude. They're here for the funeral, and we just need to be polite, let the stupid things they say roll off our backs, and get through it."

Zack's eyebrows lift, and he seems strangely amused. "Sounds like it's going to be a time. Don't worry, Mom. I can handle them." He taps his thigh a few times. "Come on, Winston. Let's go upstairs and meet some people."

Winston gets up and lethargically climbs the stairs, while I say a silent prayer that everyone will behave.

CHAPTER FOURTEEN

"So this is the big man on campus I've been hearing so much about," Lester says as Zack enters the living room. "Look at you. You look just like your father when he was your age."

Lester stands up. He's a tall man, over six feet, with broad shoulders and a deep, booming voice that most people find intimidating. I suspect that's why he's always been able to get away with such bad behavior. People are afraid to stand up to him.

"Hi, Grandpa," Zack says.

"Well, don't just stand there. Are you shy? Come over here, and shake my hand like a man."

Zack gives me a brief look and crosses the room toward Lester, who grabs his hand, pumps it hard, and pulls him roughly into his arms for a bear hug. He ruffles his hair and says, "He's not so big and tough. Captain of the hockey team, eh? What's all that for? What are you trying to prove? You probably get checked into the boards every ten seconds. At least that'll toughen you up." He turns to me. "You watching him for concussions? They say hockey and football players are getting brain damage and can't play no more."

I stand motionless, staring at him in shock. "We're keeping an eye on things."

"I saw a movie about that," Bruce adds. "But I think it's a big pile of horseshit. It's just the drug companies trying to make money."

I shake my head. "I don't think that's the case, Bruce."

Lester punches Zack in the arm. "Do you have a girlfriend?"

"No," Zack replies with an uncomfortable chuckle, rubbing his arm.

"Why not? What's wrong with you? You don't like girls? You like boys instead?"

"No. I just haven't the met the right girl yet, I guess. I'm pretty busy."

"The right girl. Humph. You oughta be sowing those wild oats while you're young." Lester regards my son with a suspicious, sinister look that causes all the little hairs on the back of my neck to stand up.

I move forward to urge Zack away from Lester toward the chair on the opposite side of the room.

Meanwhile, Winston is standing in the doorway, his head hung low, panting heavily as he watches the exchange. His behavior concerns me because it's not normal for my boisterous golden retriever to remain in a doorway when we have guests. Normally he's a tireless social butterfly and always enjoys meeting new people. I wonder if it's the pain medication that's causing him to feel groggy. Or maybe he's sore, or self-conscious about the cone.

"What in the world is that thing?" Lester asks, turning his attention to Winston. "What did he do to himself?"

Feeling instantly protective, I move closer to my dog. "He was injured in the accident with me. He was thrown out the window, actually. He had surgery that night, and he's still recovering."

"Oh, poor baby," Verna says in a saccharine voice.

I stroke Winston's back and encourage him to lie down next to me as I take a seat in the chair.

"Your mother tells me you're involved in student government," Verna says politely to Zack.

Her tone is sweet as syrup, and there's a charming sparkle in her eye. For a moment, it's hard to believe she could ever have been a loveless stepmother when Alan was a boy, but I don't doubt the truth of what Alan told me. The syrup is clearly artificial.

Zack answers her question, and I'm proud of how well-spoken and respectful he is. He also talks about his plans to attend university after high school.

"That's a good way to rack up a whole lot of debt," Lester says contemptuously. Then he hacks and coughs into his fist. "But I suppose you can afford it with two rich doctors for parents."

"It's just one parent now." Zack lowers his gaze to his lap, and I give Lester a searing look because it kills me to see my son in pain, reminded of how he's missing his father and knowing he'll never see him again.

I sit and stroke Winston's smooth golden coat and pray that Lester won't stick his foot in it again. Which he probably will.

Mom—who I swear has some form of radar when a distraction is needed—enters and lets us know that lunch is served.

We all head into the kitchen, where I do my best to keep the conversation light over big, hearty bowls of beef and barley soup with warm rolls and butter.

I suggest a few restaurants my in-laws might enjoy for dinner, making it clear that I'll be busy preparing for the gathering at the funeral home and I want them out of my hair until then. Verna asks if there's anything she can do to help, but I assure her that I have everything under control and her presence at the wake is all that's required.

My mother serves apple pie for dessert, and when we're done, we all rise from the table. Verna thanks us repeatedly, but as we make our way to the door, Lester spots one of Winston's toys—a stuffed duck that quacks—on the floor next to his food bowl.

He bends forward and picks it up. "What's this now?"

He squeezes its belly to make it quack, then biffs it into the front hall. "Fetch, boy!"

Winston lifts his head, but his ears press back under the cone.

"What's wrong with ya?" Lester asks, stomping his foot repeatedly in front of Winston's nose. "Are you a wuss? Go get it. It's a duck!"

I squat beside Winston and stroke his shoulders. "No need to get up."

Again, Lester kicks at Winston's bed with the toe of his boot to try and rouse him. "Is he a dog or a pussy?"

Despite my vow to ignore certain misbehaviors today, I can't deny a heated surge of anger. I grab hold of the toe of Lester's boot and shove it away. He loses his balance and stumbles backward.

"He just had surgery," I explain.

Lester chuckles meanly. "You're his mommy, are you? I always figured that's why Alan married you. He loved being a mama's boy."

I rise to my feet, look Lester in the eye, and speak matter-of-factly. "You should probably go now."

Verna is quick to gloss over the altercation. "Thank you so much for lunch. The soup was delicious." She moves toward the door, tugging at Lester's sleeve.

Lester and Bruce stride into the foyer, and my mother moves quickly to retrieve their coats from the closet. Winston stands up, watching intently from the kitchen, where he pants as if he's just run himself to exhaustion.

"We'll see you at the funeral home tomorrow," I say, fighting the urge to shove Lester out of my mother's house like a bouncer.

As soon as I close the door behind them, I peer discreetly out the window. Verna is slapping Lester's arm and scolding him as they move down the walk to their rental car.

I turn to see Zack leaning against the kitchen doorjamb, shaking his head. "What an ass. No wonder Dad left home and moved across the country. I would have done the same thing if he was my father."

I pull Zack into my arms and hug him tight. "Thank goodness he wasn't. You were lucky to have such a great dad."

In that moment, I think of my own upbringing and how I, too, was blessed to have a happy, perfect childhood with two kind and loving parents who never said an unkind word. Suddenly, I miss Alan desperately. How will we get through the rest of our lives without him?

CHAPTER FIFTEEN

The following night, my body feels heavy and cumbersome, as if I'm sinking into an abyss—an impenetrable fog of exhaustion and trepidation. Tonight, I will view my beloved husband in an open casket. I'll no longer be able to imagine that this is just a bad dream. It will be painfully real for all of us.

My anxiety is amplified by the fact that Zack will see Alan in the casket as well and I'll feel my son's pain on top of my own. It's impossible not to worry about how this tragedy will affect the rest of Zack's life. Up until now, he's been a well-adjusted, optimistic young man. I don't want this loss to change him or break something inside of him, but I know I can't shield him from everything. His father is dead. We have no choice but to accept it and surrender to the fact that nothing will ever be the same again.

It's a terrible chore to stand in front of the mirror and put on makeup, because my eyes are burning, my legs feel sore and weak, and honestly, I couldn't care less about how pretty I look. I stare at myself and slap my cheeks a few times to pull myself out of the haze I'm in, and then I try to force myself to care, because Alan wouldn't want me to give up on myself. He would want me to stand proudly in the funeral home and be strong. Not just today but every day afterward.

When it's time to go, I leave my bedroom and slowly descend the stairs.

Mom drives Zack and me to the funeral home, while Carla, Braden, and their daughters follow in their minivan.

We arrive fifteen minutes early to pay our respects privately ahead of the other guests. Mom pulls over in a spot across the street from the funeral home, and we get out of the car together.

It's a clear night with a full moon and bright stars in the sky. Most of the ice and snow has melted.

I notice a woman walking out of the funeral home. She wipes tears from her cheeks as she hurries down the steps, then jogs down the street to her car, which is parked at the far end of the block.

I watch her for a moment with a frown, for there can be no mistaking her. It's Paula Sheridan, the hardware store owner who called Alan in the hospital on the night of his death. What is she doing here, and why is she so upset? Unless she was making arrangements for someone of her own that she may have lost . . .

Briefly, I'm tempted to call out her name, but I don't want to cause a ruckus. This whole situation is difficult enough as it is. I can't be thinking about Paula Sheridan now. I need to focus on what matters most: keeping Zack at my side and saying goodbye to Alan.

The evening passes in a blur. People come and go: doctors we've both worked with, patients who loved Alan, and friends, old and new. They all offer the same messages of sympathy and condolence. Nobody mentions that he was drinking and driving, and for that, I am grateful.

I shake their hands and thank them for coming.

Eventually, the visitors stop arriving, the room slowly clears, and it's time for Zack and me to say our final goodbyes. Zack moves forward and kneels before the open casket. Carla and my mother chat in hushed tones, but I'm not listening to them because my heart is breaking apart as I watch my son bid farewell to his father forever.

When he returns to me, his eyes are wet as he squeezes my hand. "It's your turn, Mom."

I nod, kiss him on the cheek, and slowly approach the casket. Alan looks peaceful, but perhaps that's not the right word, because there is very little left of the man I have loved for the past twenty years. That man is long gone from this body, and it's excruciating to see him this way—so devoid of life. Part of me wants to look away, to not see him like this. I want to remember him as he was. Yet I know I can't squander this time with him, because this is my last chance. As soon as I walk out that door, I'll never see my husband again.

My breath catches in my throat, and I kneel down to whisper words of love and to share memories of special times. Eventually, Carla lays her hand on my shoulder. "Abbie . . . it's time."

No. Not yet.

I blink hard over tears that burn my eyes and run my knuckles gently down Alan's cheek, but he's so cold. He can't feel the warmth of my touch. He's not here anymore.

My hands shake, and my body trembles as I force myself to rise and step back. The whole experience leaves me weak and depleted. I have to fight to keep my emotions under control as we walk out the door—at least until I can return to my mother's house, shut my bedroom door, and allow myself to fall apart completely.

I rise at dawn the following day before anyone wakes, having slept very little through the night. Only Winston is at my side in the kitchen, with the plastic cone still fastened around his neck. He rests quietly on his bed in the corner by the table.

As I make a pot of coffee, I try to prepare myself for the church service and burial that afternoon. I just need to get through it, and then everything, I pray, will get easier.

Winston rises from his cushion and ambles to his food bowl by the back door. I realize it's empty, so I get up from my chair to fill it.

"How are you doing, by the way?" I ask as the kibbles clank into the stainless-steel bowl.

He drinks some water but doesn't have much of an appetite, so he simply follows me back to the table, where I sit down to finish my coffee. He stares at me with those big brown eyes, looking concerned.

I set down my mug. "I know. You can see that I'm upset, and there's nothing you can do about it. And you don't like wearing that silly collar. I wouldn't like it either. But don't worry. You won't have to wear it forever. Just a few more days."

He lies down and rests his chin on his paws, and I understand that it's more than just the plastic cone around his neck or a headache or pain from the surgery that's causing him to look so depressed. Somehow, he knows we're all suffering, and he's feeling it too. He's wondering where the fourth member of our pack has gone and why he's not here.

Paula Sheridan makes a sudden appearance in my mind. I realize that I was so exhausted after I returned home last night that I hadn't given any more thought to her tearful presence at the wake.

I'm still curious about why she was there. Alan was just a customer, so I don't see why she would be so upset.

Unless she knew Alan better than she let on . . .

I raise my coffee cup to my lips and think about the obvious implications of that, and then I shake my head at myself. *Stop it, Abbie. That's just crazy.*

Nevertheless, I can't help but wonder if Paula will be at the funeral service today. If she comes, will she bring her husband and stay for the reception in the church hall afterward?

I hope so, because if she tries to sneak in unnoticed like she did at the wake, I'm going to consider that to be very strange and suspicious behavior, and I can't handle strange and suspicious right now. There are enough unanswered questions on my mind, like why my husband was driving drunk on the night he died. I'm still craving an explanation for that, and the question won't leave me alone.

CHAPTER SIXTEEN

As it turns out, Paula attends Alan's funeral service, but just as I feared she might, she arrives at the last minute, sits at the back of the church—without her husband—and disappears before the organist begins to play the recessional.

Later, at the cemetery, as Alan's casket is lowered into the ground, I spot her watching from a distance, high up on the hill. Only family members have been invited to attend the burial, so I'm acutely aware of her presence while the minister reads from the prayer book.

Afterward, as we slowly make our way back to our cars, I glance toward the crest of the hill, but Paula has disappeared again. I can't help but wonder if she thinks I haven't noticed her lurking around during these times of heightened grief.

By now, I'm quite certain that she wants to be seen and she wants me to reach out to her, but I don't know why, and I don't want to suspect the obvious—that she knew my husband in an intimate way. It could be something else entirely.

Either way, my family has been through enough. We've had to deal with the press asking questions about whether Alan had a serious drinking problem and if he'd ever lost a patient under suspicious circumstances. Of course, I will continue to deny those accusations because Alan was an excellent heart surgeon, the very best in the city. I never saw him drink excessively, and certainly not a single drop when he was headed for the OR. He would have lost his license ages ago if he had done something like that.

But clearly I didn't know everything about Alan, because I have no idea why he was drunk on the road that night, nor was I aware of his connection to Paula Sheridan and the possibility of a friendship—or something more. My poor broken heart is demanding answers, and I know I'm not going to be able to simply let it go.

"It was a lovely service," Verna says to me as we reach our vehicles. She touches my arm, and suddenly I find myself wanting to lay aside my frustrations from the previous day when Lester behaved so atrociously.

This is Alan's family. They traveled a long way to be here. I should be mindful of that, and I don't want to harbor any ill will. Not today.

"Thank you, Verna," I say. "Would you like to come back to the house? We're just going to sit around and talk about happy times."

"That would be lovely," she replies. "I'll tell Lester, and we'll see you soon."

As she speaks my father-in-law's name, I wonder if I've made a mistake, but I quickly shake the worry away. Lester is Alan's father. Though he's an insensitive brute most of the time, I can't imagine that he's not grieving in his own way today, especially because of how he and Alan parted ten years ago. I suspect Lester must have *some* regrets that he keeps buried under the surface.

"We'll see you soon," I say to Verna as I get into my mother's car, feeling proud of myself for taking the high road today.

"Do you have anything decent to drink around here?" Lester asks the second we've walked through the door of my mother's house.

I glance up at him as I remove my coat. "I'm not sure. What would you like? We have wine and beer."

"No, not *that*," he replies as if I'm stupid. "Do you have any rum? Vodka? Gin?"

I feel my blood pressure rising, but I swallow hard and work to find my inner Zen. "I'm not sure. Let me check and see what Mom has in her cupboards."

Soon, I'm in the dining room on my knees, rifling through the china cabinet, where I find half a bottle of Drambuie and a full, unopened bottle of Canadian Club whiskey.

"Perfect!" Lester says, snatching both bottles from my hands. "We can make a mean Rusty Nail with these. Got any ice?"

"In the freezer." I point toward the kitchen and stand slowly, grimacing at the ache in my legs. Lester doesn't stick around to help me up, and I wonder why I'm so conscientious about being a good hostess when he has no qualms about being a terrible guest.

An hour later, he's a third of the way into the bottle of whiskey, the Drambuie is gone, and he's getting loud. I feel badly for my sister's husband, Braden, who's stuck in the kitchen with him and Bruce, listening to Lester rant about the Toronto Blue Jays. I suspect Braden is sacrificing himself just to keep Lester and Bruce out of the living room, where the women are sitting quietly with the children and Zack, talking about Alan and sipping tea.

When the sun goes down, I'm ready to call it a day. I turn to Verna and drop a few hints.

"It's been a long day," I say. "I'm ready to fall into bed."

A rowdy burst of laughter erupts from the kitchen.

Verna chuckles. "Oh, listen to those boys out there. I'm glad they're having a good time."

A good time. Sure. Let's party all night instead of remembering the man who was just lowered into the ground.

Zack, still dressed in his navy blazer and gray dress slacks, sits forward, rests his elbows on his knees, and weaves his fingers together, squeezing them tight. A muscle twitches at his jaw, and he gives me a look.

I know exactly what he's thinking—that this is a blatant show of disrespect for his father on the day of his funeral.

Winston, who is lying on the floor next to Zack, sits up and stares at me as if he can read my mind. His mouth falls open, and he begins to pant.

I nod at my son, and we share an unspoken communication. Then I turn to Verna. "I think it's probably time to say good night."

She blinks a few times. "Oh. Yes. I see." Setting her china teacup on the saucer with a noisy clink, she rises to her feet.

It's clear that I've offended her, but I don't care because Lester has been offending the entire household all afternoon with his heavy drinking and disrespect for the solemnity of the occasion. Not once has he mentioned Alan or expressed any grief or words of condolence. I don't understand why he even came. Did he think this would be a rip-roaring good time?

From the kitchen, Lester shouts the f-word in a string of angry complaints about another sports team. His deep, booming profanity causes a jolt in my body. Carla glances uneasily at her girls, who snuggle close to her on the sofa. Her youngest daughter buries her face in Carla's lap.

Zack exhales sharply. "That's it. Party's over." He stands up and leaves the room. My heart races, and I leap to my feet to follow him.

Winston follows too.

"Hey, Gramps," Zack says. "I think it's time we call it a night. We're all pretty tired."

"What do you mean, tired?" Lester shouts back at him. "The party's just getting started, boy. Go back to the living room with the ladies. Sip some tea and talk about . . ." He waves his hand dismissively through the air, wiggling his thick, stubby fingers. "Frilly things."

After everything we've all been through over the past few days, my patience is stretched to the limit, and Lester's cruel words directed at my son spark a mother's fury in me. I move fully into the kitchen to stand beside Zack. "Lester. It's been a hard day. The party's over."

Winston senses my anger and takes a stance between Lester and me, his front legs set wide apart, like a fierce guardian.

"What . . . ? Are you going to sic your crippled dog on me?" Lester asks.

"If I have to," I reply, feeling my cheeks burn. "Please, just go. Zack's right. We're all beat."

He glares at me for a few tense seconds, and I'm aware of Braden pushing away from the counter, removing his hands from his pockets while Bruce just stands there, watching in silence.

"Abbie's right," Braden says. "We should call it a night. What time is your flight tomorrow?" he asks Lester, in an obvious effort to calm rising tempers by changing the subject. I pray it will work, because I swear I'm about to lose it.

"We ain't flying out tomorrow," Lester replies. He drains the whiskey from his glass in a single gulp and slams it onto the countertop. "We fly on Thursday. But we won't be staying in this waster of a town. We'll be checking out first thing in the morning and going back to the casino, because we know when we're not welcome."

I'm fighting hard to stay calm and maintain my cool, but I feel my blood pressure rising and all my muscles tightening.

Lester staggers heavily toward me. Winston blocks him and begins to bark. I grab hold of Winston's collar to restrain him and move out of the way so that Lester can leave the kitchen and get the hell out of my house, but as he passes, he bodychecks Zack into the wall and says, "You're a little wuss. Just like your father."

A blaze of fury explodes in my blood, and all I see is red.

"Hey!" I shout, shoving Lester hard in return so he falls backward into the refrigerator. Braden moves quickly to help Zack regain his balance and get between Lester and me, and I wonder if I'm nuts to get into a physical scuffle with a man twice my size.

By now, Winston is barking madly, and it's chaos in the kitchen, but I don't care. I can't rein in my emotions anymore. The floodgates break open, and every last sour bit of my bile toward this man comes pouring out in a torrent of rage.

"How dare you speak to my son like that! You should be ashamed of yourself! And now that Alan's gone, I'll say what he always thought but was too polite to say to your face: you were a terrible father, and he couldn't stand to be around you. That's why he moved across the country—to get away from you. You're a mean, despicable bully, and I want you out of my house right now. I don't ever want to see you again."

Lester says nothing. He simply stares at me in shock, then storms out of the kitchen to the foyer. "Come on, Verna. We're leaving. Get your coat."

She scrambles from the sofa while my mother watches all of this with her mouth agape.

Carla's daughters begin to cry. She hugs them close.

No one says a word while Lester, Verna, and Bruce pull on their coats and walk out the door. As soon as they're gone, I rush forward, slam the door behind them, and lock it.

"I'm so sorry," I say to Zack, turning quickly. "I can't believe that just happened. I totally lost it."

I realize my hands are shaking.

"You did great," Zack says.

"He's always been like that," I try to explain. "Mean and crude. He's a monster, and he likes to hurt people because he thinks so little of himself. Your dad always said so. He needs to belittle others to build himself up."

"I know," Zack says. "And I'm not a wuss. Neither was Dad."

"Of course you're not. Your grandfather's a jerk, and we're never going to see him again. I'm so sorry I invited him here. I was stupid, thinking he'd be a nicer person today, just this once. I wanted to give him a chance, but he's still as rotten to the core as he ever was."

Zack shakes his head in disbelief. "I don't blame Dad for leaving home when he did. And if I ever see Lester again . . ." He gives me a dark look. "Let's just hope I don't."

All I can do is nod my head and pull him into my embrace.

I'm not normally a vengeful person, but in that moment, I wish terrible things on my father-in-law. If this had been *his* funeral today, I would hope that he'd be rotting in hell tonight and for the rest of eternity.

That night, it's not easy to relax and go to sleep. I toss and turn for hours, keeping Winston awake too, because he's curled up at the foot of my bed.

I spend quite a bit of time thinking about our altercation with Lester and all the unspeakable things he said. How was it possible that Alan turned out to be such a good father with a man like that as a role model for parenthood? How did Alan rise above it?

I roll onto my side and stare at the curtains over the window, thinking about how much I'm going to miss Alan's tenderness and how loving he was as a husband—the complete opposite of Lester. When I was pregnant with Zack, I suffered terrible morning sickness, but bless his sweet heart . . . Alan got out of bed at dawn each day to bring me crackers to eat before I rose.

I remember once when I was sick, he stood outside the bathroom door, knocking gently and asking if I was okay and if I needed anything.

Eventually he came in, picked me up off the bathroom floor, and carried me back to bed. He set me down, pulled the covers up to my shoulders, kissed me on the forehead, and called one of my colleagues to get him to cover for me in the OR that day.

Months later, my difficult pregnancy came to a head when Alan was forced to watch helplessly as I fell unconscious in the delivery room and nearly bled to death in front of his eyes. I suppose he wasn't accustomed to feeling helpless in situations like that, but this was different. I was his wife, and he wasn't permitted into the OR when they rushed me away. He waited hours while the doctors fought to save my life, and it was a close call. I was very lucky.

I remember waking up in the recovery room. He was there at my side, weeping.

"I don't know what I'd do if I ever lost you," he said.

"You won't lose me."

"You don't know that, Abbie. Anything can happen. I was so scared when they took you away."

I promised him that day that I would never leave him, and he held on to me desperately.

The memory causes my eyes to fill with tears, and I cry softly in the darkness. Winston lifts his head, moves closer, and licks the salty teardrops from my cheeks. It tickles, and I can't help but laugh at the sensation. I stroke his neck, and he settles back down at the foot of the bed.

As I recover myself, my thoughts of Alan merge into another lane. Soon, I'm thinking about the accident, and I find myself going over every word of my telephone conversation with Paula Sheridan in the hospital. I think about her hasty departure from the funeral home before anyone else arrived, and how she stood on the hilltop at the cemetery, watching Alan's burial from a distance.

My stomach does a series of flips and cartwheels because I hate being in the dark. I need to understand what's been going on.

Tossing the covers aside, I rise from bed and pad downstairs to grab my purse from the bench in the foyer. While Winston watches me from the top of the stairs, I rifle through the contents, finally locating Alan's cell phone at the bottom. I try to switch it on, but the battery's dead, so I carry it upstairs and plug it into the wall with the cord I've been using to charge my own phone.

It's torture to wait for his phone to power up, so I climb onto the bed with my back against the pillows, hugging my knees to my chest, tapping the pad of my thumb against my thigh, and feeling a twinge of guilt over what I'm about to do—snoop through his phone contacts and messages when he's not here to explain himself. Winston jumps up as well and waits patiently beside me with his chin on his front paws, the big plastic cone like a clown collar around his neck.

At last I hear the familiar chime from Alan's phone. I pick it up and search through his contacts, but Paula's name isn't listed anywhere, and there are no emails under her name either. All I have is the number she called from when I was at the hospital. I look it up, and it's not the number for Handy Hardware, but that doesn't tell me much. She may have been using her own phone to make calls to customers. I check the call history, and there are no other calls from that number, except for one earlier in the day. If there was ever any other communication between them, Alan deleted everything.

Suddenly I feel paranoid and ridiculous. *Get a grip, Abbie. Why would Alan be deleting texts and emails from the owner of the hardware store? Because you actually think there was something going on between them? Seriously?*

It's nearly four in the morning, and I know there will be no answers tonight, but I can't go on like this. I need to understand why Paula attended Alan's funeral. If she has some secret connection to him, she might be the one person who knows why he was drinking that night and driving in the opposite direction from where he was supposed to be going. I take a few deep breaths, then begin to type a text message to her from Alan's phone.

> Hi Paula. This is Abbie MacIntyre. I noticed you at the funeral home the other night and again at the cemetery today. Could we get together for a coffee and talk?

I press "Send," then slide back under the covers, hug the pillow against my cheek, and wait for morning.

CHAPTER SEVENTEEN

Alan's phone chimes at 7:00 a.m.

Winston lifts his head, stands up on the bed, and wags his tail. I wonder if he associates the distinctive notification tone with Alan and hopes that he's coming home.

Still groggy and bleary-eyed from sleep—because I haven't gotten much of it over the past few nights—I reach clumsily for the phone and swipe the screen.

To my relief, a text has come in, and it's from Paula.

I immediately tap the little yellow-and-white icon.

Hi, Abbie. I'm so sorry for your loss. I know it must be difficult, but I don't think I can be of much help. The best thing you can do right now is take time to grieve. I wish you all the best.

I shake my head in disbelief. "I beg your pardon?"

I can't help but feel indignant because Paula's text reads like the biggest brush-off of the century.

I glance at Winston, whose tongue is hanging out while he pants. I think he's expecting me to tell him that Daddy will be home at any minute. A lump forms in my throat.

"I'm sorry. He's not coming home today."

Winston lies down again, and I sense his melancholy. I try not to sink into an even deeper pit of despair.

Returning my attention to Paula's text, I decide that I simply can't let it go. I begin to type a reply.

> Hi again. Believe me, I am grieving, but I also need to understand the details around my husband's death. Could we please get together for coffee this morning?

Moments pass, slow as cold molasses. Eventually, I force myself to set the phone on the bedside table and scratch behind Winston's ears. Otherwise I'll go mad.

It's a challenge to get my fingers under the plastic cone, but Winston seems especially grateful for the attention. He bows his head and nuzzles my hand, demanding a more aggressive scratch, like Alan used to give him.

I try my best, but I know it's not the same. It'll never be the same. The phone chimes. I scramble to reach for it.

> I'm sorry, Abbie. I really don't think there's anything I can do for you. I knew your husband from the store, and I felt an affinity because I remember you from high school, but I don't know anything more than that. Who knows why things happen the way they do? Sometimes there's no rhyme or reason. Again, my deepest condolences. Please take care of yourself. And the next time we bump into each other, I hope it's under better circumstances.

I finish reading and feel a surge of anger from deep in my core because all my instincts are telling me that she's hiding something. I toss the phone onto the bed, then sit forward and scratch behind Winston's ears again until my temper cools.

"Maybe I'm just having a hard time accepting this," I say to Winston. "Or maybe the accident knocked my brain out of whack."

I realize that I never returned for a follow-up checkup with Dr. Sanders, and that's something I definitely need to do.

I set up an appointment to see Dr. Sanders that morning. He asks me all the usual questions to assess a head injury, examines the abrasion on my scalp, and concludes that I'm doing fine, all things considered. He asks how I've been feeling overall. I confess that I've been excessively fatigued at times and that I find it difficult to stay awake but I can't get a good night's sleep either.

He says that's to be expected, given what I've been through. He advises me to get as much rest as I need and not to feel guilty about taking a short nap in the afternoon if that helps.

I thank him, leave the hospital, and return to my mother's car, where I get into the driver's seat and grip the steering wheel with both hands. I stare straight ahead like a robot, barely blinking, because my cuts and bruises may be healing, but I'm a widow now—a widow who can't escape the feeling that her husband may have been keeping secrets.

A sickening knot of dread forms in my belly as I contemplate this new reality, full of doubts about our relationship. And it's not just that. He's gone now. From this day forward, there will be nothing but an empty pillow beside me when I wake in the mornings. Alan won't be around to book family vacations for us or fix the internet when the Wi-Fi kicks me off. I'm a complete numbskull when it comes to technology. He was always there to take care of those things and so many others.

And what about growing old? I'd always imagined we'd take care of each other when the aging process began and the inevitable health problems descended upon us—like hearing loss and not being able to see the tiny print on the pill bottles in the cupboard. Knowing us, we would have joked about it and made fun of each other. Just like my mom, we would never have surrendered our sense of humor.

But now, I'll have to read the pill bottles myself and always keep a magnifying glass handy. There will be no one to make fun of me and make me laugh when I'm eighty and can't find my teeth.

Suddenly I burst into tears, and I realize it's the first time I've had complete privacy to sob openly, without constraint, where no one can hear me. The flood is torrential—a massive tsunami of grief and rage. I scream and cry and pound the steering wheel over and over.

Why, Alan? Why were you on the road that night, and what in the world were you up to?

Five minutes later, I'm driving to the hardware store because I've made up my mind to talk to Paula. I can't begin to move forward until I do, and I need for her to understand that.

I drive all the way across town, thinking nonstop about what I'll say to her when I arrive. My blood is fired with adrenaline because this time I'm determined not to take no for an answer. I'm going to demand that she explain why she snuck into the funeral home before the wake began and why she was skulking around the cemetery during the burial.

When I reach the store, I pull into the parking lot, find a spot, and shut off the engine.

For a few seconds, I hesitate, because I feel like a woman obsessed, but I know that if I don't see this through, I'll lie awake again tonight—and every night for the rest of my life—tossing and turning until dawn, wondering what the hell really happened to my husband that night.

I unbuckle my seat belt and walk into the store.

"I'm sorry. She isn't in today," the young clerk at the customer service desk tells me. "She's home sick."

My head throbs, and I rub at the back of my neck. This feels very anticlimactic, and I want to grit my teeth together and scream. But it's not this young girl's fault, so I fight to keep it together. "I see. Thank you."

Taking a few deep breaths, I walk out of the store and try calling Paula's cell phone as I cross the parking lot. She doesn't answer, and I can't help but suspect that she's ignoring my calls. I suppose I shouldn't be surprised. I'm being a pain in the ass.

When I reach my car, I get in and sit for a while, watching customers come and go.

Maybe I *am* going crazy. Maybe there was a perfectly reasonable explanation for why Alan was driving under the influence. Maybe there was some sort of medical emergency, and he had to make a choice.

If so, what was the emergency? And did it have anything to do with Paula? Was that why she called him on a Sunday night, hours after the store had closed? On her personal cell phone?

Had she even been at the store?

I blow my nose, pick up my cell phone again, and google Paula's home address.

It's kind of scary how easy it is to find out where a person lives. It's even scarier that I've been moved to do what I'm doing.

A few minutes later, I'm driving up her street like some sort of stalker.

CHAPTER EIGHTEEN

I get out of my car, sling my purse over my shoulder, and gaze up at the house where Paula lives with her husband. It's a modest split-level home with pale-blue vinyl siding, located in a small subdivision on the edge of town.

For a brief moment, I consider changing my mind and going straight home, but I decide to bite the bullet. I walk up the steps and ring the front doorbell.

A pretty young woman answers. She has blonde hair and appears to be in her early twenties.

"Yes?" she asks but balks slightly at my appearance. Suddenly I remember that my face is still black and blue and my eyes are no doubt puffy from crying. On top of that, I'm dressed in baggy gray sweatpants, sneakers, and an ugly parka. I probably look like a homeless person, which is not like me at all. I usually make an effort when it comes to my appearance. I wear makeup and do my hair and dress fashionably—but I suppose I've been knocked around a bit lately. Looking put together isn't at the top of my priority list.

"Hi," I say in a warm and friendly tone, hoping to put her at ease. "I'm looking for Paula Sheridan. Is this where she lives?"

"Yeah, she's my stepmom," the girl replies with some apprehension. "But she's not here right now. She's at the store."

I feel my eyebrows pull together in a frown, and I'm immediately suspicious. "I just went there looking for her, and they said she was at home today. That she was sick."

The girl shrugs a shoulder. "Maybe the clerk got it wrong, because she's not here."

I can't very well push my way past her and search the house, so I simply thank her and turn to go.

She stops me. "Would you like to try her cell phone?"

I face her again. "I already did, but she didn't answer. I'll try again later. Thanks."

She shuts the door, and I walk down the cement path but stop halfway when I hear the door open again.

"Abbie MacIntyre?"

I immediately turn and look up.

An older man steps outside. He looks to be in his midfifties. He's handsome, trim, and fit, dressed in jeans and a blue wool pullover. I realize how pathetic I must appear with my bruised face and unwashed hair.

"Yes," I reply.

He regards me coolly. "I'm Paula's husband, Michael. I'm sorry about your loss. I saw it on the news. Paula says she went to high school with you?"

"That's right."

He takes another step forward. "Well . . . she showed me your texts, and I'm not sure what to say. I'm sorry for what you're going through, but I'm not sure why you think Paula can help you."

"I'm not sure either," I hear myself replying.

He studies my face for a moment. "You should know that Paula felt badly, because your husband was a regular customer at the store. She said he was always very nice. It's a terrible thing that happened, but . . . you need to find a way to move forward that doesn't involve my wife."

We stand in silence for a brief moment, and I wonder if he thinks I'm a nutcase. I feel like one at the moment.

"If you could just tell Paula that I came by . . ." I begin to back away. "I'd appreciate it."

"I will," he says. "Take care. And again, I'm sorry for your loss."

Paula's husband disappears inside, while I hurry to my mother's car, wondering if I'm not behaving rationally. Maybe he's right. Maybe I just need to accept Alan's death as a freak accident and try to begin the healing process. Maybe I need to take a step back and focus on what I have left.

When I arrive back at the house, Zack and the girls are in the basement watching a movie, and Mom is upstairs napping. I ask Carla if she'll come for a drive with me because I need to get a lot of stuff off my chest. My sister takes one look at me, sees that I've been crying, and grabs her coat.

"Why didn't you tell me about Paula before?" she asks a few minutes later as we leave town, heading toward the highway because, for some reason I can't explain, I need to see the place where Alan and I collided with each other. I'm desperate for clarity, and I don't know where else to look for it.

Carla is behind the wheel. Not me.

"I'm not sure," I reply. "All I know is that Paula has been floating around since the moment Alan landed in the ER, and I have a weird feeling about it because it doesn't make sense to me—that a store manager would care so much about the death of a customer she claims she barely knew. And why won't she talk to me?" I pause. "I keep thinking about all the things Lester said . . . about encouraging Zack to sow his wild oats and get around. Is that how he raised Alan? Did he make it seem like he needed to prove his manhood that way?" I meet Carla's gaze directly. "Or maybe I'm looking for answers where there are none. Maybe I'm paranoid and irrational. Or not. What if there *was* something going on between Alan and Paula?"

"Oh, Sis." Carla's tone is sympathetic. "Don't let Lester do that to you. He's a mean-spirited jerk. You've always known that."

"I do, but . . ." I turn to her. "Do you think there could be any truth to this? Could there have been a side to Alan I didn't know? A side that Lester created?"

Carla lets out a laugh of disbelief. "You were happily married for twenty years. If Alan was having an affair, there's no way you wouldn't have suspected it. But you didn't, because it's not true. I think you're just trying to deflect the pain you're feeling."

I continue to stare out the window, feeling suddenly unsure of everything.

"Maybe I *did* suspect something was off," I say with a small shrug of defeat.

Carla's gaze shoots to my face. She flicks the blinker and pulls onto the shoulder of the road, shuts off the engine, and faces me.

"What are you talking about?"

I take a deep breath. "I never told anyone this, but sometimes lately I worried that . . . that he wasn't attracted to me anymore."

"What made you think that?"

I exhale heavily. "What can I say? We were married for two decades. The honeymoon phase was long over."

"But you *were* making love, right?" Carla asks.

I glance out the window and force myself to answer the question. "Over the past few years, not very often. We used to do it more, but we both got so busy with our call schedules, working late in the OR. By the time we finally fell into bed, we were exhausted. At least I was. I only felt guilty about it once in a while, whenever I realized how much time had gone by since the last time we'd been physical. Then I'd get my act together, plan a romantic date night, or we'd go for an overnight getaway somewhere."

I feel suddenly defensive. "But he never complained. He told me he loved me all the time."

She studies me carefully, and I find myself rambling. "It wasn't *always* like that. The first few years were very passionate. I guess things started to change after Zack was born. But that's normal, right? Having a baby is like throwing a hand grenade into the romance department."

"I won't argue there," Carla replies. "It's not easy to feel sexy when you're up to your elbows in dirty diapers and you're sleep-deprived all the time. All you want to do is collapse. I think every mother knows that feeling."

And yet I can't help but feel that with Alan and me it was far more complicated than that—that there were other issues at play. I remember waking up in the recovery room after I'd hemorrhaged on the delivery table while giving birth to Zack. I'd never seen Alan weep like that. Not ever. Not before or since, and nothing was quite the same after that.

"Sometimes, when Zack was little," I tell Carla, "I would catch Alan staring off into space, and I'd ask him if everything was okay, and he'd snap out of it and give me a kiss, look me straight in the eye, and tell me that everything was perfect. We both knew how close I'd come to dying when Zack was born, and sometimes I felt like a part of him had pulled away from me a little."

"Did you ever talk to him about it?"

"We did, that first year after Zack was born. He often told me how grateful he was that we both survived. He'd get emotional about it. But then we moved on because it was painful to talk about." I pause, reflecting on some of the conversations we'd had. "A few times we discussed adopting a second child because we'd always intended to have two or three, and I wanted a sibling for Zack, but Alan was just so thankful for what we had. He didn't want to upset the perfect balance. It was almost as if he felt like it would be greedy to ask for more. He would say, 'Do you know how lucky we are? Let's not tempt fate.'"

I look down at my lap. "I wish it could have been simpler. I wish I'd been able to get pregnant again and that it could have gone smoothly the second time around."

Carla reaches for my hand. "At least you had Zack, and he's an amazing kid. And we were *all* lucky you survived that day. As for Alan, I know he loved you and Zack. He was a good man. I think you're just upset and confused because of what happened. Your whole world has just been turned upside down. You're traumatized."

"Maybe you're right."

We sit for another few minutes. Then Carla pulls onto the road, and we continue toward the accident site.

We reach the main highway and drive for about a mile before I ask Carla to slow down. I peer out the window and search for the spot at the edge of the forest where my SUV landed after rolling down the embankment.

Nothing looks the same in the daylight, but soon I catch a glimpse of skid marks on the pavement and bits of metal and glass on the shoulder. A rush of panic shoots through me as I relive the crash—the terrifying instant when Alan's car struck mine. I feel the total loss of control as I fishtail on the pavement and can't right the steering wheel. I tumble down the embankment. Glass smashes. Steel collapses. The noise is deafening, and I can't stop the world from spinning . . .

I have to wrench myself out of the horrific memory, and I wonder how long it will be before I won't feel nervous in a car on the highway.

"This is it," I say, fighting to take a few deep breaths, to slow my pounding heart. "Can we stop?"

Carla checks the rearview mirror and carefully pulls over. She shuts off the engine.

We both get out. I leave the car door open as I look down the embankment to the rocky bottom, where I had been trapped in my SUV.

"Lord Almighty," Carla says as she puts her arm around my shoulder and pulls me close. "You're lucky to be alive."

"Yes. Me and Winston both."

We continue to stare.

"Should we go down there?" I ask.

"Why?"

"I don't know. I feel like I need to search around. Maybe some of my stuff is down there. I never did find my sunglasses."

But do I really care about my sunglasses? What I truly want is clarity. Would I find it by wandering around in the ravine? Probably not.

"It looks dangerous," Carla says.

Just then, a cell phone chimes from inside the car. I recognize the sound. It's Alan's phone.

My pulse quickens, because every time I hear it, I think it's him and I feel a nonsensical thrill that he's back. But the feeling only lasts for a fraction of a second, and then disappointment comes crashing down as I remember that he's dead and he'll never send texts to me again.

Nevertheless, I move quickly to check the phone. I dig it out of my purse and swipe the screen.

"It's Paula." My blood races as I read her message. "She's changed her mind. She wants to talk to me."

Carla's forehead crinkles. "Really? When?"

"Right now. She wants to meet for a drink."

My heart begins to pound faster and harder.

"What are you going to do?" Carla asks.

"Say yes, of course."

Immediately, I text a reply.

I hit "Send" without hesitation and hope that the memory of my happy marriage isn't about to be shattered as easily as everything else was when Alan and I crashed into each other.

CHAPTER NINETEEN

It's the middle of the afternoon.

Paula asked me to meet her in a bar in the neighboring town of Bridgewater, about a twenty-minute drive from my mother's house in Lunenburg. This leaves me a brief window of time to go home and change my clothes and explain to Zack that I'm heading out to meet an old friend who also knew Alan.

A half hour later, I arrive at a sketchy-looking tavern on the outskirts of town. At first, I'm not sure I'm in the right place because it's situated at the back of a large parking lot in an industrial area. The sign reads PAT'S PLACE, and the building is painted black, including the windows. There are only a few cars parked around back—a couple of rusty old clunkers and a pickup truck. I feel a bit like Alice about to fall down the rabbit hole.

After a moment's deliberation, I decide to take my chances. I get out of the car, approach the front door, and walk in.

Based on my first impression of the exterior, the inside is exactly as I imagined it would be. It's dingy and dimly lit, with low ceilings, fake wood paneling, and a pool table. There's a noticeable stench of stale beer in the air.

My breathing accelerates, and I break out in a sweat, because I'm not the sort of person who frequents dive bars like this, especially not alone. At least there's no rowdy biker gang in here this afternoon.

There are only a few patrons at the bar—weathered-looking old men, sitting forward with their hands cupped around mugs of beer. They sit apart from each other, watching an old box TV with a snowy picture. It sits on a shelf behind the bartender, who wears a tight, dirty gray T-shirt that barely covers his bulging belly.

Swallowing uneasily—and still not entirely sure I'm in the right place—I move beyond the entrance. My feet stick to the floor. Every step sounds like Velcro.

In that moment, I decide I'll do whatever it takes *not* to have to use the washroom while I'm here.

I don't see Paula anywhere, but there are a few tables around a back corner, so I venture deeper into the shadows. At last, I find her alone at a table near the washrooms, surrounded by empty wineglasses. Her head has fallen forward onto her arms on the table. She appears to be asleep. Or passed out.

I clear my throat.

Slowly, she lifts her head and meets my gaze with bloodshot eyes and smeared mascara. "Abbie. What are you doing here?"

"You texted me and told me to come."

Seconds pass while she blinks up at me, struggling to comprehend my words. "Did I?"

"Yes."

She wets her lips and leans back in the chair. "I shouldn't have done that."

"Well, you did, and here I am."

Sitting down on a rickety chair across from her, I clutch my purse on my lap. The bartender walks by and pushes through the door to the men's washroom. A terrible odor wafts out as the door swings shut, and I press the back of my hand to my nose to keep from gagging.

"Do you often come here?" I ask, because I still can't believe she chose this place for us to meet.

Paula can barely hold her head up. It's obvious that she's drunk. "I know . . . it's pathetic, but it's the only place where I'm sure I won't bump into anyone I know."

Paula reaches for her wineglass, tips it back, and swallows the entire contents in a single gulp.

I shake my head at her. "You're not planning on driving anywhere, I hope."

"Definitely not." She sets the glass down, slides it away, and burps like a trucker, then glances toward the bar. "Where did he go? I need another one."

The doctor in me can't help but try and talk some sense into her. "If you keep this up, you're going to be sick, or worse. I'm sure you know that people die of alcohol poisoning. You should drink some water."

Her glassy-eyed gaze meets mine, and she merely shrugs.

I notice her clammy skin and greasy honey-colored hair. I doubt she's showered since the night I saw her at the funeral home. Nevertheless, despite her poor personal hygiene, she's still a naturally beautiful woman with a dewy complexion and big blue eyes—the type who doesn't need makeup. Personally, I have to work at my appearance, and this contrast makes my insides squeeze like a fist.

"Where's your car?" I ask, remembering the clunkers I saw in the parking lot.

She gestures inelegantly. "That way."

"You'll have to leave it, wherever it is. I'll take you home. We can talk while we drive."

She shakes her head. "No. I'm not going home."

"Why not?"

Her speech is so badly slurred I can barely make out a word she says. "Because my husband can't see me like this." She reaches for the empty wineglass, picks it up by the stem, peers inside, and tries to suck out a few remaining drops. "Thanks to you."

"And why is this my fault?"

"Because you went to my house, and now he's suspicious. Not that he wasn't suspicious before. He probably was."

My stomach muscles clench tight with dread. "Suspicious of what?"

Paula looks up at me drunkenly, as if I'm a fool. "What do *you* think? It's the reason you're here, isn't it? The reason you've been texting me. The reason you went to my house." She sits back and waves a hand through the air. "Because you've figured it all out. You know what was going on between Alan and me."

I feel a bit sick, because she appears to be admitting flat out that she and Alan were having an affair.

I'm not sure what to say or do. I'm in shock, and I can't speak.

"I need another glass of wine," Paula says, squinting toward the bar.

At this point, I could probably use a stiff drink too, but I resist the urge because I need to keep my wits about me and get the whole story out of her.

"I think you've had enough," I say.

"You're probably right." She tries to get up but staggers sideways and almost knocks over the chair.

I leap out of my seat to grab hold of her. Just then, the bartender exits the washroom. "If you're done, Paula, and I really think you ought to be, you'll need to settle up at the bar."

Swaying on her feet, Paula reaches for her purse and fumbles with the zipper. She pulls out her wallet and hands it to me. "Pay my bill, will you? Use cash."

I take the wallet from her limp grip, move to the bar to ask the amount she owes, and hand over a wad of twenties. Paula can barely stand, so I return to help her. The bartender sees me struggling, comes over, and helps me get her to the door.

"Do you have a car here?" he asks me.

"Yes."

As soon as I push the door open, bright winter sunlight blinds me. I'm forced to squint as we drag our drunken cargo to my mother's vehicle.

We manage to get Paula settled in the front seat. Then the bartender says, "I don't know who you are, but go easy on her, all right? She's going through a rough time. She just lost someone."

I want to scoff, because I'm the one who lost someone. Paula's someone was never really hers to lose. Or maybe I have that backward. I don't know anymore.

I buckle Paula's seat belt, shut the car door, and face the bartender.

"Where are you planning to take her?" he asks as I begin to dig through my purse for my keys.

"Home."

The bartender regards me hesitantly, then follows me around to the driver's-side door. "You can't take her there. Not like this."

I stop and stare. "Why not?"

I have no intention of hauling her to my mother's house to sleep this off. Not with my family there—my mother, my son, and my nieces.

The bartender rubs at the back of his neck. "Her husband can be a jerk sometimes. Alan had a place here in town, just a few blocks away. That's where she'd want to go."

"A place . . ." *Alan had a place?* "Can you give me the address?"

Again he hesitates. He studies me painstakingly. "Jesus. Are you Alan's wife?" He points at his own face and draws a circle in the air with his finger. "I'm guessing because of the bruises. You were in the accident . . ."

This is unbearable. I feel like I'm the only person in the world who knows nothing. "You knew Alan?"

He nods and looks down at the ground. "Yeah. He was a good guy. Came here a lot. He helped me last year. He noticed a lump on my neck and told me I should have it looked at. I doubt I'd be here today if he hadn't pointed that out to me. So . . . I'm sorry about what happened. It's a real pisser."

By this point, I feel like I might throw up, because it's just been confirmed that my husband was cheating on me and this man seems to know more about his extracurricular activities than I ever did.

The bartender's cheeks flush with color, as if he's realizing only now the enormity of what he's just revealed to me. I imagine what he must be thinking: *Don't kill the messenger.*

I might not want to kill him, but I sure as hell would like to yell at him and shake him until his teeth rattle, just to vent some of my anger, because I feel like a pressure cooker with the lid about to fly off.

He glances over his shoulder. "I gotta get back inside."

He gives me the address of an apartment in town. Apparently it's within walking distance, a few blocks away. Not that Paula's in any condition to walk. She's passed out cold.

I look in at her and feel an extreme antagonism building up inside of me. I don't think I've ever felt so outraged by anyone. Not even Lester.

I get into the driver's seat and can't think about inserting the key into the ignition because I'm angrier than a bull. All I can do is stare at Paula—she's so gallingly pretty—and wonder about the lies my husband must have been telling me over the past few years. Or maybe during our entire marriage.

Was Paula the only one? If he had a place of his own in this town, there might have been others.

I have no idea what to do or how to go on living the life I thought I knew. That life is over, not only because my husband is dead but also because my marriage to him wasn't what I thought it was. He was a stranger, a cheater, a liar, and he betrayed me.

How could I not have known? And how can I possibly grieve for him now? Part of me wishes he were alive so I could kill him myself.

Suddenly I feel like I'm hanging upside down by my ankles and I don't know which way is up. It takes all my concentration to turn the key and start the car, because I want answers from the woman passed out in the seat beside me and I'm determined to get them.

CHAPTER TWENTY

"Come on—get up. You have to walk," I say to Paula as I open the passenger-side door, unbuckle her seat belt, and try to wake her by tugging at her arm.

Her head swivels like it's on one of those bobblehead toys, and she looks up at me in a daze.

"That's right—time to walk." I pull her to her feet. "Do you have a key to the front door?"

"Pocket," she drawls, seeming unable to retrieve it on her own. I'm forced to slide my hand into her coat pockets to find it.

A moment later, she's staggering up the walk in her camel-colored wool coat and jeans, making her way to the entrance of a run-down three-story brick apartment building with dilapidated wooden balconies. It's a far cry from the expensive South End home Alan and I shared in Halifax. Nor does it hold a candle to Paula's tidy little house in the Lunenburg subdivision full of families.

She opens the door to a security entrance with an intercom to each unit. I glance at the names and see "Sedgewick" handprinted in ball-point pen on a little piece of white paper. My stomach burns. If this is Alan's secret love pad, how long did he have it, and how was he paying for it? Was he using our retirement fund? Or did he have a private bank account I didn't know about? Where did the secrets end?

It takes a moment for me to focus my attention on finding the right key to let us in, while Paula leans against the wall with her eyes closed.

At last, I unlock the door, pull it open, and gesture for her to follow me. She pushes by and makes a beeline for the elevator, and we ride up to the third floor in silence. As soon as the doors open, she takes the keys from me, walks out, and lets herself into an apartment at the end of the hall, leaving the door open for me to follow her inside.

She goes immediately to the bathroom, and I remain just inside the door, looking around the small space. The walls are beige and full of stains. The brown wall-to-wall carpet smells musty—it probably hasn't been changed in twenty years—and the sofa looks like something someone picked up on the side of the road on garbage day.

Alan certainly wasn't trying to impress anyone. He probably chose this place because he could stay hidden here. Like Paula said, they didn't expect to run into anyone they knew in this neighborhood. And the costs were probably low enough not to affect our financial situation. I wouldn't have noticed. Hell, I *hadn't* noticed.

Or maybe he had a hankering for the world he knew as a child, because according to the stories he told me, his family had sometimes lived below the poverty line.

I hear the toilet flushing and water running in the bathroom, so I steal the opportunity to poke around in the living room in this secret place Alan kept hidden from me. I figure I've earned the right.

I let the shock settle in while I look at things. On the end table next to the sofa, there's a framed photograph of Alan and Paula together on a whitewater rafting adventure. He must have taken her with him when he went away for a medical conference somewhere, which makes me feel jealous and angry. How could I not have suspected anything?

Swallowing uneasily, I force myself to do the unthinkable. I wander to the bedroom, but I can't bring myself to step over the threshold. All I can do is stare at the bed covered with masculine gray and black bed linens and contemplate the fact that my husband made love to another woman in those sheets.

I'm afraid I might throw up.

Paula emerges from the bathroom and collapses on the ratty sofa. "I'm sorry. I shouldn't have texted you. Thanks for the ride, but you should go now."

I return to the living room and shake my head at her, because I came here for answers and I'm not leaving without them.

"Thanks, but I think I'll stay awhile."

She offers no reply, so I set my purse on the hall table, remove my jacket, and text my sister to let her know where I am.

Eventually, Paula staggers to the kitchen to fill a glass with water. She takes a few sips, then shuffles back to the sofa and sits down.

"I guess the cat's finally out of the bag," she says, and I can't help but wonder if she's glad about that.

I sit on a tattered upholstered chair, facing her. "If you're talking about your affair with my husband, then yes, the cat's running all over the damn place."

I consider all the questions I want to ask her. She'd better be sober enough to answer them. At least there's a coffee maker on the counter. I'll do whatever it takes.

"You're not doing yourself any favors," I say, "by going on a bender like this. It won't bring Alan back, and it won't take away your pain. It'll just add a whopping headache on top of it."

"I know."

We sit in silence for a moment until she finally meets my gaze. "You must really hate me right now."

"I can't say that I *like* you. I just want to know what was going on between you and Alan, and for how long." I glance around the room. "Obviously, if you had this place together, it must have been serious."

When she speaks, there's a sudden hint of rancor in her voice. "It wasn't serious enough to get him to leave *you*, even though I tried my best to convince him to."

The jealous, aggrieved wife in me wants to scratch her eyes out for trying to take my husband away from me.

And she's blaming me for her unhappiness? Seriously?

I have to fight to stay cool, only because I want more information. "Just tell me how you met him."

She won't look at me when she talks. "He came into the hardware store to buy a furnace filter. We didn't have the kind he needed, so I had to special order it. I asked for his number so that I could call him when it came in."

"How long ago was that?"

"Three years ago. It was summertime."

I shift uneasily in my seat. "How soon after that did you start the affair?"

"Pretty soon after." She meets my eyes with a look of pure misery. "When he came in to pick up the filter, it was my birthday, and he was *so* nice."

There's a hot pounding in my ears, and my body begins to tremble with rage. "Just tell me how it happened."

She keeps her eyes fixed on mine, and I can't decide if she's full of grief and remorse or if she wants to rub this in my face like sandpaper. "We flirted and started texting each other, and then we met for a drink."

As I imagine all of this happening, my stomach turns because I can't imagine Alan—my darling Alan—falling under the spell of another woman. A woman who was married herself and obviously had no qualms about flirting with a married man with a teenage son. I want to scream and hit something, but there's no way in hell I'll let this morph into an episode of *Jerry Springer* in which we start screaming and throwing chairs at each other. I want to keep my cool.

"Were you married back then?" I ask.

"Yes. Just for a year or so."

"That seems a bit soon to start cheating."

She shakes her head with something that might be regret, but I can't be sure. "Michael isn't the easiest man to live with. He can be controlling sometimes. I probably shouldn't have married him. But then Alan came along, and he was the opposite. He was so kind and caring."

I wonder which of them was the instigator in all of this. The part of me that still loves my husband wants to believe it wasn't his fault—that he was seduced and manipulated by a beautiful woman who was desperate to escape her own imperfect marriage. But I don't know anything anymore. For all I know, Alan could have recognized that she was vulnerable and in need of a hero, and maybe that was what he couldn't resist.

"Who started it?" I ask plainly. "You or Alan?"

"I don't know," she replies. "We both did, I guess. The attraction was intense."

I look away, because hearing about their attraction makes me want to scream.

It also makes me feel inadequate—like a failure as a wife for not recognizing that our marriage was in trouble or for not working harder to keep the romance alive in the first place. But I was so busy with work, doing a lot of night shifts. I didn't always have time for him. I certainly didn't need him to be my hero. I prided myself on being a strong, independent woman, and I always made it clear that he wasn't responsible for my happiness. I didn't want to put that on him.

Was that the problem? Did he not feel needed? Was that why he'd had an affair?

Or was that when he stopped wanting me sexually? When he already had Paula on the side?

And how often did they come here? Was she better than me?

No. Abbie, don't go there . . .

I turn and look at Paula again. She starts to cry, but I have no desire to comfort her. After a moment, she collects herself and slides her drunken gaze to meet mine. "I should have known he was never going to leave you. You should feel happy about that."

Happy? Was she serious?

I'm breathing heavily now. It feels almost like a panic attack.

"Do you and Michael have any children of your own?" I ask, taking a few deep breaths.

"No," she replies. "I wanted kids, and he knew it. But as soon as we were married, he told me that he'd had a vasectomy years ago."

"God." As much as I don't want to feel sympathy for her, I can't help thinking that that kind of trickery was wrong of him.

Paula turns to me. "I'm not going home tonight. Michael and I had a really bad fight on the phone after he talked to you, which is why I'm here and not there." She watches me for a moment. "I suppose I should thank you for getting me out of that bar in one piece."

"I didn't do it for you. I came here because I wanted answers, and I still want to know what happened on the night Alan died. I don't understand how he could have gotten behind the wheel when he was drinking. Now that I know he was having an affair with you, I'm wondering what else was going on that night."

She lowers her gaze. "He was very upset that weekend."

Her reply hits me like a brick in the head. I sit forward in the chair. "Tell me what you know."

She hesitates, and it feels like she's keeping quiet so that she can feel superior and wallow in the fact that she knew my husband better than I did.

At last, her eyes lift. "There's no point keeping it to myself, because you're probably going to find out about it anyway, when you get the autopsy report."

I rest my elbows on my knees and frown. "Autopsy report? Jesus, Paula. What do you know?"

She covers her face with her hands and starts sobbing inconsolably.

Oh God, stop it! Maybe it's cruel of me, but I feel only impatience and hostility. I want to shake her until she breaks apart and squeeze the truth out of her once and for all.

Paula can't stop crying, so I go to the bathroom and get a roll of toilet paper. I hand her a few squares to wipe her tears and blow her nose.

She finally collects herself, takes a deep breath, and begins to explain. She dumps it on me so fast I nearly lose my balance.

"On the Friday before the accident, Alan found out he had cancer."

I blink a few times. "*What?* That can't be true. He would have told me."

But I should know better than to presume anything. At this point, nothing is out of the realm of possibility.

But how could he have told Paula first, while keeping it from me? Did that mean it was true love between them? Not just sex?

She rises from the sofa and goes to the kitchen. I follow, but I give her a moment before I ask another question. "When did he tell you this?"

"Friday afternoon. As soon as he got out of the doctor's office."

I'm trying to digest this news—that my husband had cancer—but I can't seem to get past the fact that when he learned of it, he called Paula and not me.

Where was I that night? I was in the OR.

Then I try to remember if he was different over the next two days, and I recall that he seemed tired on Saturday afternoon. When I asked if he was okay, he brushed it off and said he might be coming down with something. I made him a cup of tea, and he seemed to perk up after that. He was obviously very good at keeping me in the dark.

"What can you tell me about the diagnosis?" I ask, digging deep for the doctor in me, not the wife who has never felt more betrayed or more like a failure as a woman.

Paula stares at the floor. "I don't know. It wasn't good. All I know is that he went to see his doctor about a mark on his shoulder that he thought looked suspicious. Then he found out it was cancer, which started in his kidneys and had already spread everywhere . . . to his lungs, liver, and bones. There were hardly any symptoms other than the mark on his shoulder. The doctor gave him three months to live."

I feel suddenly breathless and cover my face with my hands. Hot tears fill my eyes.

Paula doesn't let up. "He called on Sunday to tell me that he wanted to end it between us and spend whatever time he had left with you. I tried to change his mind, but I couldn't. So you won in the end."

I look up. "I beg your pardon?"

She stares at me with bitterness. "He wanted to spend his last days with you and Zack. So there you go, Abbie. Congratulations."

I stare at her in shock. "Are you kidding me? You think I should feel triumphant? As if the past three years of lies and infidelity never happened?"

She turns away from me, staggering slightly because she's still intoxicated. "This is messed up."

"You're damn right it is." I follow her. "I'll never really know if he would have spent his last days with Zack and me. Was he coming here to see you on Sunday? Had he changed his mind?" I realize I'm shouting now, and I try to cool my temper. "And why the hell was he drunk driving, regardless?"

"I'm not sure, but he was angry with me because I threatened to tell you everything. The last time I spoke to him was on Sunday afternoon, and he was upset. He hung up on me, and I think he must have gone to a bar or a liquor store after that."

"What do you mean exactly, that he was upset?"

She shakes her head. "I don't know . . . he said he screwed everything up, and he begged me not to tell you about us. He went on and on about what a bad person he was and how he was sorry for ruining my life. I told him I wasn't going to just disappear and leave him to die alone. I said I wanted to be by his side until the very end, but that just made him even more angry. He reminded me that he wouldn't be alone. He'd have you. Then he told me to stay away, that it was over between us." Her voice shakes while she fights not to cry. "I was begging him not to end it, and that's when he said he'd be better off dead if I told you the truth, and he hung up on me."

My eyebrows pull together in a frown. "Better off dead? Wait a second . . . was he suicidal?"

She sobs. "I don't know! Part of me wonders if he was coming to see me because he'd changed his mind, or maybe he was coming here to threaten me in person, to make sure I'd keep quiet. Now I'll never know for sure. And neither will you."

I stand up because I can't listen to any more. I don't want to be in the same room with the woman who was sleeping with my husband and tried to keep him from me in his final days. Does she truly believe that I beat her in the end? That I feel victorious because Alan wanted to devote himself to Zack and me and not her? I didn't even know that I was a player in this game until this very moment.

She follows me to the door, where I grab my jacket and shove my arms into the sleeves.

"Wait, Abbie," she says. "Please, don't go."

"Why not? I got what I came for. You told me everything I need to know. There's no point in beating a dead horse." I look around for my purse.

"I'm sorry I kept this from you," Paula says, sounding a little less drunk now, "but Alan made me promise never to tell you, and after the accident, I felt so guilty . . . that it was my fault he was on the road that night. And then I figured . . . what would be the point in telling you? It couldn't change anything, and you'd only be in more pain."

"Then you shouldn't have come to the funeral," I reply. "You should have stayed away."

But would I have preferred to live the rest of my life in ignorance? I honestly don't know the answer to that question. Maybe I would have.

"Despite how this must seem to you," Paula continues, "you should know that Alan loved you."

I hold up a hand. "Please. Don't patronize me."

"I'm serious," she replies, sounding desperate. "I was the one who was jealous of you, because I knew he'd never choose me. He didn't want to break up your family. It was always that way. He was very clear about it."

I find my purse and shake my head at her. "I don't want to hear any more."

I walk out the door, but she won't stop. She's like a tenacious terrier, following me down the hall to the elevator.

I press the button, the doors open, and I step on. "Please don't contact me again. We're done now." The doors shut between us.

A moment later, seated in my mother's car, I insert the key into the ignition with trembling hands and start the engine. My tires skid on the pavement as I pull away.

I make it less than a block from the apartment building before I pull over because I need to have a meltdown. I squeeze my eyes shut and pound the steering wheel multiple times with my fist.

God in heaven. Alan had cancer. And on the day that he died, he may have been trying to put an end to his affair. Or maybe his life . . .

But why didn't he call me right away when he found out about his diagnosis? I'm a doctor. Did he not think I could handle it? Maybe I could have helped him somehow. There might have been hope, a better prognosis . . .

I force myself to sit back and take a few breaths.

Why should I even care whether Alan had a terminal disease? He'd been cheating on me for three years. Maybe longer. There could have been others before Paula. And if he *was* suicidal, was he just being a coward because he didn't want to face me when the truth came out?

I squeeze my fists around the steering wheel, flex my fingers, and look up at the roof of the car. I need to let this anger flow out of me, because I can't go home and see Zack like this, with poison in my veins.

After a moment, I dig into my purse for my cell phone. I dial my sister's number, and I'm relieved when she answers.

"Hello?"

"Hi, Carla. It's me."

"Finally," she replies. "I've been waiting to hear from you. What happened?"

I bite my bottom lip and fight back the tears. Alan doesn't deserve them.

"Paula told me that she and Alan had been having an affair for the past three years and that Alan found out he had cancer on the Friday before he died."

"What?" Carla replies. "Are you serious?"

I continue on, explaining everything I know. "He didn't have long to live, and that's why he was drunk on Sunday—because Paula was pressuring him to leave me, and I guess he couldn't deal with any of it." I pause. "He might even have been suicidal, but I doubt we'll ever know for sure."

There's a long pause on the other end of the line. "Oh my God."

"But that was no excuse for him to get behind the wheel when he was drunk," I continue. "He could have killed other people. I can't feel sorry for him, Carla. Not after all this. He deserved what he got."

I regret my words the instant they pass my lips, and I cup my forehead in my palm. "Oh, I didn't mean that. I'm just really upset right now."

"Of course you are," she gently replies. "And you have every right to be. I can't imagine how I'd feel if I were in your shoes and found out that Braden was keeping secrets like that from me."

I sit in the car, in the glow from the dashboard lights, tapping my thumb against the steering wheel and staring straight ahead—not really seeing anything beyond the glass.

I feel as if my seemingly perfect life was never anything but a fragile house of cards. I had no idea that a sudden, unexpected gust of wind would blow it all down.

"Are you okay?" Carla asks. "Will you come home now?"

I inhale deeply. "Yes. Has Zack been asking about me?"

"Don't worry about him. He's fine. He and Braden just took the girls to a movie, so he won't be back for a while. I thought it would be good for them to get out of the house."

"Yes," I reply. "And listen, don't say anything to him or Mom about this. I don't know how I'm going to handle it, if I should tell them or not."

Carla hesitates. "But you have to tell Zack."

"About the affair?" I consider that for a moment and feel a strong resistance to the idea. "No, I can't do that. He loved his dad. I don't want him to start questioning those feelings or believe that he comes from a long line of dishonorable men. This anger and confusion I'm feeling right now is . . . it's not healthy. Part of me wishes I'd never found out."

She ponders my reasoning. "Maybe you're right. But you don't have to decide anything tonight. Take time to think about it. In the end, you'll know what's best."

"I hope so." Feeling dazed and tired, I realize I haven't eaten all day. I glance at the dashboard clock. "I should come home now. What about supper? Should I pick something up?"

"Don't worry about a thing. Mom's already cooking. Just come home, Abbie. We'll take care of you."

"Okay, I'll see you soon."

I end the call, slap my cheeks a few times—*hard*—to try and wake myself up from this unbelievable nightmare, and pull onto the road leading back to my mother's house, since the home I knew with Alan doesn't seem to exist anymore.

CHAPTER TWENTY-ONE

When I arrive, I smell something delicious cooking on the stove. After what I've just been through, the company of my sister and mother does wonders to soothe my spirits, and I want to hang on to that feeling of security.

Letting my eyes fall closed, I breathe deeply and remind myself how blessed I've been—until now. I can't let myself lose sight of all the good things, even though all I want to do is scream and hit something.

I'm hanging up my coat when Carla walks out of the kitchen to greet me. Without a word, she wraps her arms around my shoulders and holds me tight.

"Thank you," I whisper in her ear. "I don't know how I'd be getting through this without you."

"At least you know the truth now. You don't have to wonder. You know exactly where you stand, and you can deal with it head-on."

Head-on. Such strong, fighting words, but I'm not sure I'm up to it. I don't know how to be a widow. I don't know how to manage these feelings of betrayal that complicate the grief I should be feeling over my husband's death, which is a tragedy all on its own. If only it were that simple, that contained.

Carla and I go to the kitchen, where I find my mother standing at the stove, stirring a pot of something. I work hard to hide the fact that I've just learned something shocking and heartbreaking about my husband and that it feels like my perfect world has been completely annihilated.

I give her a kiss on the cheek. "That smells great. Is it chicken fiesta soup?" One of her specialties.

Mom takes one look at me and frowns with concern—probably because it's obvious that I've been crying.

But that's to be expected, right? It's the day after my husband's funeral. What woman wouldn't be crying?

She asks no further questions, so I sit down at the table, already set for the three of us, with a green salad, a basket of soft rolls, and a selection of dressings in bottles. There's a bottle of white wine too, and I can't wait to pour myself a great big, gigantic glass.

Mom serves the soup, we pour the wine, and I'm so hungry I devour a full bowl before I realize that Winston is not at my feet. This is unusual when there's a meal on the table, not to mention the fact that he didn't greet me at the door.

I glance around and listen for sounds in the quiet house. "Where's Winston?"

Mom and Carla pause with their soup spoons in midair. They look at each other questioningly.

"I don't know," Mom finally says, setting down her spoon. "He was in the basement with the kids earlier, before they went to the movie."

I immediately push back my chair.

"Winston?" I hurry downstairs, reach the rec room, and don't see him anywhere. "We're having supper!" I call out to him. "It's chicken soup!"

My body floods with alarm, and I start to wonder if I'm anxious about everything because I have PTSD from the crash. Or maybe I'm turning into a crazed woman who can't relax about anything because her life is exploding and she knows there will be nothing but chaos from this day forward.

"Winston!" I shout, my gaze darting from one corner of the rec room to the other.

At last, when I flick on the fluorescent light in the unfinished section of the basement, I find him under a table by the storage shelves. He's curled up, sleeping, still wearing the white plastic cone around his neck. Normally, he would be on his feet by now, tail wagging, but tonight, he's not responding.

I run to him and drop to my knees on the cement floor. He doesn't open his eyes.

I place my fingers under his nose to check his airways, and I touch his belly. He's still breathing, but he feels feverish.

"Winston!" I shout.

He opens his eyes at last and blinks a few times, but he still doesn't lift his head.

"What's wrong, baby?" I ask in a gentler voice. "You don't feel so good?"

I roll him gently onto his back to check his incision. There's redness and swelling around the stitches, which, together with the fever, is a clear sign of infection.

"*Shit.*" I blame myself for being so distracted over the past twenty-four hours. I should have made sure someone was keeping a closer eye on him today.

Stroking his silky fur, I bend down to kiss his cheek.

I can't lose this dog.

"I'm going to call the vet," I tell him. "You stay right here. I'll be back."

I rush upstairs to get my cell phone, which has the vet's number listed in my contacts. Mom and Carla watch me with alarm as I skid past the dinner table.

"Is he okay?" Carla asks.

"His incision is infected." I pick up my phone and scroll through my list of contacts. "I'm calling the vet right now."

As soon as I find Dr. Payne's number, I hit the call button and run back down to the basement.

The receptionist answers. "Oceanview Animal Hospital. Ruby speaking."

"Hi, Ruby. This is Abbie MacIntyre. Winston's mom."

"Oh yes," she cheerfully replies. "How's he doing?"

"Not good, actually." I speak calmly and give her the information she needs. "His incision is infected, and he has a fever."

"Oh dear," she replies. "Stay on the line. I'll connect you with Dr. Payne."

There's a click, followed by elevator music. I pace around the chilly basement corridor, chewing my thumbnail while I wait for him to answer.

"Hello, Abbie?"

"Yes. I'm here."

"What's going on?"

I kneel next to Winston, sit back on my heels, and pat him. "I went out for a while this afternoon, and I just got home to find Winston asleep and lethargic. He has a fever, and his incision is showing signs of infection."

"Is he conscious?" Dr. Payne asks.

"Yes, but lethargic. He opened his eyes when I shouted his name, but he barely lifted his head. He's very weak."

Before giving Dr. Payne a chance to reply, I begin to ramble. "Please, you have to help me. We can't lose him, not after everything we've been through. Seriously, I need him to be okay."

"Don't worry, Abbie. Can you bring him in right now?" Dr. Payne asks.

I quickly consider the logistics. "I'll have to carry him to the car. My son's not here, but I'm sure I can get my sister to help me."

"No, no . . . don't do that," Dr. Payne replies. "Just stay put. Don't move him. I'll come over."

"Thank you."

"It's no problem. Tell me your address?"

I give it to him, and he promises to be here in ten minutes.

Dr. Payne arrives wearing jeans and a sweatshirt and carrying an old-fashioned-looking black leather doctor's bag.

I show him downstairs to the basement, and he follows me to where Winston is curled up under the table. Dr. Payne kneels beside him and lays a hand on his belly. "Hey, buddy, how are you doing?"

Winston's eyes open at the sound of Dr. Payne's voice, and his nose twitches as he sniffs the air. I hope he's not frightened.

Dr. Payne pulls a penlight out of his bag and uses it to examine Winston's incision. He then withdraws a stethoscope and listens to his heart. He presses on his belly to check for pain or swelling.

Dr. Payne looks up at me. "There's definitely some infection around the incision, and you're right—he has a fever. I'm going to give him some antibiotics, but I'd like to take him to the clinic for the night, maybe cut a couple of stitches to let the wound drain, do some blood work and an x-ray, and keep an eye on him. Is that okay with you?"

"Of course," I reply, even though I can't bear the thought of being separated from him again. "I just don't want him to be uncomfortable or in pain. Please don't let him suffer."

I realize I'm preparing myself for the worst. It seems impossible to think positive thoughts when everything good in my life has fallen straight into the crapper over the past few days. I'm not sure how much more I can take.

Dr. Payne frowns at me with concern. "Are you okay, Abbie?"

Suddenly, the room is spinning. There's a tingling in my head that mutates into a heavy fog. I feel an overwhelming desire to close my eyes.

The next thing I know, I'm on the floor, blinking up at Dr. Payne, who is leaning over me, cradling my head in his hand. "Just relax. Take a few deep breaths."

I stare up at him, confused. "Oh God. Did I just pass out?"

"Yes, you fainted."

He must have caught me on the way down.

"This is so embarrassing." I move to sit up, but I'm feeling weak and groggy, so I lay my head back down on the cement floor. "How long was I out?"

"Not long. About ten seconds." He listens to my heart with his stethoscope and watches my face intently. "Your heart's beating pretty fast, Abbie," he tells me. "But you probably already know that."

"Yes. I think . . . maybe it was a panic attack."

"Have you ever had one before? Have you ever fainted?"

I shake my head. "No, but it's been a rough few days. I seem to be falling down a lot lately. I collapsed in the ER when Alan was . . ." I can't finish the sentence. "And I didn't eat much today."

Only then do I realize that Winston is no longer curled up under the table. He's sitting up, leaning over the top of my head. I tip my head back to look up at him, and he bends forward and licks my eyelids. I laugh and cup his big, furry, coned head in my hands. Thank heavens he's strong enough to move.

"Good boy," I say. "I'm glad one of us is feeling better. You gave me a good scare."

My heart rate settles, and I manage to sit up. Winston lowers himself to the floor and rests his chin on his paws.

Dr. Payne pats him on the back. "I'd still like to take him overnight, if you don't mind."

"Of course."

With Dr. Payne's help, I rise to my feet. He cups my elbow with his hand and doesn't let go.

"Are you sure you're going to be okay?" he asks.

"I'm fine."

He hesitates. "You should probably get checked out, just to make sure. You've been through a lot, Abbie. I think you should see your doctor."

I know he's right, but I can't think about that right now. I'm worried about Winston, and I'm still reeling over what I learned about Alan today.

Dr. Payne finally lets go of my arm and turns to Winston. "What do you say, buddy? Do you think you can walk to the limo?"

"That sounds fancy."

The corner of Dr. Payne's mouth curls up in a small grin. "Even with the animals, *limo* usually gets a better reaction than *ambulance*."

Either way, Winston shows no interest in getting to his feet.

"I'll get his leash," I say. "That usually starts his tail wagging."

I run upstairs, but when I return, Winston is lying on his side again, eyes closed, and Dr. Payne is listening to his heart with the stethoscope.

My anxiety returns. "Is he doing okay?"

Dr. Payne removes the ear tips and drapes the instrument around his neck. "He's the same."

I squat down and hook the leash onto Winston's collar, but he doesn't even lift his head.

"I'll carry him," Dr. Payne says. "Would you mind getting my bag?"

"Not at all." I pick it up, then stand back to give him room. He gently scoops Winston into his arms and carries him up the stairs.

Seeing Winston like this breaks my heart. He's so weak in the vet's arms.

We reach the kitchen, and Mom and Carla rise from the table.

"Is he okay?" Carla asks.

"I don't know," I reply. "He's pretty weak. Dr. Payne is taking him back to the clinic for the night."

I lead Dr. Payne to the front door. It's below freezing outside, and I can see my breath on the air as we make our way to the van. The interior is equipped with oxygen, a folded-down gurney, a backboard, a large wire cage, and first aid supplies.

Dr. Payne strains to lay Winston down on the carpeted floor. Then he climbs into the back and moves him into the cage that's bolted to the side wall. He closes the door and secures the latch.

Winston lies unresponsive, which causes a knot to form in my stomach.

"Mind if I come with you?" I ask Dr. Payne as he hops out and shuts the double doors. "You said your clinic was closed for the day. Your technicians must be gone. You might need some help?"

He stares at me for a moment, unsure.

I continue to plead my case. "Listen . . . I just really need to be with him right now. This has been the worst day of my life, which is saying a lot, and I know I won't be able to relax if I stay here. I'll be thinking about him the whole time and trying to resist calling you every ten seconds."

Dr. Payne nods at me. "Okay then. I'll need my jacket, though. It's nging in your front hall closet."

"Great. I'll go get it." I hand him his vet bag and run back up the stairs.

Quickly, I explain the situation to Carla and my mother as I rifle through the closet. I also ask if Carla will pick me up at the clinic later.

She says yes, and I ask them to explain everything to Zack when he gets home.

"He can call me on my cell."

I realize I never told either of them that I fainted in the basement, and I'm glad I didn't, because they'd only worry more. They'd try to convince me to go to the ER tonight, when I need to be with Winston.

A moment later, I hurry out the door and hop into Dr. Payne's vehicle.

He shifts into reverse, and we back out of the driveway.

CHAPTER TWENTY-TWO

Dr. Payne's Victorian home is brightly lit, with lights on in every window, but the clinic is dark. As we pull into the veterinary hospital parking lot, I wonder how often this sort of thing happens, and I hope his family is understanding.

I get out of the car and watch him slide Winston out of the van on a gurney. He hands me the keys to the clinic. "Would you mind unlocking the door?"

"Sure." I lead the way while he wheels Winston across the paved lot.

A moment later, we enter the treatment area at the back. Dr. Payne switches on the lights and computers. He rolls Winston on the gurney toward a bank of white cabinets and locates what he needs to take a blood sample. Next, he takes Winston into a small digital-imaging room and turns on the x-ray machine.

"Can I do anything to help?" I ask at the door.

"No, I've got this," he replies. "But if you'd like a cup of coffee, feel free to help yourself." His hands are busy, so he tosses his head to gesture toward a door beyond the row of computers. "There's a small staff room right through there."

"Great. Would you like a cup too?"

"That would be great."

Happy to feel useful, I remove my coat, set my purse down on a chair, and head into a small, newly renovated lunchroom with a stainless-steel fridge, a stove, contemporary white cupboards, and an antique pine table with four chairs. The coffee maker is one of those Keurig machines, so it's easy to find everything and make two cups.

I peek my head out the door and see that Dr. Payne has already finished in the x-ray room. Winston is resting quietly on the gurney beside him while he sits on a stool and works with the blood samples he just took.

"Dr. Payne, do you take cream or sugar?"

"Black is fine," he replies. "And call me Nathan."

"Nathan."

I return to the coffee maker and brew a second cup, and then I carry both mugs out to the main treatment area and set his down beside him.

"Thanks." Seeming intensely focused, he takes a quick sip, then wheels his stool to a computer workstation and begins typing. "Would you like to see the x-rays?"

"I'd love to."

I move closer to stand over his shoulder.

"Everything looks good to me," I say, bending forward to look more closely. "What do you think?"

Nathan sips his coffee. "I don't see any issues. But I still want to monitor that infection and see how he responds to the antibiotics. I'd like to keep him overnight."

"Sure," I reply. "But . . . should I stay as well?"

"You don't have to."

I glance over at Winston on the gurney. "I know, but I'd rather not leave him, and to tell you the truth, I'd prefer not to go home just yet."

Nathan swivels around on his chair and looks up at me. "Is everything okay at home?"

I don't know how to answer the question—how to tell him that I'm afraid to face my son because I'm keeping a secret from him and I'm a terrible liar. I'm afraid he'll know that I'm hiding something.

Nathan stares at me for a few seconds, then bows his head and shakes it. "I'm sorry. That was a dumb question. Of course everything's not okay. You just lost your husband."

In more ways than one.

Still not sure how to respond, I turn and approach Winston. I stroke his head and rub behind his ears. "It wasn't a dumb question."

I hear Nathan rise from his chair. He circles around the gurney to stand on the opposite side, with Winston between us.

"I know what it's like," he says, "when everyone keeps telling you that they're sorry for your loss or that it'll get easier in time. There's nothing anyone can say, really."

I glance up. "Have you lost someone?"

"My wife," he replies. "Three years ago."

My head draws back slightly. "Oh. I'm sorry. I didn't know." I shake my head at myself. "There it is again. That word. *Sorry*."

"If I only had a dime . . . ," he says.

"For every time you heard it." I let out a sigh. "Me too, and it's been less than a week since . . ."

I can't bring myself to finish the sentence, so I don't. I just leave it there, hanging in the air between us.

"And you have children?" I remember Ruby mentioning something about him needing to pick up one of his daughters at school the last time I was here.

"I have two girls," he explains. "Twelve and nine."

"Who's taking care of them now?"

"My parents," he replies. "This is their house." He gives me a play-ful, sheepish grin. "Yes, I'm a grown man who lives with his parents."

I return the smile. "Well, there are worse places you could be. Did you grow up in Lunenburg?"

"Yes."

"Did we know each other?" I ask. "Because I grew up here too. What year did you graduate from high school?"

"Ninety-seven."

"Ah. I was there before your time. I graduated in 1991."

He nods and pats Winston.

"Was your wife from here as well?" I ask.

"No, we met at vet school in Toronto. We opened a clinic there together, and that's where we were living when she got sick."

I glance up at him, wondering . . .

"Breast cancer," he tells me.

"Ah." I nod soberly.

"After she was gone," he continues, "it was difficult, trying to raise two young daughters on my own and keep the clinic going at the same time. Her parents didn't really want to be involved. They were older and had just retired to Florida the year before, so my parents convinced me to come home and open an animal hospital here."

"It's a wonderful place to raise children," I say with certainty.

"Yes, and it was their idea to renovate this place, since they had more space than they knew what to do with. They're seniors now, so I pay them rent, which helps them out financially, and they want nothing more than to spend time with their grandkids, so everybody's happy." He gives me a sympathetic look. "Listen, it does get easier. It may not seem like it now, but it will."

"That's good to know. Because it's hard to imagine anything ever being easy again. Not in this lifetime."

He runs his hand down the back of Winston's head. "Just make sure you ask for help when you need it and say yes when people offer. Like if a neighbor offers to mow your lawn, they *want* you to say yes. It makes them feel good to know they're helping somehow. It's just as much for them as it is for you. Let them help."

"I'm sure that's true," I reply, "but I don't think anyone can truly help me with the worst of my problems. I'm dealing with bigger issues than just taking care of my lawn."

He considers this. "You're talking about the big bottomless pit of grief? The loneliness?"

My eyes lift, and I find myself wanting to vent all my woes. Maybe it's because this man is an outsider—someone unbiased who never knew Alan and me as a couple. "Not exactly."

He inclines his head, curious.

"I learned something today," I finally tell him as I stroke the soft fur around Winston's neck. "Although maybe I always knew there was something wrong. I just didn't want to face it."

"What was that?"

Winston opens his eyes, looks up at me for a few seconds. I bend forward and kiss the top of his head, and he closes his eyes again.

"Today I learned that my husband was having an affair."

Nathan's eyebrows lift. "Oh God, that's awful. How did you find out?"

"Well . . . after he got behind the wheel with a blood alcohol level of 0.33 and nearly killed me on the highway—and Winston too—his secret lover decided it was a good idea to sneak in and out of the funeral home before the wake and then skulk around at the burial, basically alerting me to the fact that he was leading a double life."

Nathan shakes his head in disbelief. "Did she tell you who she was?"

"No, but I already knew her from high school, and my spider senses were tingling. Today she confessed everything."

"Wow."

"I know, right? It was going on for three years, and he managed to keep it secret the whole time. I didn't suspect a thing, which makes me feel like a complete fool. Now I'm questioning everything about our relationship. Oh, and on top of that, he recently found out that he had terminal cancer. He didn't tell me that either."

I don't mean to sound glib, but that's how it all comes pouring out, and I feel like I'm describing a soap opera on TV. The fact that this is my life is surreal, especially to me.

I glance up and discover that Nathan is watching me with a frown. Almost immediately, my eyes fill with tears, and I back away from the gurney. I press my fingers to my lips to try and stop the floodgates from opening again, because I've done enough crying. I'm tired of blubbering, and I don't want to fall apart anymore.

I move to a chair and sit down.

Nathan drags another chair to face mine and sits down before me. "I've heard of bad days before, but this really takes the cake."

"I should get a prize."

"You deserve one."

He leans forward and takes hold of both my hands. "All that and Winston too. No wonder you fainted."

I say nothing for a moment, and then I express what's at the top of my mind. "The problem is . . . I don't know what I should tell my son. I'm afraid that if I don't say anything, he's going to find out somehow or see right through me. That's why I prefer not to go home right now. It's hard enough for him to accept that his father was drinking and driving, because that's not something he would ever do—or so we thought. And Zack's such a good kid. We raised him to be responsible and obey the law. Drinking and driving . . . there's just no excuse for that. It's unforgiveable, right? I was shocked that Alan did that, and I wanted answers. But this—the lies about his three-year affair . . . how do I hide that from my son? And should I?"

"I don't know," Nathan says. "I mean . . . is this something he needs to know?"

I inch forward slightly. "No, I don't think so, because it would only cause Zack more pain, and I want to protect him from that. But what if he finds out somehow?"

I glance away, toward the surgery suite behind a wall of glass, where the lights are turned off. "I'm feeling Alan's betrayal along with the pain of losing him in the accident, and it's been hell. I wish I'd never found out about the affair. Now that he's gone, what's the point? It's not something we can ever work out. He can't explain himself to me or apologize or make me feel better about our relationship, which was something he was always so good at doing. Despite what you might think, we had a happy marriage. We never fought, and he was my best friend. We were an amazing team as parents. We were always on the same page. We wanted the same things out of life. At least I thought we did."

Nathan shakes his head. "I can't even imagine what you must be going through right now. Losing a loved one is hard enough, but to pile all this crap on top of it. Seriously, Abbie . . ."

"I know. It sucks."

Nathan sits back and glances at Winston. "You're welcome to stay here longer if you want to. There's a sofa in the staff room, and I can get you some blankets. But if it's Winston you're worried about, don't be. You can sleep well tonight, knowing he'll be fine." He meets my gaze again. "But I think what you really need to do is go home and be with your family. Does anyone else know about this? Have you told anyone at all?"

"My sister," I reply. "I told her everything today."

"Good. You need to have someone you can confide in. Someone you can trust."

I let out a sigh. "You're probably right. Thanks for listening. I'm sorry for dumping all that on you."

"Don't be."

I inhale a deep breath and slap my knee. "Well. I should probably go home now. Clearly I need to get some rest."

We stand up, and I move to say goodbye to Winston. I run my fingers through his soft golden fur, bend forward and kiss his cheek, and whisper in his ear. "Get some rest, angel. I'll be back for you in the morning."

I thank Nathan again, then call Carla to come and pick me up.

CHAPTER TWENTY-THREE

I can't deny that a small, petty part of me wants to reveal Alan's infidelity to Zack—for no other reason than to exact revenge.

Think of it. I have the power to make my cheating husband pay for his betrayal by posthumously eroding the love his son feels for him.

But no.

Of course I would never do such a thing, because it would hurt Zack more than it would hurt Alan, because Alan is dead. Besides, I'm not a vindictive woman. At least I'm trying not to be. This is my anger talking. I need to beat that spiteful little devil down with a big fat Oprah stick.

When everyone is in bed, Carla pulls two of Mom's best crystal snifters from the top shelf in the dining room and pours us each a brandy from the bottle we picked up on the way home. We sit down at the kitchen table to talk, and I tell her all the sordid details about my day—the things I didn't reveal when we spoke on the phone, like how I practically carried Paula out of the bar and what the bartender said.

None of it seems real to me now as I sit across from my sister in my mother's cozy kitchen, where Alan and I created so many happy memories together. We came here every weekend, ever since Zack was a baby, and for all those years, I truly believed that I was blessed to have the most loving, devoted, loyal husband a woman could ever dream of.

Now I have to accept that for him the lure of this town in recent years was not my mother's delicious Sunday dinners or the fun we had as a family. It was Paula Sheridan and whatever they did together. Whatever plans they made to meet up with each other in secret.

By now, I've lost count of how many times Carla has refilled our glasses. I let my forehead fall forward into my hand and squeeze my eyes shut. "How could I not have known? Am I really that stupid? That blind?"

Carla reaches across the table and takes hold of my hand. "Abbie, you're not stupid. You're a good person, and you see the best in people. You're trusting because you have faith that people are decent and honorable. You believed in Alan because you're an optimist. Don't let this change what I love most about you."

I feel drunk and sleepy. My body feels like a heavy slab of iron. I can barely lift my head.

"You're looking at the glass half-full," I say. "You see me as an optimist, but maybe I'm just naive. I don't know which is better. To be blind and optimistic—to wear rose-colored glasses and allow yourself to be vulnerable—or to be realistic and cynical? To be prepared for someone to disappoint you? To have your guard up and not be taken by surprise?"

Carla sits back. "Being an optimist doesn't make you blind. A cynic can be blind too—in even worse ways. A cynic can miss out on something wonderful because they only see the dark side of it, so they steer away from a good thing because they expect it to go wrong eventually."

I've had too much to drink, and I can't fully comprehend what my sister is saying to me, although I know it's very wise.

We sit in silence for a long time.

"It's nearly two in the morning," Carla says. "You should get some sleep."

I nod in agreement. Though I still haven't decided what I'm going to tell Zack—if anything. The problem is that if I don't tell him, I'm going to have to learn how to become a better liar, better at hiding things, like Alan was, and I don't like the thought of that.

But I'm in no condition to make any important decisions tonight. I just need to get some rest so I'm not so tired tomorrow.

As soon as I wake the next morning, I call the veterinary hospital. Ruby tells me that Winston is doing much better and I can pick him up anytime. I take a couple of Tylenols to take the edge off my brandy headache, and then I ask Zack if he wants to come with me. He says yes.

I don't see Dr. Payne that morning because he's out back performing a canine dental extraction, which is just as well because I feel a bit awkward about our conversation the night before. It's not my habit to reveal the skeletons in my family's closet to perfect strangers, and I certainly don't want Zack to sense that I've shared something private with a stranger before I've told *him* about it.

Thankfully, those worries fall away when the door opens from the treatment room and Ruby leads Winston out to the reception area. Though he still wears the cone around his head, he's on his feet, tail wagging, excited to see us.

Zack and I make a big fuss over him, and then I pay the bill, and we take him to the car. He jumps into the back seat, just like his old self, delighted about a ride in the car.

"He seems a lot better," Zack says as we buckle in and pull out of the parking lot.

I glance at Winston in the rearview mirror. He's smiling from ear to ear, tongue hanging out while he trots back and forth from one window to the other, barely able to contain his excitement.

"Maybe we should take him for a short walk today, down to the waterfront."

"That sounds good."

We drive in silence for a moment, and then Zack turns to me and asks tentatively, "Mom, when are we going to go home? I mean . . . now that the funeral's over."

I glance at him briefly. "You don't want to stay another day or two?"

"I've already missed a lot of school."

"I'm sure your teachers won't expect you to come back right away. They know what happened. They'll make allowances for that."

"I know," he replies, "but I'd still like to be at home. Sleep in my own bed. I want to start figuring out how we're going to live."

"You mean . . . without your dad." My stomach turns over with dread because I'm not sure I'm ready to face this new future.

Zack gazes out the window at the houses as we pass. "It's going to be weird. Especially when we walk through the door the first time. But I want to get through it, you know?" He turns to me. "Don't get me wrong, Mom. I love being with Gram and Aunt Carla and the girls, but I keep thinking about the fact that Dad's sneakers are by the front door. I noticed them when Maureen came to pick me up, but I couldn't bring myself to move them. I'm kind of dreading seeing his stuff when we get home—like his clothes in the closet and his medical magazines on the coffee table. It's hanging over my head."

I understand exactly what he's saying because I'm dreading it too. "You want to face it head-on."

Those were Carla's words to me.

"Yes," Zack replies. "Let's just get it over with. And after we get through all that hard stuff, I was thinking . . . maybe we could do something special for Dad."

My stomach starts to actually hurt, because I'm not sure where Zack is going with this, and doing something special for my lying, cheating husband isn't exactly at the top of my priority list right now. I just want to figure out how to get up in the mornings without wanting to smash our framed wedding portrait against the corner of the kitchen table.

"What do you have in mind?" I ask, wrestling my true feelings into submission.

"I don't know. Maybe we could brainstorm. But I was thinking about a scholarship fund for students in need. Maybe for kids who have abusive parents. Or even foster kids. I think Dad would approve of that because of how he grew up. He was lucky to get away from Grandpa and go to college and live a better life. I mean . . . seriously, Mom, we had a perfect life."

A perfect life.

I bite my lip because I feel as if I'm being ripped in half, straight down the middle. Part of me is proud of my son for recognizing the challenges his father faced as a child, for wanting to do something to help other kids in the same position, and most of all for reminding me how rough Alan had it growing up. I can't ignore the fact that he was raised by a cruel and heartless man who probably played a significant role in Alan's need to feel adored. Maybe he genuinely needed the adulation Paula gave him when I was too busy at work or fielding Zack's activities.

Another part of me doesn't want to spend a single second of my time analyzing why Alan needed Paula—because he had a wife at home who loved him—nor do I want to expend effort to create a lasting legacy in Alan's memory, where he will be honored for years to come . . . revered as a generous, courageous, loving family man.

Yeah, right.

There's a heavy pounding in my ears, and my stomach burns.

"That might be awkward," I say, "considering he was a drunk driver."

The heated words fly out of my mouth before I can stop them. I want to take them back, but I can't.

Zack darts a look at me, and my cheeks flush.

"I'm sorry. I shouldn't have said that."

"No, it's fine," he replies. "You're right. I didn't think of that." He's quiet for a moment. "Why was he drunk, Mom? It makes no sense. I never thought he would ever do something like that."

There are a lot of things I never thought Alan would do, but here we are.

We've almost reached my mother's house, but I decide I should keep driving and continue this conversation. I flick my blinker and head up the hill toward the old Lunenburg Academy.

"There's something I haven't told you," I say. "Something I found out yesterday."

"What is it?"

I pull over onto the side of the road and shut off the engine, then find myself becoming very selective about what truths I wish to reveal. I suspect I'll have to tweak certain details.

"On the Friday before the accident," I say, "Dad found out he had cancer."

Zack's mouth falls open. "*What?* Cancer? And you didn't know? You only found out yesterday?"

I nod my head. "That's right. He didn't tell me. I'm not sure why. Maybe he was planning to, but I think that's why he was drinking that day. He was upset."

Zack stares at me, mouth agape. "What kind of cancer was it?"

"It started in his kidneys, then it spread quickly to his lungs, liver, and bones. I'm told there were no symptoms. Apparently he went to see his doctor about a mark on his shoulder, which he thought looked suspicious. That led them to the root of the problem, and by then it was too late. The cancer was very aggressive, and they didn't expect him to live more than a few months."

Zack frowns in disbelief. "So he was going to die anyway?"

"Yes." My voice breaks.

Zack turns away, covers his eyes with his hand, and weeps.

It kills me to see him in pain. I want nothing more than to make everything better, but that's not possible. His father is dead, and it's tragic. There's no escaping it. All I can do is lay my hand on Zack's shoulder and wait for him to get over the shock of what I just told him.

"How did you find out?" he asks.

My heart lurches because I can't possibly tell him the truth. Not yet. Maybe not ever.

"The doctor told me," I lie.

"Because of the autopsy?" Zack asks.

We don't even have the autopsy results yet. We won't have them for at least another week, but Zack doesn't know that. I simply nod my head.

"Why didn't you tell me last night?" he asks, sounding hurt and incredulous.

I scramble for a reply. "I'm sorry. It was late when I got home from the vet, and I was barely keeping it together after what happened with Winston. I just needed time to sleep and put myself back together. I was a wreck. I'm so sorry, honey."

At least that much was true.

I'm relieved when Zack accepts my explanation. He reaches for my hand and squeezes it. "It's okay, Mom. You've told me now."

I raise his hand to my lips and kiss the back of it. "I'm so sorry you have to go through this. I wish everything could be normal again."

"Me too," he replies, "but it'll never be normal again. We just have to get used to it. Are *you* going to be okay, Mom?"

I love him so much for thinking of me when he has his own grief to manage.

"I don't have much choice, do I? I'll have to be."

We hug each other tightly. Then I sit back and think about what to do next.

"If you want to go home, we'll go home," I say. "Winston's okay now, and Carla and the kids are leaving tomorrow anyway."

Zack nods at me. "Can we go today?"

"That soon?"

"Yeah, I'm restless here, Mom. I can't sleep. Even though the funeral's over, I still feel like the worst is ahead of us. I just want to deal with it."

I stare at him for a moment. "Okay," I say reluctantly. "We'll pick up a rental car, pack up our stuff, and go after lunch."

And just like that, ready or not, I am back on the road, heading for home. The only problem is . . . it doesn't feel like home anymore, and I don't know if it ever will.

CHAPTER TWENTY-FOUR

I'll never forget the first time I laid eyes on the house that would become our family home. Alan and I had been hunting for weeks but couldn't find anything that felt right. Then a new property came on the market. When we pulled up in front of it to meet the real estate agent for a viewing, the exterior was strangely familiar to me, as if I'd already lived in it, or maybe I recognized it from a dream. I'm still not sure where the feeling came from, but I just *knew* that this was meant to be our house.

It was a century-old Tudor revival with a multigabled roof and decorative half-timber framing in the elegant, upscale South End of Halifax. Alan and I both fell in love with it instantly, and we shared a look as we got out of the car. This was two months before Zack was born, and he was kicking in my belly as we climbed the steps to the front door. We made an offer the same day, even though the house was run-down and in desperate need of an update.

We spent the next few years tidying up the ivy-cloaked exterior and renovating the inside with a modern, updated kitchen and fresh paint on every wall, while we retained all the gorgeous Renaissance-style embellishments we loved—like the arched board-and-batten front door with hefty metal hardware, the exposed ceiling beams in the main living area, and the leaded-glass windows with diamond-shaped panes.

And when Zack was three, he loved trains, so we decided to redecorate his room with a steam-train wallpaper border. But first, we had to repaint the walls blue, so we were up early one Saturday morning, dressed in our painting clothes and caps, with a plastic tarp spread across the floor. I remember—just as if it were yesterday—how thrilled Zack was by the crinkling sound it made when he jumped on it. His sweet cheeks flushed bright red as he laughed and bounced across the floor.

"Hey, buddy, do you want to do some painting?" Alan asked, kneeling low and offering Zack the brush.

I was busy with the roller, but I paused for a moment to watch.

Zack went still, and his eyes grew wide. He moved forward to take the brush from Alan, who led him to the center of the wall opposite the window and helped him dip the brush into the paint can.

"Great job," Alan said as he held Zack's hand and gently guided the brushstrokes up and down. "What do you think of this? Do you like painting?"

"Yes, Daddy. I wuv it."

"It's fun to paint together, isn't it? You, me, and Mom. The Three Musketeers."

I remember the intense rush of love that coursed through me as I watched my husband look at our little boy with unbridled joy and adoration. Tears of happiness filled my eyes, and I couldn't believe how lucky I was to be married to such a good man and such a loving father to our son.

As Zack and I pull into the driveway, for one blissful moment, my anger toward Alan dissolves as I recall how happy we were. Then it all comes charging back when I think of Paula Sheridan and their secret love nest.

Zack presses the button on the remote control to open the garage door. The door slowly lifts, and I drive the rental vehicle inside.

It's only been a week since I was last here, but it feels like a lifetime ago. I'm not the same woman I was when I drove off with Winston in the back seat of my SUV. I was so content and eager to spend the day with my mother, oblivious to my husband's infidelity. Little did I know that my so-called perfect life was about to be blown to smithereens.

I shut off the engine, and Zack presses the button again to close the door behind us. Winston is beside himself with anticipation, pacing in the back seat, impatient to jump out and run inside—to see Alan, no doubt, the fourth member of our pack, who threw the tennis ball farther and faster than anyone.

The mood is somber as Zack and I get out of the car and open the trunk to retrieve our suitcases. Neither of us speaks a word, while Winston jumps against the inside door to the laundry room, wagging his tail and whimpering.

I lug my bags out of the trunk and open the door to the house. Winston darts inside and disappears into the kitchen, then runs from room to room, up the stairs, all around the house, sniffing and searching.

Zack and I share a look.

"He's going to be disappointed," Zack says.

I set down my bag, then make my way to the kitchen and turn on some lights.

The house feels like a tomb. I glance over at the computer desk in the family room, where Alan used to sit while Zack and I watched television. His water bottle is still there, half-full, standing on a bunch of papers—bills and such that will need to be taken care of. I wonder suddenly if Alan ever sent messages to Paula from that chair, when I was only a few feet away.

Winston trots down the stairs and completes a second sweep of the ground floor, then the basement—to no avail. When he comes back up the stairs, I approach him, drop to one knee, and place my hands on his cheeks.

"Sorry, baby, he's not here. You're going to have to get used to it being just the three of us."

Oddly, I believe he understands. He's searched the house from top to bottom. Somehow, he knows. This is final.

I give him another pat on the head, then rise to my feet and go check what's still good in the refrigerator. Winston follows me like a shadow.

Over the next few days, Zack and I try to ease ourselves back into some of our normal routines, but it's not easy. Each morning I wake up, glance over at the empty pillow on Alan's side of the bed, and feel a giant, gaping hole in my existence. The early part of the morning seems so quiet. It's strange not to hear Alan in the shower or ask him what time he'll be home from work as he gets dressed.

During the day, I can't go anywhere in the house without being reminded of Alan because his personal possessions are everywhere—his bicycle in the garage, his shoes piled in the front hall closet. It hurts to look at them, and when I do, I find myself staring in a daze, not knowing what to do with his things or how not to feel this pain, which is more confusing than ever now that I'm home, because I'm so angry with him for cheating on me, yet I can't bear his absence and wish he were here.

I'm not ready to return to work yet because I still feel completely drained and worn out from the accident and getting through Alan's funeral. Zack is more resilient than I am, and he goes bravely off to school.

When he comes home after his first day back, he tells me that the guidance counselor pulled him out of class to ask how he was coping. She encouraged him to seek help if he needed it—whether that meant talking to someone or being granted an extension on a project. He was both surprised and touched by how caring everyone was, asking him how he was getting along and expressing how sorry they were.

As for me, I spend the next four days on the sofa, feeling lethargic and depressed. There are moments when I hate Alan for destroying our beautiful life together. How could he have done it? How could he have squandered it all?

Then I cry like a baby because I miss him so much and want him back. I sleep a lot. And I call Carla, and we talk and talk. She wants to come and stay with me for a while, but I don't let her because she has a family she needs to take care of.

The only thing I manage to accomplish that first week, besides taking Winston for a daily walk after lunch, is a trip to the grocery store to buy food so that Zack and I won't starve or be forced to eat toast and canned beans night after night.

But shopping for groceries only makes me feel more depressed. I move through the store like a zombie, and people stare at my bruised face as I slowly push my cart up and down the aisles. What makes it worse are the festive holiday decorations that start to appear in the stores on the first of December. Songs like "I'll Be Home for Christmas" are piped through the overhead speakers. The lyrics make me want to grab a jar of salsa off the shelf and smash it on the floor because my husband won't be home for Christmas this year—or ever. I resist the urge to destroy nonperishables, however.

Later in the week, I try to ignore Alan's things in the same way that most of us don't see clutter after living with it for months or years, thinking that will help. I force myself to glance unseeingly over his books on the shelf and his power tools in the basement, which is much easier than making a decision about when I'm going to get rid of everything—including that apartment in Bridgewater.

I tell myself it's going to take some time before I'm ready, and I just need to be patient. Time heals all wounds, right? But every once in a while, when I go into our closet, I flirt with the idea of burning his belongings in a massive pile in the backyard and spitting on the ashes. Or I could wait for the simmering anger to pass and rummage through every item lovingly, thinking carefully about where it should go and to whom.

Will that day ever come? Will the anger ever pass? I have no idea.

After a week of pure wretchedness, I watch Zack leave for school and decide that it's time for me to pull myself together too. First, I need to cancel the lease on Alan's disgusting apartment. Then buy a new car with the insurance money from the accident and get rid of the rental. Zack will be thrilled to help me pick something out. Then I'll need to return to work. It'll do me good to be around people again, because I can't stay at home forever feeling sorry for myself and avoiding my responsibilities.

I drink two cups of coffee and examine my banged-up face in the mirror—it's looking somewhat better. A thick coat of foundation hides most of the scars and what's left of the bruises.

Then I look down at Winston and realize he's doing much better too. I kneel down and give him a scratch behind the ears. "I think we're over the hump, buddy—at least physically."

He sits still while I examine his incision, which appears to be completely healed. "That looks really good. In fact, I'm going to text the vet and give him an update."

Rising to my feet, I pull my cell phone out of my pocket, find Nathan in my list of contacts, and begin typing: Hi there. I just wanted to let you know that Winston is doing really well and his incision is healed. Thank you again for everything you did for us last month.

I'm pleased when Nathan texts me back immediately. Hi, Abbie. It's nice to hear from you. I'm glad Winston is on the mend. How are you doing?

I smile and respond, Oh . . . you know . . . pretty good, all things considered. Taking it day by day.

His reply comes in a few seconds later. That's all you can do. Just remember not to put too much pressure on yourself to feel normal again. That will take time.

Don't worry, I reply. Normal is not in my periphery at the moment.

He replies, LOL.

I smile and send one last text: Have a nice Christmas if I don't talk to you, and say hi to Ruby for me.

He responds, I will. Take care, Abbie!

You too, I reply.

With renewed purpose, I search through my list of contacts again and call the chief of surgery at the hospital to let him know I'm ready to return to work.

"Are you sure, Abbie?" he asks. "Because if you need more time . . ."

"No," I reply. "It'll do me good to get out of the house. I need to be with people."

Especially with the holidays coming. The distraction will be good for me.

He admits he's overjoyed to hear it because a number of cases have been bumped over the past few weeks. I've been sorely missed.

I take a long shower and feel thankful that I have a challenging, rewarding career that I love. I pray that it will help to bring me back to the world of the living.

CHAPTER TWENTY-FIVE

Zack and I decide that we'll keep Christmas low-key this year. Personally, I would have preferred to skip it altogether and start fresh next year, but I can't do that to Zack, so I force myself to get a tree at the farmers market on a Saturday afternoon, drag it home, and stick it in the metal stand.

Together, we agree to keep up the tradition of opening a box of chocolates and listening to holiday music while we hang the lights and decorations, but it's impossible to act cheerful when every ornament we touch is a reminder of Christmases past.

The "World's Best Dad" trophy is especially disheartening, because Zack gave that to Alan just last year.

As soon as we hear the song "Have Yourself a Merry Little Christmas" by the Carpenters, we exchange a look. Zack nearly trips over a box of garland as he scrambles to shut off the speaker, because we both know that Alan had a secret childhood crush on Karen Carpenter, which we used to tease him about every time this song came on.

"How about I turn on TV instead?" Zack says.

"That's a great idea."

He picks up the remote control and tunes in to the Weather Channel. "This should be safe."

We continue hanging ornaments while Winston lies on the carpet with his chin on his paws, looking depressed as he watches us. So much for being merry.

"So have you made any decisions about college next year?" I ask Zack, feeling a somewhat desperate need to talk about something other than our Christmas memories.

Zack bends to withdraw a little wooden snowman from a box and turns to hang it on the tree. "Actually. I'm thinking I might just go to Dal and live at home."

I gape at him in shock. "Dal. But I thought you wanted to go to Queen's or Western."

It has always been Zack's dream to go away to college and live in a new city, on his own. Dalhousie is an excellent school, but it's just down the street.

"What changed your mind?"

He glances at me briefly before he bends to pick up another ornament. "I don't know."

"C'mon, Zack. We're always honest with each other." *Well . . . maybe not always.* "What's going on?"

"We just lost Dad. And I . . . I don't want you to be all alone."

While I hate the idea of my son feeling responsible for my happiness when he should be excited about his own, I'm proud of him for thinking of others and not just himself.

Then suddenly, I wish that we'd had another child so that Zack wouldn't feel as if he were deserting me now.

It isn't the first time I've wished I could have gotten pregnant again. Certainly when Zack was little, he often expressed his desire for a baby brother or sister, but it just wasn't in the cards. But now, with Alan gone, I see how much pressure this puts on Zack, my only child, to be the center of my world. It's a lot of responsibility for a seventeen-year-old.

"Don't worry about me," I assure him, since the last thing I want is for him to sacrifice his dreams because he doesn't think his mother can handle solitude. "I have Winston to keep me company, and you know how busy I am with work. I have a full life, Zack. It would break my heart if I thought I was holding you back."

"You're not holding me back," he replies without looking me in the eye as he combs through the box for another ornament. "Lots of my friends are going to Dal, and Dal has a really good science program."

I know he's doing his best to convince me—and himself—but I can't let him do this.

"But you always wanted to go away to school."

"Yeah, but things are different now. I just want to stay put for a while."

I hang a tiny golden reindeer on the tree and then go to the kitchen to refill my glass of eggnog. "Well, you don't have to decide anything right now. You have plenty of time to think about it, and you might feel differently in the new year. I just want you to be happy, and if that means you going away to college, then that's what I want too."

Yet a part of me relishes the idea of my son staying home for another year because I love him desperately, and after losing my husband, the thought of saying goodbye to Zack is like another knife in my heart.

If not for my mother, waking up on Christmas morning and opening gifts without Alan would have been pure torture for Zack and me, but she arrives on Christmas Eve with a festive cherry cheesecake, a giant can of caramel popcorn, and a bag full of gifts. Winston leaps up from his lounging position on the rug, runs to the door to greet her, and wags his tail happily. It's a welcome distraction.

Then we all sit together on Christmas Eve and watch *The Sound of Music*, which again distracts us from the fact that this is, without a doubt, the worst Christmas on record. All we want to do is get through it.

On Christmas morning, we open gifts without much ceremony, as we agreed to keep presents to a minimum and avoid giving each other anything too sentimental. I couldn't help myself, though. I've overcompensated for what we've lost and bought Zack all new hockey equipment and a new cell phone, which occupies him for a while as he sets it up. He gives me a lovely silk scarf, while my mother presents me with a basket full of jams, chocolates, and coffee. Zack receives a fifty-dollar bill from her, along with socks and a new shirt.

As soon as the gifts are unwrapped, we move away from the tree and focus on cooking a gigantic breakfast. After the dishes are washed and put away, Zack texts some of his friends on his new phone and goes to Jeremy's house to hang out in his basement and play the new video game he got from Dave and Maureen.

I'm glad he's keeping busy and spending time with friends. As for me, I just want to forget that it's Christmas and move past it as quickly as possible.

Somewhere between Christmas and New Year's, in the middle of one of those endless nights, I awake groggily to the sound of the garage door opening, then a thump downstairs and the crashing clatter of something tipping over.

Zack pounds repeatedly on my bedroom door. *"Mom!"* He rattles the doorknob. *"Someone's in the basement!"*

Panic sweeps through my bloodstream. I'm so frightened I can't move a muscle. I can't even make my voice work to call out to him.

Alan. Why aren't you here?

My body feels made of lead. I try to scream, but it comes out as a mournful moan.

Winston jumps onto the bed and stands over me on all fours. He licks my eyelids, and suddenly I'm free from the terror paralysis, and I'm able to move. My eyes fly open. I grab hold of the fur around his neck and stare into his face to anchor myself in wakefulness.

Was I dreaming? No, there was definitely a noise in the basement. Someone's in the house.

Zack.

I leap out of bed and run out of the room. The house is dark and quiet, except for Winston, who jumps off my bed and hurries down the hall ahead of me like a heroic four-legged defender. Head low, he runs to Zack's room, peers in the door, then dashes down the stairs, barking viciously—and he's not normally a barker.

I worry that Zack has already gone downstairs, and what if the intruder has a knife or a gun? I stumble slightly in my rush to get to his room, but when I enter, I find him sitting up in bed, switching on the light, which seems odd, considering he was banging at my door just now. Or was he?

Winston is barking somewhere downstairs, and my insides wrench at the thought that he's down there alone, trying to protect us.

"Someone's inside the house, for real," I whisper, dashing to Zack's phone on his bedside table. "I'm calling 911."

Zack tosses the covers aside and rises from bed. His wild gaze darts around the room and fixes on a hockey stick leaning against the wall.

While I wait for the call to connect with emergency services, Zack picks up the stick and starts for the door.

"No, don't go down there!" I whisper. "I'm calling the police."

"But Winston's down there," Zack replies.

"He'll be all right."

I say these words even though I'm not sure he will be.

Then it occurs to me that a moment ago, I thought Zack was banging on my bedroom door, warning me about the intruder, but when I entered his room, he was still in bed.

Nevertheless, I know what I heard. It happened. It was real.

"Did you bang on my door a few minutes ago?" I ask.

"No."

"Did you hear the garage door open?"

Again, he shakes his head.

Winston has stopped barking, but I hear him running all over the house, searching every room, including the basement.

Someone answers my call. Though I'm suddenly feeling doubtful that I actually heard something—maybe I *was* dreaming—I don't want to take any chances, so I explain that I heard an intruder enter my home through the garage. The dispatcher instructs me to stay on the line and remain upstairs with the door closed and locked and to wait for the police to arrive.

I convince Zack to wait with me, while my mind works through what just occurred. As I begin to feel more wakeful, I wonder if I might have indeed been dreaming, because Zack insists that he never knocked on my door.

But I'd swear on my life that I heard the garage door opening, and obviously Winston heard it too. It was too real to be a dream. It happened. I'm certain. Someone entered through the garage, knocked something over, and might still be in the house.

I want Winston to come back upstairs. I'm worried for him.

When the police arrive, they do a full sweep of the house and inform me that the garage door is closed. Winston is stressed from all the activity and strangers combing through our house in the middle of the night. He sits at my side, panting heavily, while I speak to the officer in charge.

I explain again that I heard noises and Winston heard them too. But at this point, I'm starting to wonder if I'm going crazy.

If it wasn't real, I'm too embarrassed to admit it, even to Zack.

After the police leave, I try to go back to sleep, but it's not easy. Zack's nervous too, so I suggest he sleep in the king-size bed with Winston and me. Then I hurry downstairs to get a frying pan, return to bed, and slide it under my pillow.

What a night.

Despite all the lies and betrayals in my marriage, I miss Alan more than ever and wish he was here with us. I always felt safe with him in bed beside me.

The following day at the hospital, I'm exhausted from sleeplessness, and I drift off at the lunch table in the doctors' lounge.

A nurse finds me with my face resting next to my salad bowl, and she shakes me awake for my next surgery.

I'm mortified and apologize profusely, but she understands when I explain what happened the night before. She is kind enough to bring me a strong cup of black coffee, but as I sip on it, I can't help but wonder if there's something seriously wrong with me. One minute I miss my husband, and I'm devastated over the loss of him. The next minute I want to strangle him with my bare hands for what he did to us. And now I'm falling asleep at work in the middle of the day, in plain sight of everyone.

Is this normal? Or am I totally losing it?

CHAPTER TWENTY-SIX

Somehow, Zack and I manage to make it to the new year, and I'm sitting in the bleachers watching his hockey game, relieved to slide back into some semblance of my old life. My nose is cold, and my rear end is numb, but I revel in the company of the hockey moms and dads, all of whom I've come to know very well over the past few years through sports dinners and fund-raisers, games and practices. On top of that, the blaring music, the noisy scrape of the players' skates across the ice, and the refs' shrill whistles create a cacophony that rouses me from the recent deadness of my life.

Not long after the first period, my cell phone vibrates in my coat pocket. I reach in with my thick woolen mitten to check the call display.

OCEANVIEW ANIMAL HOSPITAL.

I get up from the wooden bench and climb down the bleachers to take the call. "Hello?"

"Hi. Is this Abbie?"

It's Nathan's voice, which comes as a surprise. "Yes. Hi, Nathan. How are you doing?"

"I'm good. How about you?"

I walk along the boards, past the plexiglass barrier, to the lobby. "Well, you know . . . as good as can be expected."

He's quiet for a few seconds. "Yeah. I thought about you over Christmas. I wanted to call you, actually, just to see how you were doing, because I know what it can be like, but I didn't want to intrude."

"You wouldn't have intruded. I would have liked to talk to you because you've been where I'm at right now, and sometimes it feels like Crazy Town."

He chuckles. "I know the feeling. You can call me anytime, you know. You have my cell number."

"I do, and thank you. I appreciate that." I take a deep breath. "I'm just glad the holidays are over." Moving to a chair in the lobby, I sit down.

"So how's Zack getting along?" Nathan asks.

"Pretty well. Better than me, but I suppose he isn't working with all the information I have, so it's more of a normal grieving process for him. As for me, I still feel like I'm being tossed around inside a washing machine." I stop talking and press the heel of my hand to my forehead. "I'm sorry. I'm sure you didn't call to hear me whining about my life."

"Actually, that's *exactly* why I called."

I laugh, and he pauses. "So you haven't told Zack anything."

"No. I've talked to him about the drunk driving because the whole world heard about that, and I told him about Alan's cancer diagnosis but not about the affair, and I'm still not sure I ever will tell him. At least he has a good support system at school. The teachers and his coaches have been terrific."

"That's good to hear. Are you back at work now?"

"Yes, and it's been good for me to get back into a routine, to have a reason to get up in the mornings."

"It definitely helps. Just remember what I said. It *will* get easier. I promise."

"I hope you're right."

Beyond the doors to the rink, a whistle blows, and the music blasts through the speaker system.

"Are you listening to 'We Will Rock You?'" Nathan asks.

"Yeah. I'm at a hockey rink. Zack's playing tonight."

"What's the score?"

"Three to one right now. They're winning."

"Good stuff," Nathan says. "I'll root for him."

A few high school girls enter the community center through the main doors. It's below freezing outside with fresh snow on the ground, but they're wearing short skirts and ballerina flats with no socks on their feet. I watch them giggle and check their phones as they push through the inside doors to the rink.

"So you're probably wondering why I'm calling?" Nathan asks.

"Aside from your interest in high school hockey?"

He chuckles. "Yeah. I wanted to check and see how Winston was doing. Before Christmas, you mentioned that his incision looked good, but I'd still like to see him for a final follow-up appointment, just to make sure everything's okay."

"Of course. Zack and I go to my mom's place for dinner most Sundays. Are you open on weekends?"

"Not usually, but I'll make an exception if that's the only time you're in town. Are you coming this Sunday?"

I pinch the bridge of my nose, struggling to remember my call schedule for the week. I'm pretty sure Sunday is open.

"Yes, that'll work," I say.

"Great," he replies. "What time is good for you?"

"How about late afternoon?"

He takes a moment to check his schedule as well, then suggests I come by at four thirty.

I thank him again, end the call, and return to the game.

Late on Saturday afternoon—following a long night in the OR with a complicated hernia case—I take a nap on the sofa in the living room.

I've just drifted off when I'm awakened by the sound of a key in the front door.

Zack walks in, but I'm so tired I don't bother to move or get up. I continue to lie there, stretched out on my stomach with my arms wrapped around the sofa pillow.

Zack goes straight to the kitchen to get something to eat. He's not gentle with the microwave door, which he slams shut, and then I hear the beep of the buttons and the hum of the machine when he presses start. He sets a plate down on the granite countertop with a noisy clink that echoes off the ceiling. Everything seems amplified, especially the chip bag he rips open with a vengeance. I can hear him crunching loudly.

I want to tell him to be quiet, but I let it go because I just want to keep sleeping.

He eats standing up in the kitchen, and I hear him speak softly on his cell phone to someone.

"Yeah, she's asleep on the couch . . . no, she still hasn't cleaned out the closet yet . . . I don't know . . . I think she's nuts. She won't talk about him, and she won't say why she hates him so much . . . he's dead, and he can't defend himself . . . sometimes I just want to shake her because she won't move on. I can't wait to get out of here in the fall. I swear to God I won't look back."

Stunned and hurt by how my son talks about me, I fight not to cry. I don't know what to say to him or how to deal with this right now, so I pretend to be asleep as he leaves through the front door.

Zack doesn't come home again that day. He texts me later to tell me he's going to a party and plans to sleep over at a friend's house.

I decide to give him some space until I can figure out how to deal with this in a calm way, but I'm deeply hurt and troubled by what he said on the phone. I can't believe it. He's never spoken that way before, with such bitter disdain for someone, at least not when I was within earshot. I feel wounded and anguished, and I worry that Alan's death has affected him more than he's letting on. I feel like I'm losing everything I love . . . that it's all falling apart . . . and my house feels colder and emptier than ever.

The phone rings, and it's Maureen. I tell her about what Zack said.

"Oh, Abbie. Teenage boys can be so insensitive sometimes," she says, "but it doesn't mean anything. He's a great kid, and he loves you."

I'm tempted to let everything spill out about Alan's infidelity—because Maureen is one of my closest friends and so far I haven't told her anything about his cheating—but I'm afraid Jeremy might find out, and I can't let Zack learn about it from anyone but me, so I bite my tongue. Carla and Nathan remain my only confidants.

Maureen and I chat about other things, and then we talk about catching a movie that night with a few of the other hockey moms, since the boys are going to a party anyway.

"I'll call Gwen," she says, "and you can call Kate."

"That sounds great."

It all works out, and Maureen picks me up at six, and we meet the other gals at the theater. It really helps for me to laugh with some friends at an outrageous chick flick. It feels good to get my mind off things, at least for a little while.

Later, when I return home, Winston is waiting at the door for me. I let him out the back door, and then we curl up on the sofa together to watch the news.

Winston. Like an angel, he rests his head on my lap. I rub behind his ears.

When we finally go upstairs to bed, he jumps up and sleeps on Alan's side, which is unusual for him, as he normally prefers his own fluffy cushion on the floor.

I like how it feels to share the bed again, even if it's only with my dog. I suspect Winston knows how much I appreciate it, because he's amazingly intuitive.

The following day, Zack and I get into the car to drive to my mother's house for the afternoon. As soon as we're outside the city, I feel ready to bring up what I overheard him say on the phone the day before, although I don't want him to know that I eavesdropped.

I glance across at him. He's staring down at his phone, texting.

"How was the party last night?" I ask.

He finishes what he's doing, then looks up at me. "What?"

I repeat the question.

"It was okay. And it wasn't really a party. There were only twelve of us."

"I see. So enlighten me. If twelve doesn't qualify as a party, what number does?"

He thinks about that for a few seconds. "Oh, I don't know. Twenty? Twenty-five?"

He leans forward and switches on the radio.

"Listen, Zack," I say, turning the volume down slightly. "I wonder if we could talk about something."

"Sure." He gazes out the window.

I clear my throat and dive straight to the point. "Remember when you came home yesterday afternoon and you thought I was asleep on the couch?"

He turns toward me and frowns, but I continue, undaunted.

"I didn't mean to eavesdrop, but I heard some of the things you said when you were talking on the phone, and I was really hurt. I had no idea you felt that way."

"What are you talking about?" he asks, and I sense he's about to deny everything.

"I heard you say that you were disappointed that I haven't removed your father's things from my closet, and that you think I hate him—which I don't—and that I'm not moving forward like I should be, and that you can't wait to move out in the fall. Is that true?"

His cheeks flush red, and he stares at me with a look of pure horror.

"I'm not angry, honey. I just want to talk about it, because I hate to think that you're unhappy at home. Or that you think I'm nuts. If there's anything you want to ask me, I promise I'll answer it honestly."

His eyebrows pull together with alarm. Finally, he speaks. "Mom. I never came home yesterday."

I dart a glance at him. "What do you mean? Yes, you did. You made yourself something to eat, and then you left again."

He shakes his head. "No, I didn't."

"Yes," I insist. "I heard you talking on the phone. And you cooked something in the microwave and ate chips."

He faces me more directly. "I swear to God, Mom, I didn't come home. I was with the guys all day. We had hockey practice at three, and then I went straight to Greg's house and texted you that I was going to spend the night there. I know you got my text because you replied to it."

My heart begins to pound. "But I heard you talking. I heard the microwave."

Then suddenly I remember waking up and going into the kitchen and being surprised that there wasn't a mess. Zack had cleaned up all his dishes and put everything away. The kitchen was spotless, but I realize I never heard him running water to wash up.

"Are you okay, Mom?"

"I don't know." I wonder briefly if I should pull over because I'm afraid I might be delusional, but I take a few deep breaths and keep driving. "Did I dream that?"

Zack watches me with concern. "You probably did, like you dreamed about the intruder that night."

"But that was real," I say. "I swear it was. Even Winston heard it."

"Well, whatever you think happened yesterday didn't, because I never came home."

Despite my concerns that there might be something wrong with me, I'm relieved that my son never said those awful things. "So you never said you can't wait to move out?"

"No. I swear on my life, Mom. I didn't."

I reach to take hold of his hand and squeeze it. "Oh, I'm so glad. I thought you hated me. I was heartbroken. I hardly slept a wink last night."

"No, Mom. I love you more than anything, and I want to live at home next year. I told you, I don't need to go away."

I start to laugh and cry at the same time, even though I'm afraid I might be going insane with these bizarre dreams that seem like reality.

"Maybe you should see a doctor," Zack says. "I've noticed you've been sleeping a lot lately."

It's true. I've been falling asleep at the strangest times and have been having trouble staying focused. I've been gaining a bit of weight too.

"I will see someone, but it's probably just stress," I say to Zack, not wanting to worry him—or myself. "It's been a rough few months."

We drive for a while in silence. "But do you really think I should be ready to clean out the closet by now?"

He lets out a heavy sigh. "First of all, I never said that. And you'll be ready when you're ready, Mom. There's no need to rush it."

My son makes me feel so much better. I'm glad I have him in my life.

CHAPTER TWENTY-SEVEN

Shortly after four, while Zack is helping my mother chop vegetables for dinner, I zip out to take Winston for his appointment with Nathan.

Nathan meets us at the door and shows us in to one of the small private examination rooms. He checks Winston over, asks me all sorts of questions, and finally delivers a clean bill of health. "He's a trouper. Tip-top condition. A-plus in terms of a recovery."

"At least one of us gets an A," I reply with a touch of humor as I bend to hook Winston's leash onto his collar.

Nathan leans back against the counter and studies me for a moment. "Everything okay?"

I wave a hand dismissively through the air. "Yes. It's nothing."

"I'm sure it's not nothing. You look tired. Are you sleeping okay?"

I realize this man is very good at reading people—or maybe he's just good at reading me. It's not surprising. I never quite managed to master the art of the poker face, which is why I'm so worried about messing up everything with Zack. This whole situation feels like a ticking time bomb.

"Actually, sleep's been a bit of a challenge lately," I admit. "I've had a few strange dreams. But I can't keep pouring out all my woes to you every time I see you."

"I don't mind. What kind of dreams?"

Winston sits down, and I pat him on the head.

"Well, first I dreamed that someone broke into my house through the garage. I was so scared I was literally paralyzed. To be honest, I'm still not sure it didn't actually happen. I called the cops and everything, and Winston went completely ballistic. He ran all over the house barking—like a very good guard dog—so I thought he heard something too, but maybe he was just sensing my fear. I don't know. Anyway, the cops came and said there was no one in the house, and no sign of forced entry. I even thought I heard Zack banging on my door to warn me about the intruder, but he said he didn't do that. So maybe I did dream the whole thing. It just felt so real."

"Jeez."

"I know, right? It was scary. And then yesterday, I fell asleep on the sofa and thought Zack came home to fix himself something to eat. I asked him about it today, but he said he never stopped by after school. So that didn't even happen." I angle my head slightly. "Did you ever have dreams like that after you lost your wife? Dreams that seemed real? Maybe they're what they call lucid dreams."

He considers that for a moment. "Come to think of it, I did have a recurring stress dream. It was always some variation of the same thing—that I'm performing surgery on a dog or a cat and something goes wrong, like the power goes out or my instruments aren't clean, and I have to do the surgery anyway. The dreams eventually stopped after I moved home and opened up the clinic here." He appears pensive. "Gosh, I haven't had a dream like that in two years."

"Well, that gives me hope." I pat Winston again, pleased that he's so polite and patient while we're talking.

"Still . . . ," Nathan says, "you should probably see your doctor if something feels off. And remember, you fainted that time. Best not to take chances."

"You're right. I'll make an appointment."

Nathan gives Winston a light scratch behind the ears. "Otherwise, you're doing okay?"

I shrug. "Some days are better than others. There are just so many details to take care of, like banking issues or Alan's magazine subscriptions that need to be canceled. Every day, something comes in the mail that I need to deal with. And I want to clean out the closet and get rid of his stuff, which is starting to collect dust, but part of me can't bring myself to do it, while the other part of me just wants to burn it all because I'm still so mad at him. That said, I don't want Zack to see an angry display and suspect something's wrong, beyond the obvious—that his father is dead."

I speak the words harshly, and my stomach turns over with disgust that I can sound so cavalier and bitter about my husband's passing. What sort of woman am I becoming? I don't want to be bitter.

Tears spring to my eyes. I work hard to blink them back.

"That came out wrong," I say, looking down at the floor and shaking my head. "You must think I'm a terrible person."

"No, I don't think that at all. I think you're shouldering a lot—more than most people could handle. I'm amazed, actually, that you're keeping it together as well as you are."

"Well," I say with a hint of mockery, "you didn't see me flip out at my father-in-law after Alan's funeral. Or pound the steering wheel after I found out the truth from Alan's mistress. I'm doing everything I can to keep calm for Zack, but I assure you, deep down, where no one can see . . . there's a lot of running and screaming."

He chuckles at that. "I know the feeling. I think it's part of being a parent. Sometimes you just want to go hide under a rock somewhere, but you have to stay strong for your kids, to keep *their* world upright."

"Exactly. That's it, in a nutshell."

Hearing him say those words feels like an epiphany, but it isn't. As a mother, I've always known it was like that, but I never heard Alan say it. I suppose when it came to our son, I was always the soldier who never left her post, while Alan obviously felt free enough to dash off and take care of himself when he needed to, knowing I'd be there, holding down the family fort. Maybe Nathan's wife was a dependable soldier too, but she's gone now, and he's on his own, taking full command of the troops. Like me.

"I'm discovering very quickly," I say, "that when you're a single parent, you can't afford the luxury of falling apart, because there's no copilot to take over for you. But maybe that's a good thing. It makes us strong." I pause. "But still . . . there are days when I would love to have a record-breaking meltdown. There are a lot of days like that, actually."

Nathan nods, then reaches out and rubs my upper arm with sympathy.

His touch catches me off guard and stirs an awareness in me—maybe because it's been more than twenty years since any man other than Alan has touched me with tenderness or intimacy. But this isn't sexual. That's not what's happening here. It's something else—support and understanding—and I find myself wanting to fall into it.

Then I feel a rush of guilt because I'm accepting comfort from a good-looking man who isn't my husband and in my heart I'm still Alan's wife. I may be angry with him for what he did, but I can't stop loving him. I'll *always* love him, despite everything. And I miss him. I wish he were still alive, that none of this had ever happened and we could simply go back to the way things were.

But of course, that's not possible.

"I should probably go." I fumble to open the glass door of the exam room.

Nathan follows and escorts Winston and me down the hall to the reception area. I walk past the front desk, then stop in my tracks and turn. "Wait. I need to pay you."

I realize I'm a bit frazzled.

He holds up a hand. "No. Please don't worry about it."

"But it's a Sunday. You opened the clinic especially for me. I can't *not* pay you."

He shakes his head. "It's not a problem. Besides, Ruby's not here, and she's the one who handles payments. So as you can see, my hands are tied."

I swallow uneasily. "Okay. Have her send me a bill then?"

He shrugs a shoulder and grins, as if to say he probably won't.

I let out a breath and take in the features of his face.

He truly is a handsome man. I hadn't actually noticed before today. I suppose I've been walking around in a daze. It's nice to know something in me is still awake and breathing.

Shaking my head to clear it, I turn to go and lead Winston across the reception area. Nathan follows and holds the door open for us. "Good night, Abbie. Get home safely."

"I will. And I'll see you later. Thanks again."

I lead Winston to the car, and he leaps into the back seat and turns a few circles, tail swishing back and forth, as if something fun and exciting is about to happen. His enthusiasm is infectious.

"What are you so happy about?" I ask, laughing and rubbing his head.

As I get into the driver's seat and start the car, I realize I'm still smiling. Maybe it's because I'm starting to believe there might actually be a light at the end of this dark tunnel, and that I'm going to be okay . . . eventually, like Nathan. I just have to keep getting out of bed each day and putting one foot in front of the other. Like all good soldiers must.

Later that night, after Zack and I return home to Halifax and I'm in my pajamas in bed, a text comes in. It's from Nathan. Hey there. Did you get home safely?

I quickly thumb a reply. Yes, we're home safe and sound. Thanks for checking on us.

I hit "Send," then wait to see if he'll respond. After a few seconds, my phone chimes. A message is waiting. No prob. It was nice to see you today. Glad Winston's doing well.

I smile and type, It was nice to see you too. You always make me feel better about things.

His reply comes in a moment later. Happy to help. You just have to hang in there, and call if you ever want to talk. I'm a good listener.

I take some time to think about how I should respond. Eventually I text, Thank you. I will.

Sitting up on the pillows, I stare at my phone and wait for his reply. Finally, a message comes in: Have a good night.

I smile again and respond, You too. Sleep well.

We end it at that, and I turn out the light.

CHAPTER TWENTY-EIGHT

The following day, I make an appointment to see my family doctor about the dreams I've been having, as well as my fatigue. The receptionist asks me to come in that afternoon at four. I thank her and hang up. Then I scrub in for my next surgery.

"Scalpel, please. Skin blade," I say when things are underway.

The scrub nurse, as she's done so many times before, places the instrument in my hand.

"Okay to start?" I say to the anesthetist.

"Yes," she replies. "Patient's asleep with good paralysis."

I lean in with the scalpel and steady my hand, preparing to make the first cut. My vision is a bit hazy, so I hesitate.

"Are you okay?" asks Dr. Moore, the junior surgical resident assigned to me this month.

"Yes, I'm fine," I say with a forced air of confidence and proceed with a one-inch cut above the patient's belly button.

"S retractors and sponge, please," says Dr. Moore.

He carefully makes his way down to the fascial layer.

"Suture, please," I say as I prepare the first of two anchors for the laparoscopy port. Deftly cutting a small opening into the delicate tissue,

I dissect deeper and reach the peritoneum. "Hasson trocar, please. Gas on. Camera off standby, please. Let's have a look."

I slide the camera through the Hasson into the abdominal cavity. The liver looks ratty and lumpy. Probably advanced cirrhosis. "Damn, I wasn't expecting this."

The gallbladder is distended and swollen and looks like it's ripe and ready to pop. "This isn't going to be easy."

I add a couple of extra ports and use graspers to grab the gallbladder, but it's plastered against the liver and small bowel.

I pause for a moment.

Dr. Moore can read my mind. "We're going to have to open?"

"Not sure," I say, dissecting a bit more, only to realize I've torn into a small pumping bleeder. The spray covers the camera lens.

"Damn! Take out the camera, and clean the lens. I'll need clips quickly."

With a clean lens and a few clips, I finally manage to stop the bleeder. "Let's convert to open."

We remove the laparoscopy equipment, and I make a large standard incision below the right lower rib cage. At least we'll be able to see.

All the while, I feel a fog rolling into my head, growing denser by the second. I want to lie down and take a power nap, but I can't possibly surrender to that temptation when I have an anesthetized patient lying with an open abdomen on the table in front of me.

I fight through the haze and squeeze my eyes shut every few seconds, then open them wide and blink hard to stay focused.

"Are you okay, Doctor?" one of the nurses asks. She sounds a bit concerned.

Dr. Moore glances up from an artery he's clamping and waits for me to respond.

"My eyes are a bit dry," I explain, even though there's a tingling sensation in my brain, like some sort of electric impulse, and it's making me uneasy because I've never felt anything like this before and now's not a good time for a headache, when I'm holding a patient's life in my hands.

Relief floods through me when I finally clip off the cystic artery and cystic duct and painstakingly dissect the gallbladder off the liver bed. Everything looks dry, so we start closing as nurses count sponges and instruments.

"Double-stranded PDS to close fascia, please."

This is it. I'm on the homestretch now as I close the wound. I just need to stay awake for another half hour or so, and then I can go collapse somewhere.

"Stapler to Dr. Moore and two pickups to me, please."

Suddenly, alarms start going off. I glance at the monitor. The patient's BP is dropping fast, and his pulse is racing ever faster.

Adrenaline sparks in my veins, which is not unusual at a time like this, but today it causes my knees to buckle. The surgical instruments fall from my hands, and I go down hard with a tremendous thump on the floor.

My eyes are closed, but in my mind, I'm conscious of the sounds and activity around me. The surgical team takes charge of the situation and moves around the table.

"I got this," the resident says, while a nurse runs for the door and calls for help.

Machines are beeping everywhere. All I want to do is scramble to my feet and save the patient's life—or at least supervise the resident—but I can't move. My body refuses to respond to my brain's commands. In my head, I'm screaming, *Get up!* But I'm paralyzed.

A nurse, Corinne, crouches beside me, finds the pulse at my neck, and drags me away from the table to give others room to work. She rolls me onto my back and speaks close to my face. "Dr. MacIntyre, can you hear me? You fainted. Hello!"

I know I fainted! But I'm awake now! I just can't move. Please, make sure the patient is okay. Check the arterial clips. He's probably bleeding!

I'm thinking these things in my brain, but I can't get my mouth or vocal cords to work.

The anesthetist works with the resident, who is barking instructions to the nurses. "We got a pumper at the liver edge. Clamp, please. Suction! I can't see!"

It's driving me mad that I can't do anything to help, and I don't understand what's happening to me.

Is this real? Am I dreaming again?

Or am I dead?

A gurney bursts through the doors to the OR.

Corinne says to whoever is pushing it, "She passed out. She's unconscious."

I'm not unconscious! I hear everything you're saying!

I'm still listening to what's going on above me . . . the resident is focused . . . alarms are still screaming . . .

I'm as limp as a rag doll, but I feel every movement, every hand on my body as they lift me onto the gurney, extend the wheels, and roll me out of the OR. My heart thunders in my chest. I want to tell them what's going on—that I'm still here—but I can't. I'm trapped inside this physical shell that won't move.

One of my colleagues—Jack Bradley, an ER doc—helps push the gurney somewhere. I don't know where they're taking me.

"She collapsed in the middle of a surgery?" he asks with disbelief.

"Yes," Corinne replies. "She just passed out without any warning. Went down like a ton of bricks."

"Did she complain of chest pains or anything beforehand?"

"No, but she said her eyes were dry. She was squeezing them open and shut as if she was having trouble seeing."

The gurney swings around and comes to a halt. All I can do is lie there like a corpse while they place an oxygen mask over my face and wrap a blood pressure cuff around my arm.

"All right—stat glucometer, and let's get a twelve-lead EKG, put her on O$_2$, and get her on a heart monitor. We'll need a full lab panel and a pregnancy test. Abbie, can you hear me? It's me, Jack."

He lifts my eyelids and shines a penlight at my pupils.

Inside my head, I'm screaming and shouting, desperate for someone to hear me and understand that I'm conscious! I fight for the strength to move—please, just a finger or toe—but it's no use.

And I don't need a pregnancy test, for Christ's sake! I had a hysterectomy, not to mention the fact that I haven't been sexually active in months.

Then something happens. I manage to push through the physical resistance. My hand is limp, but I can lift my wrist, then my fingers. My plea for help finally escapes my lips, though it comes out as a low, weak, pathetic-sounding moan.

"She's waking up," Corinne says.

My eyes flutter open, and the first thing I see is Jack leaning over me. He's a young ER doc, known for his passion for surfing. "Can you hear me, Abbie?"

I nod my head and take in a deep breath as my muscles begin to work again. I lift both hands, wiggle my fingers, and try to sit up.

Jack eases me back down, which is just as well because I feel like I've been hit by a truck. All I want to do is go to sleep.

"Do you know who I am?" he asks.

I know the routine, so I answer everything he's about to ask me. "Yes, you're Jack Bradley, and my name is Abbie MacIntyre." I swallow heavily and fight for the strength to continue. My voice is weak, and I can't speak very fast. "It's Monday morning, and I just collapsed in the OR. But I'm okay now."

"Let me be the judge of that. Can you tell me if you had any symptoms beforehand? Dizziness? Chest pains? Corinne said you were blinking, as if you were having trouble focusing. You said your eyes were dry?"

I lay my open palm on my forehead. "Yes, but that wasn't the real problem. I felt sleepy, and I was trying to stay awake. I've been sleeping a lot lately, taking frequent naps in the day. I have an appointment to see my doctor about it this afternoon. But I'm not pregnant. I had a hysterectomy years ago."

"Okay. Good to know. How long has this been going on?" Jack asks.

I try to think. "Since my accident, I guess. I thought the fatigue was stress related, but lately I've been having some strange dreams that are more like hallucinations, and this is the second time I've passed out—although I didn't actually pass out just now. I was completely conscious and awake. I could hear everything that was going on around me. I just couldn't move my body or open my eyes or speak. It was total paralysis."

"Okay . . ." Jack stalls for a few seconds while he mulls over everything. "And this started happening after your accident?"

"Yes."

He turns to one of the other nurses. "Let's get someone down here from neuro. Tell them who the patient is, that it's Dr. MacIntyre."

"Really . . . ," I say, "I don't want any special treatment . . ."

The nurse goes to a phone to make the call, and Jack touches my arm. "You're not on anything, are you? Any medications? Alcohol? Illicit drugs? I need to know."

I shake my head.

"Then tell me more about how you felt in the seconds just before you collapsed. Describe the experience to me."

I pause. "Okay, but first, can you tell me what's going on with the gallbladder patient? Is he okay?"

"We'll check on that for you." Jack makes eye contact with another nurse, who leaves the room.

I take a deep breath and think back to how I felt just before I collapsed.

"I was tired," I tell him, "but that's nothing new. Like I said, I've been sleeping a lot lately. But then I felt a tingling sensation in my head. I thought it would pass and that I was going to make it through the rest of the surgery, but then the patient's blood pressure dropped, and alarms started going off. I felt a rush of adrenaline, and that's when my knees gave out, and I couldn't hold on to the instruments. My whole body just wilted. It was like all my limbs turned to spaghetti, and that's why I fell. But like I said, I was conscious the whole time. I was fully aware of everything that was happening in the room. I could hear the resident and the anesthetist taking over, and then I felt myself being lifted onto the gurney. I heard Corinne tell you that I was blinking a lot and that I said my eyes were dry."

Jack frowns at me. "Was it like . . . an out-of-body experience?"

Of all the doctors I know, only Jack would ask that question.

"No, I was very much inside my body, and my eyes were closed, so I couldn't actually see anything, and yet I could see it in my mind. It was like I was trapped, and I wanted to break free from the paralysis, but I couldn't."

He nods at me. "You say your knees buckled when you felt the panic from the alarms going off?"

"Yes."

A nurse returns with news about my patient in the OR. "Everything's fine," she says. "They're just closing up now."

"Thank God."

Jack glances toward the door to the trauma room and pats my arm. "I'll be right back. Just stay put, okay?"

Even though I have plenty to do in the hospital and another surgery scheduled in an hour, I don't put up a fight because all I want to do is sleep. As soon as Jack is gone, I close my eyes and fall into a fitful slumber in which I dream that I'm skiing fast down a snow-covered mountain, unable to slow down because it's too steep. I'm terrified I'm going to plummet to my death.

Then suddenly I'm being chased by a mugger in a city neighborhood. I dash into an alley, search for a place to hide, but there's nowhere to conceal myself, so I just keep running, leaping over bags of garbage . . .

Someone touches my shoulder and shakes me hard. I wake with a gasp.

The head of neurology is standing over me, watching me intently. I'm surprised to see him, and I worry that I might have been moaning or talking in my sleep, none of which is terribly professional.

At least this time, I know I was dreaming. I have no illusions that I was actually skiing down a snowy mountain or running from a thief who wanted to hurt me.

I try to sit up, but I feel weak and groggy. "Dr. Tremblay . . . how long was I out?"

"About ten minutes," he tells me. "How are you feeling now?"

"Rotten," I reply, leaning up on my elbows. Then I decide it would be best to rest my head on the pillow before adding, "And exhausted. Like my body is made of lead. I'm just so tired."

He ponders that and nods with understanding. "Dr. Bradley told me what happened. He described your symptoms to me, but I'd like to hear it from you. Can you tell me everything you remember, leading up to the moment you collapsed? And anything else you think is relevant about your health."

"Of course." I explain my fainting episode again and the level of awareness I had, along with the strange dreams I've had at home over the past few weeks. And my car accident.

Dr. Tremblay listens attentively.

I also mention that I've put on a few pounds.

When I'm finished telling him everything, he asks, "Are you aware that you were dreaming just now?"

"Yes. Was I moaning? Or tossing and turning?"

"No, but your eyelids were fluttering. You've been in a state of REM since the moment I entered the room."

He raises an eyebrow, and I understand why he's telling me this—because we both know it's not normal to enter the REM phase so quickly after drifting off. It should take anywhere from eighty to a hundred minutes.

"So . . . what do you think is going on?" I ask him, and I feel inadequate because I don't know the answer myself. I'm a physician. Shouldn't I know what's wrong with me?

Dr. Tremblay glances away briefly. "I can't be absolutely sure without performing some tests," he says, "but I suspect that what happened to you in the OR just now was cataplexy."

Cataplexy. I know that disorder, and it's not something I want to hear.

"What you've just told me," he continues, "about the dreams you've been having and your increased fatigue and sleeping during the day is consistent with the condition of—"

"Narcolepsy," we each say together.

I stare at him with wide eyes, suddenly feeling very alert.

He nods, knowing that he doesn't need to explain to me that narcolepsy is a neurological condition that causes disruptions in sleep patterns and excessive sleepiness during the day. The afflicted person can sometimes nod off involuntarily.

Another symptom is sleep paralysis—which is normal for most people during a state of REM, probably because our brains want to prevent us from acting out our dreams. But with narcolepsy, this paralysis can occur when the person is falling asleep or waking up, and it can be accompanied by vivid hallucinations that seem real.

Cataplexy is an add-on I really don't need as a surgeon. It's a loss in muscle tone while the person is awake. It's usually triggered by a strong emotion, like panic. Even laughter can bring it on. Some episodes can be barely perceptible, with only a slight muscle weakness—a drooping eyelid, for example—but a more severe attack can result in a full physical collapse, like what just happened to me in the OR when the alarms started going off.

"But why?" I ask him. "I was fine before. Is this because of my accident?"

All the anger I have felt toward Alan pales in comparison to the blistering fury I feel now, because if I have acquired this condition because of his drunk driving escapade on his way to see his secret lover, I will never be able to forgive him. This isn't something I can get over eventually, like the heartbreak from his affair. This is my whole future.

I'm a surgeon. How can I operate if I might drop instruments or fall down without warning? How can I handle sudden stressful situations if I have cataplexy? My career will be over. My life will never be the same.

If there was ever any chance of forgiveness, it's slipping away now, fast as blue blazes.

Dr. Tremblay speaks plainly to me. "Narcolepsy is a mysterious condition, Abbie, and it may have any of several causes. It could be autoimmune in nature, or it may be genetic. Symptoms can take a while to fully manifest, so we can't be sure it was your accident that caused this, at least not yet." He holds up a hand. "But let's not jump the gun. I'd like to do a full physical to rule out other things, then send you to a sleep clinic for some tests before we attach a diagnosis to this."

I shut my eyes and nod my head, because I know how this works. We can't presume anything at this stage. We need clinical test results and analysis to be sure.

"When can we do that?" I ask as I glance at the clock on the wall. "I have another case in less than an hour."

He gives me a sympathetic look. "You'll have to reschedule or get another surgeon to cover for you. And I advise you to stay out of the OR until we have this figured out."

I lie back on the pillow and blink up at the ceiling. *Great.* The last thing I need is more time on my sofa in my bathrobe, watching daytime television. I thought I was past that.

What's next, Lord? What else do you have lined up for me? I'm chomping at the bit to find out.

CHAPTER TWENTY-NINE

Despite the fact that I told my colleagues I didn't want special treatment, Dr. Tremblay fast-tracks me into the sleep disorder clinic for overnight testing the following week. In the meantime, I'm not permitted to perform any surgeries, although I'm allowed to see patients in my office for diagnoses and follow-ups, and I continue to do rounds in the hospital.

While I wait to be tested, I research the heck out of my suspected condition and all the latest developments and treatments. My symptoms seem to grow worse, but I suspect that's not truly the case. I'm simply more mindful of them now that I understand what's wrong with me. When the fog enters my brain, I recognize it immediately, and I surrender to the urge to fall asleep, somewhere safe and appropriate for a nap.

On Sunday, after Zack's hockey practice, he and I take Winston and drive to Lunenburg for dinner with my mom. While Zack is helping her set the table, I disappear into the bedroom for a few minutes to make a phone call, because there's someone who's been on my mind and I've been channeling him even harder since being in town.

"Hi, Nathan? It's Abbie. I hope I'm not calling at a bad time."

"Not at all," he replies. "The girls are watching a movie. I'm glad you called. How are you?"

"I'm doing okay. I'm at my mom's place right now." I move to the window and look out at the backyard. "How have you been?"

"Great," he replies. "Work is good. We're heading into dental health month at the clinic, so that's keeping me busy. Girls are doing well. Marie just got a part in the school play this week."

"That's wonderful. What's the play?"

"It's a kid's version of *Macbeth*. She's playing the nurse."

"How exciting."

"Yes, it's going to be fun. What's up with you?"

I sit down on the edge of the bed and inch back against the pillows. "Funny you should ask. A lot's happened, actually, since the last time we spoke, and that's kind of why I'm calling. Remember when I told you about the dreams I was having, and you suggested I see my doctor?"

"Yes, of course."

"Well, I made an appointment, but before I could get there, I passed out during a surgery."

"Oh no. Are you okay?"

I pause and run my finger along the braided trim on the comforter. "Not exactly. On the upside, the surgical patient is doing fine, thank goodness, but it turns out that I might have narcolepsy."

"Narcolepsy." Nathan whistles. "Isn't that where you can fall asleep unexpectedly? Even if you're standing up?"

"That's about the gist of it." I cross my legs at the ankles. "I'm going for tests next week, but I'm pretty sure that's what's wrong with me. I thought you might like to know."

He lets out a breath. "Gosh, Abbie, I'm really sorry to hear that. What kind of tests will they be doing?"

"It's an overnight clinic where they'll attach electrodes to my head and take measurements of brain activity while I'm sleeping. But the worst part is that I can't perform any surgeries until we get this figured out. It's too risky. So I'm just puttering around in my office at work. Not the best scenario right now, when I would prefer to be busy."

"I totally get that."

We're quiet for a moment.

"But enough about me. How's everything else? You said Marie's in the school play. How about Jen?"

He laughs. "Oh gosh . . . let me just say that last night was not fun for me as a parent."

"Why? What happened?" I glance at the clock and wonder if Zack is missing me yet and if he's going to knock on the door anytime soon. I hope not, because I really want to hear about Nathan's night.

"Jen had a friend sleep over," he explains. "This is a new friend who moved to town recently, and she struck me as a bit rebellious. But anyway, they were watching movies in the basement, and I stayed up until about midnight just to make sure they were settled, but after I turned out the light to go to sleep, it seemed too quiet down there. And I can't explain it, but I had a bad feeling because of a few looks they exchanged—like they were planning something."

"This sounds bad."

"It was. Although I suppose it could've been much worse. Anyway, I went to check on them at about one a.m., and the lights were out in the basement, as if they were sound asleep. But get this—those two little rascals had piled pillows under the blankets on the sofa bed and snuck out the back door."

"Oh my gosh! What did you do?"

"Well . . . first I thought I was going to have a coronary. I was ripping mad but also terrified because I didn't know where they were or what they were up to. Then I called Jen's cell phone, and surprisingly, she answered. Sounded pretty nervous, though. I don't think she expected me to get up and check on them."

"Where was she?"

"Just down the road at the playground," he tells me. "Perfectly safe. They thought it would be fun to go hang out there in the middle of the night without anyone knowing."

"What did you do next?"

"I ran out to get them, of course. I brought them home, and we had a serious talk about how dangerous that was. Then I said the sleepover was over, and I drove her friend home and had to explain to the girl's parents what happened. Not a fun moment. They were pretty good about it, but they grounded her, and she went to bed in tears. Then I took Jen home and banned sleepovers for a while. She feels pretty bad. I can tell. She's normally such a good kid. She's not the type to break rules, and she doesn't like disappointing me. She apologized about a dozen times today."

"That's good, at least. Oh, Nathan. That's rough."

"Yeah. So there we have it. What a weekend. I can hardly wait for the teen years. More of this to come, no doubt."

I push a lock of hair behind my ear, remembering what it was like with Zack. Of course, I wasn't a single parent back then. I feel for Nathan, heading into that territory on his own.

"I won't lie," I say. "It's not easy. You just have to do your best to love them through it."

"Love them through it. I'll try to remember that."

The conversation soon meanders into the subject of kids with cell phones and how to manage that particular hornet's nest.

I jump when a knock sounds at the bedroom door. I whisper to Nathan, "Just hold on a second." Then I cup my hand over the mouthpiece and call out, "Yes? Come in!"

Zack opens the door and peers in at me. "I thought you were asleep."

"No, I'm just talking on the phone," I explain.

"Okay."

He watches me for a few seconds, as if he wants to ask who I'm talking to.

I pray that he won't ask that question, which makes me squirm inwardly, as if I'm doing something wrong by sneaking into the bedroom to call Nathan about something personal.

"Dinner's almost ready," Zack finally says. "You should come out to the kitchen."

"Sure," I say with some relief that he's not going to interrogate me. "I'll be right there."

He shuts the door, and I try to shake off my unease before I return my attention to Nathan. "I'm sorry. I have to get going. It was good talking to you, though."

"It was good talking to you too, Abbie. I'm glad you called. Have a nice visit tonight."

"I will."

I quickly end the call and go take a seat at the kitchen table, where I ponder the fact that I felt like I had something to hide when Zack caught me on the phone with Nathan just now. I tell myself there's no need to feel guilty. We're just friends. But I'm not sure Zack would understand that. I'm not even sure I understand it myself. It makes me think about how Alan behaved over the past few years. How he kept so much hidden from me. I can see now how it was possible, and I don't like how that makes me feel.

The following week, I report to the sleep lab for my overnight analysis. Electrodes are attached to my head and body to measure things like heart and respiratory rates, electrical activity in my brain, and nerve activity in my muscles. The tests reveal exactly what we suspected: significant abnormalities in my sleep cycle, with REM occurring at inappropriate times.

Upon my next meeting with Dr. Tremblay, he shares the results with me. He is somber as he explains that I am indeed afflicted with narcolepsy.

Seated in a chair on the opposite side of his large desk, I take a moment to digest this news. I close my eyes, rub at my temples, and can think of only one thing, which I say out loud.

"I want to *kill* my husband right now, but unfortunately for me, I can't because he's already dead."

Dr. Tremblay says nothing, and I realize it was a harsh statement and he's probably shocked. But I don't care because I'm mad as hell. And he doesn't know the half of it.

I let my hands drop to my lap and clasp them together. "I suppose we should start talking about treatments."

He agrees and launches into a long description of all the medications available, what they can do to help improve my symptoms, and what side effects I can expect.

He also informs me that I should stop driving until we get everything under control, because statistically, people with untreated narcoleptic symptoms are ten times more likely to get into an accident. He assures me that it's only temporary, because once we find the right balance of medications, I'll be as safe and capable as anyone else on the road—outside of philandering husbands who are lying to their wives and driving drunk, of course.

I'm only half listening to Dr. Tremblay, because I can't get past the anger I still feel toward Alan, and now the fog is rolling into my brain again. I find it difficult to concentrate. Some of what the doctor says goes in one ear and out the other, but it doesn't matter because I've already researched all the recommended medications and side effects and statistics about accidents. I know everything inside out, and I already know which drugs I want to try first.

We settle on what my treatment will be, and I leave his office, knowing I won't be able to return to the OR anytime soon. As I ride the elevator down, I can't help but think of the terrifying split second when Alan's car clipped the back end of mine on the highway and sent me tumbling down the embankment, totaling my SUV, nearly killing me and our dog, and possibly causing this irreversible neurological condition.

I'm so angry with him I want to hit something. There's a pounding in my ears, and I fear I'm going to collapse again because of this intense anger I feel. But I don't collapse. The rage flows through me, my muscles remain strong, and the elevator doors slide open. I step off without incident.

As I call a cab to take me home, I realize it was sheer force of will that kept me on my feet just now, because I don't want to give Alan the power to hurt me anymore. I want to live, and live happily, and in order to do that, I need to do my best to stop fixating on his betrayal and the anger I feel. I need to focus on how I'm going to manage this condition and move on with positivity and determination, not vitriol, which will only bury me in ugly emotional muck. That won't help me at all.

I know this because I'm still stuck in that muck, and I want to be free of it.

CHAPTER THIRTY

A few weeks later, I come home after work to find Zack on the sofa watching television. Winston greets me at the door, tail wagging, and I bend to give him a pat. "Hey there. How are you doing?"

He licks the back of my hand and follows me eagerly into the kitchen, where I drop my keys into the bowl on the counter.

"How was your day?" I ask Zack.

"Okay, I guess."

"Just okay?" After seventeen years, I can read my son's moods like a book, and it's obvious that something's on his mind. I take a seat beside him on the sofa. "What's up?"

Winston jumps up between us, and Zack rubs behind his ears. "Jeremy just got into the premed program at Western."

My eyebrows lift. "Wow, good for him. That's a tough program to get into."

Zack stares at the television. "Yeah, he's pretty pumped."

I watch my son for a moment, and I know exactly what he's feeling because I'm feeling it too. I know him too well, and his pain is my pain. His joy is my joy.

"What about you?" I ask, picking up the remote control and muting the TV. "Are you not pumped about going to Dal?"

We had this conversation at Christmas, and I knew then that Zack would feel like he was missing out if he had to stay at home because of me.

He merely shrugs. "It'll be fine."

"Really? I don't think so. It's only five blocks away." I reach out and squeeze his shoulder. "Listen, you know I'll be okay if you go away to school. I'll miss you of course, but I have Winston to keep me company." I stroke the fur on Winston's back. "And it's not like you and I would never talk to each other. We could text every day. Seriously, Zack, if you want to go away, I'm all for it. It's not too late to apply. I don't know when the deadlines are for scholarships, but—"

"I already applied," he tells me, meeting my gaze with a look of unease, "just to see what would happen."

My head draws back slightly. "Oh, you did. And . . . ?"

"And . . ." He hesitates, then finally spills the beans. "I got accepted to Western and Queens. Full scholarships at both."

A swell of pride washes over me. "You're joking! How could you not tell me this? That's amazing! I'm so proud of you."

He exhales heavily. "Thanks, but I don't want to go, Mom. Especially with what's been going on with your health lately. And I know how much you miss Dad."

I do miss Alan—the husband I once knew. But that man doesn't exist anymore.

I quickly shake my head at Zack. "Sweetheart, if you want to go to Western or Queens, that's what I want too. Honestly, I'd be incredibly proud of you, and so would Gram. I really think you should go. It's what you've always wanted."

He stares at me for a moment, then bows his head. His voice shakes when he speaks. "You've been through so much, Mom. I can't just leave you."

I slide closer and pull him into my arms. "You won't be leaving me. Like I said, we'll text every day, and you can come home for summers and Thanksgiving and Christmas. I'll be fine. I've got big plans of my own, you know."

He draws back. "You do?"

"Of course." I scramble to come up with something, because I can't let him believe that I'm just going to lie down and die when he goes off to college.

Which I have no intention of doing. That's not going to happen. I don't know what exactly *is* going to happen, but I've got plenty of time to figure it out.

"Well . . ." I sit back and rest my arm along the back of the sofa. "The first thing I'm going to do is accept that I'm never going to hold a scalpel again. I can't keep waiting around for that day to come."

Zack hangs his head. "Mom, please don't give up . . ."

"I'm not giving up. I'm just being realistic. All these medications are working well, but they come with side effects, and I'm not as steady as I need to be." I hold up my hand to show him. "Sometimes I get the shakes."

He rests his head on the back of the sofa. "So what are you going to do?"

"I don't know. I'm still a doctor. I have practical knowledge, and you'd be surprised how many job opportunities are out there. I just need to figure out what direction I want to go in now. I loved being a GP before I became a surgeon. I could go back to that, or I could do another residency and learn a new specialty, something where I'm not holding a scalpel. Or I could move into research. It's kind of exciting, actually, to think about a fresh start with something totally new."

A whole new life. Something to set my sights on.

Zack smiles at me. "You're smart, Mom. You can be anything you want to be."

"Except a surgeon," I say with a chuckle, as an unexpected bubble of joy rises up inside me. "And thank you for the vote of confidence. I raised you well."

"You and Dad both."

I feel the smile drain from my face because of how Zack idolizes his father, while I'm finding it harder and harder to cherish Alan's memory in any way, shape, or form.

Zack reaches for the remote control to unmute the television. As he sits forward, I notice the scar on his elbow from the skateboard accident he had when he was fourteen, and it reminds me of Alan.

He was delivering a guest lecture at the medical school when Zack fell off the skateboard and hit his head, and in a state of pure panic as a mother, I called and asked the organizers to interrupt the class and send Alan to the hospital, because I remembered what had happened on the day Alan's mother died. Lester hadn't pulled him out of class, and he never got to say goodbye to her.

Zack's injuries were serious. There was swelling in his brain. I couldn't take any chances.

When Alan arrived, he was very distraught and asked me all sorts of questions about what had happened. He demanded to see the x-rays, discussed the prognosis with the neurologist, and stayed in the ICU with me until Zack finally turned a corner.

But then Alan said he couldn't do it anymore.

"Do what?" I asked.

"I can't see him like this. I can't bear it."

Alan walked out of the hospital, leaving me standing there, dumbstruck, in front of the nurses' station, watching him storm off without looking back. It was so unlike him.

Thankfully, a few hours later, he returned. Not that I ever doubted he would. I knew he just needed some time alone.

When he walked into the ICU, he went straight to Zack's bedside. They had a brief conversation, and then Alan turned to me and pulled me into his arms.

"I'm sorry," he whispered in my ear. "I shouldn't have walked out on you like that."

I was so happy that he had come back to me. "It's okay. I understand."

We held each other, and I felt no resentment toward Alan for that brief spell of weakness. I knew it was because he loved us more than life itself. There was never any doubt about that. Not at the time.

So maybe what I need to do now is find a way to look at my son and acknowledge the fact that my marriage wasn't a total waste. Alan gave me Zack and was a loving father to him—the polar opposite of his own.

Will that be enough to make up for what he did? Will I ever be able to answer that question in the affirmative?

Zack's phone rings, and he checks the call display. "It's Jeremy," he says. "Mind if I take this?"

"Go ahead. I need to get supper started anyway."

Winston follows me to the kitchen, where I check to see what's in the freezer. I hear Zack laughing on the phone. His voice is animated because he's excited to share the news that he'll be going to Queens or Western.

Suddenly I imagine living here in this big house without him. It's going to be very quiet. I take a moment to let that sink in and remind myself that it's still many months away.

February 14 rolls around, and though I would prefer not to wallow in misery over the fact that it's my first Valentine's Day without Alan, I can't help but feel the weight of his absence as I remember how he used to bring me flowers and take me out for dinner at a nice restaurant. Often, he gave me jewelry. Every woman's dream, right?

But then I find myself racking my brain, struggling to recall the details from the last few years, when he must have been seeing Paula at the same time. Last year, he gave me a charm bracelet and took me to Café Chianti. Did he take Paula out to dinner too? Perhaps the weekend before or after? Did he give her a charm bracelet as well, and if so, what were the tokens that symbolized their relationship? Were they romantic and personal?

Deciding that I'm just torturing myself by wondering about these sorts of details when nothing can change the past, I'm tempted to send a text to Nathan—the only other widowed person I know besides my mother—just to say hi, because he probably has a hard time with this cruel, wicked day too. But I recognize that I'm feeling bitter toward Alan, and I don't want this to be about vengeance, so I set my phone aside.

Later that night, it chimes on the kitchen counter anyway. I pick it up and read a text from Nathan: Hey you. Happy Valentine's Day. Most romantic day of the year, right? Having fun yet?

I smile and let out a breath that releases all the tension in my neck and shoulders. I quickly type a reply: I swear you must be my alter ego. I was thinking about going for a flying leap off the Macdonald Bridge just now, but your message has cheered me up. :)

I hit "Send" and wait for his reply.

Avoid the bridge. Water's too cold this time of year. Instead, I recommend a big bottle of cheap whiskey. Works for me.

I laugh and type, Perfect! Wish you were here so we could drown our sorrows together.

He doesn't respond for a moment, and I wonder if that was an inappropriate thing to say. It's Valentine's Day, after all, and it's been only three months since I buried my husband. I don't want there to be any misunderstandings about this friendship that's been growing between us.

Finally, a message comes in. He says, Me too.

I sit down on the stool at the kitchen island and start to feel a bit uneasy. What if Zack picked up my phone and read these messages? What would he think?

Nevertheless, it's been a rough day, and I'm grateful to be able to express at least some of what I'm feeling. Nathan is one of the few people who truly understand.

I decide to text another message: Three months in and I'm feeling pretty angry at the universe, but mostly at Alan. Especially today. It's hard to remember the good times.

There's a long pause. Do you want to give me a call?

I consider that, and part of me wants to, but another part of me is afraid of confiding in this man too much more than I have already. He's generous and kind, smart and handsome, and he's alone on Valentine's Day. It feels a bit dangerous.

Inhaling a deep breath, I type a reply: I would love to talk, but I probably shouldn't. Zack's waiting for me to watch a movie. I'll insist on an action thriller of course, with lots of car chases and fistfights.

None of that is true. Zack is at Jeremy's house, and I'm here alone. But it gets me off the hook without my having to explain my feelings.

Nathan texts back, Good plan. I recommend Jason Bourne. Or King Kong has a certain appeal on Valentine's Day. It's a love story, sort of, so you won't feel like you're practicing total avoidance.

I chuckle. Then I marvel at Nathan's gift for lightening my load at any given moment. Those are excellent suggestions. Thank you. Have a great night :).

You too. TTYL

I like how he ends the message with "Talk to you later." It's nice to know that the door remains open.

I set down my phone and start to walk away with a smile but immediately return to it and delete that entire thread of texts, just to be safe.

A few days later, I sit down with the chief of surgery to talk about the future. I explain to him that I'm feeling better with the medications Dr. Tremblay has prescribed and I can function very well throughout the day and have no trouble meeting with patients, but I inform him that I can't continue to wait around to return to the OR. I need to make plans for the future.

"I need to find another way to be a doctor," I tell him, "and I'm sure you'd like to bring in another surgeon to replace me permanently."

Dr. Richards regards me with sadness and compassion. "I'm so sorry, Abbie. You know how hard it is for me to hear you say that. You were a terrific surgeon. I hate to lose you."

"Thank you, John."

"But I respect and appreciate your decision, and I agree that it's for the best. Do you have any idea what you're going to do next? Where you'll go from here?"

I think about his question and look down at my hands on my lap—no longer the hands of a surgeon.

"Not yet, but I'm considering going back to being a regular GP, maybe joining an established practice that needs an extra doc. Daytime hours only."

"There are plenty of those in the city," he says. "I'm sure they'll be fighting to get you. And you know you can rely on me for an excellent reference."

"Thanks." I rise to my feet and shake his hand. "It's been a pleasure working with you these past few years. I mean that."

He makes a slight grimace. "Wait a second. You're not planning on quitting today, are you? Because there's still plenty of work around here—follow-ups and consults—and I haven't even begun to look for your replacement."

I smile at him. "Don't worry. I'll stay until you find someone. I'd never leave you in the lurch."

He wipes the back of his hand across his forehead. "Phew."

I laugh, and we chat for a few minutes. Then I return to my office to work on some files. Eventually, I feel an overwhelming urge to lay my head on the desk and close my eyes. Thankfully, it's a good time of the day for it. I have a full hour before my next appointment, so I get up, close my door, lock it securely, and lie down on the sofa to take a quick power nap.

A short while later, I wake to the sound of a knock at the door. It's my receptionist, Janine.

"Dr. MacIntyre, are you in there? Please answer. Your door's been locked for two hours. Are you okay?"

Oh God, has it really been two hours? I missed my appointment?

I try to get up, but I can't move, and this time, I know exactly what's happening.

Janine knocks again. "Dr. MacIntyre?"

I want to answer her, but I can't even lift my hand off the leather sofa or open my eyes or call out. All I can do is lie there like a corpse, listening to the sound of her rapid knocking on the door.

Her voice grows more panicked. "Dr. MacIntyre! Are you in there? I know you are. Please answer me, or I'm going to get security to open the door."

Please don't do that. Just give me a minute or two. The paralysis will pass soon . . .

But it doesn't pass, despite my intense efforts to push my eyes open and roll off the sofa.

I hear keys jingling and Janine talking to someone, and I prepare myself for the security guard to walk in and find me drooling on the sofa cushions.

The lock clicks, the door opens, but it's not the security guard. It's Troy—the young firefighter who rescued me from my vehicle on the night of the accident and later found Winston in the ice storm. He's wearing heavy gear and carrying the Jaws of Life. Despite my embarrassment, I'm overjoyed to see him because he saved my life and Winston's too.

And that is the moment I know that I'm dreaming.

He kneels down beside the sofa. "Dr. MacIntyre, can you hear me? Just try to relax. You're going to be fine."

I want to tell him that I'm already fine. I know exactly what's happening to me. It's just narcolepsy.

He reaches for my hand and squeezes it. "Don't be afraid. We're going to get you out of here. We're just setting up the equipment. Can you hear me?" He presses his fingers to the pulse at my neck and says to Janine, "She's alive. But barely. We just need to get her out of here."

No! I'm fine! And you don't need to get me out of here. Just wait a minute or two. I'll be able to move soon.

And you're not even here.

Two more firefighters come running into my office to operate the Jaws of Life. Troy tosses a heavy blanket over my head to protect me from flying glass and steel. I feel panic and fear.

The noise is deafening, and my heart is racing. Then it occurs to me that maybe I'm not here at all. Maybe I'm back in the wreck, and all of this agony in my life has been a nightmare, just like I imagined it was on the night Alan died. Maybe none of it's real. Maybe I'm truly dying. Maybe I'm already dead. Is this the afterlife?

Please, don't let it be that. I don't want to die. I want to live.

Suddenly my strength returns, and I can move my fingers and toes but not the rest of me.

Am I stuck under the dashboard? Is that the weight that's pressing down on my legs, or is it just the paralysis? Am I truly unconscious?

I draw in a quick breath and force my eyes open.

It's bright.

The middle of the day.

I'm staring at the ceiling in my office.

The room is quiet and empty. The door is closed. Troy isn't here, and Janine isn't knocking at my door.

But my heart is pounding like a drum, and I can't stop shaking as I try to sit up.

It was just a dream, Abbie. You're not back in the ravine, trapped in your car. You're not dying.

But it felt so real . . . the sound of the machines, Troy's voice in my ear, the fear of death. I truly thought I was back there.

I wasn't, thank heavens.

I survived the wreck, and I'm still here.

I'm here. I'm alive. And I'm so grateful for that.

Slowly, I sit up and try to work some strength back into my limbs. I rest my elbows on my knees and rake my fingers through my hair, shake my head to try and clear away the fog.

I glance at the clock on the wall, worried that I've missed my appointment, but evidently I've been asleep for less than twenty minutes, not two hours, although it feels like ages.

My body is heavy as lead, but I manage to drag myself off the sofa and move to my desk to send Dr. Tremblay an email. I want to tell him about this latest hypnagogic hallucination.

He responds immediately to let me know that it's unlikely I'll ever be completely free of hallucinations during my daytime naps, but the sedative at night should at least allow me to get the sleep I require and lend some normalcy to my life.

Life.

Normalcy.

By some miracle, I survived the accident, and I have my entire future still ahead of me. I didn't die that night, like Alan did. How lucky I was! I feel so happy and relieved I'm completely breathless.

Leaning back in my chair, I cover my face with my hands and begin to weep. These are tears of joy and gratitude—passionate tears that flow like a waterfall down my cheeks as I laugh and cry at the same time. I feel an exhilaration I never imagined I would ever feel again. I am positively euphoric, and I can't believe how lucky I am to be alive. I feel reborn. Who ever knew that my narcolepsy could turn out to be such an unexpected gift?

The exhilaration continues into the night. I feel euphoric again when Zack skates past the center line and passes the puck to a teammate, who scores a fast goal. I cheer and clap with my mittens on, jumping up from my seat in the bleachers while the game horns blare and the other hockey parents cheer alongside me. Maureen and I high-five Gwen and Kate and shout over the boards, "Way to go, Citadel!" Rock music shakes the arena while the players congratulate each other, and the referees give the signal to start another play.

The game ends with a score of three to two, with Zack's team coming out on top, and I feel lighthearted as I exit the arena with Zack beside me, hauling his giant equipment bag over his shoulder. I'll definitely miss the excitement of these games when he goes off to college in the fall, but he plans to try out for the team at Western, so it's nice to know there may be more hockey in our future. But even if there isn't, I'm happy today.

Later that night, as I settle into bed, I scroll through messages on my phone and feel an urge to text Nathan, just to tell him about the game. Nothing more.

Hey there. Just got home from the rink. Zack's team won and they're going on to the finals. A good day!

Nathan responds a few seconds later. That's great! Cheers to more good days ahead. And I'd love to see him play sometime.

Suddenly, there's a disturbance in me, because I can't imagine inviting Nathan to one of Zack's hockey games. How could I introduce him to the other hockey parents who sat in chilly arenas beside Alan and me for years? What would they think of that, so soon after Alan's death?

And how would I explain to Zack why Winston's veterinarian—who just so happens to be a very handsome man—is sitting in Alan's place, watching and cheering?

I don't respond to the text. Later that night, I toss and turn in bed. I flip from side to side, thinking about my friendship with Nathan and wishing I could be a normal grieving widow who wouldn't feel the confusing desire to send personal text messages to a man she barely knows and reveal intimate details about her marriage. And then feel guilty about it.

Why can't I just be the kind of widow who idolizes her late husband and believes he was the best man in the world? But I'm not that kind of widow because that's not the hand I've been dealt. I'm still angry with Alan, and if anything, I wish he were still here, if only so that I could tear a strip off him, tell him how badly he hurt me, and then kick him out of the house. Or at the very least banish him to the sofa until he comes groveling and begging for my forgiveness, telling me he made a terrible mistake with Paula and it's over forever. Then I may or may not take him back.

But I probably would, because despite everything, I still love him, and I would do anything to have our life back.

The following day, I stare at my phone on my desk at work, and I can't stop thinking about Nathan's message: I'd love to see him play sometime.

That simply can't happen. Not now. I'm doing well, so much better lately, but I'm not ready to bring another man into my life, even as a friend, because I need to respect these stages of grief. I need to get through it all, not just for my own sake but for Zack's and for everyone else who loved Alan.

With a sigh, I pick up my phone and begin to type a long-winded message to Nathan:

Hi again. I have something to say, and I'm not sure how to say it. But first I want to thank you for being so kind to me, and especially for saving Winston's life. You've become someone who lifts my spirits during the darkest moments, and I am grateful that you've been a part of my life these past few months. But I'm going to be honest. I have to confess that I feel uncomfortable with how much I like you. Sometimes I feel uneasy when we text each other because you make me feel happy, and that makes me feel guilty, because it's only been a few months since I said goodbye to Alan, and I shouldn't be feeling happy and excited when my phone chimes with a text message from a man I can't help but care for. Is this making any sense? I guess you can probably tell that I'm still an emotional disaster, and I don't want to screw up my friendship with you. I'm afraid that I will—that in a moment of weakness or insecurity or loneliness, I'll cross a line and do something, or say something, that I'm not ready to do or say. I'm also terrified that Zack will see our messages and get the wrong idea. I need to think of him and put him first, so I can't be forming friendships—however innocent they may be—with handsome new men. Zack wouldn't understand it. And he's leaving in the fall, so I don't want to do anything that might cause upheaval in our relationship, or arguments during our last few months together. I want to help him get over the loss of his father, not create heartache or confusion for him. This is hard, because I like you so much and I enjoy talking to you. You're like my secret happy place. But I have to think of Zack. I hope this is making sense and you don't hate me.

I reread the message, edit a few words and phrases, and hit "Send" before I change my mind. Then I sit back and stare at my phone, wondering if Nathan has received it yet.

As I imagine him reading it, my stomach erupts into butterflies because I've just confessed that I like him more than I should and that I find him handsome. That was very bold, but it's easier to be bold in a text message. I'm not sure I would have the courage to say all those things if I were standing in front of him in his office.

A little while later, my phone chimes, and my pulse quickens. I pick up my phone and begin to read.

Hi Abbie. Thanks for being so honest about how you are feeling, and don't worry, it makes total sense and I don't hate you. Since we're being honest, I'll confess that I like you too, so I can't pretend that all our encounters have been innocent. I've found you attractive since the first moment I laid eyes on you sitting with Winston in my ICU. So there you have it. It's out in the open. But I totally understand where you're coming from and that you need to think of your son and that you're still grieving. It's like we said that day in my clinic—when you're a parent, you can't enjoy the luxury of putting your own needs first. But our kids are worth it, aren't they? I sure do love my girls, more than life itself.

So I'll say goodbye now. But please know that if you ever need to talk, I'm always here. Take care of yourself, and keep on hanging in there.

Nathan

When I finish reading his message, my eyes well up with tears because he has been so unbelievably kind and understanding, and I can't deny that I feel a pulsing little thrill to hear that he finds me attractive. After everything I've learned about Alan and Paula, it's nice to know I'm not a total loser. But what moves me most is the way Nathan ended his message, the same way he has ended so many others—with a door that continues to remain open.

CHAPTER THIRTY-ONE

September

This is it—the moment I've been dreading for months. Zack gets on a plane today and will fly halfway across the country to start university. I won't see him until Thanksgiving.

We've never been apart that long before, and he'll no longer be my little boy. There will be no more school lunches or chauffeuring him to hockey games and parties on weekends. No more calling up the stairs to wake him on a Saturday morning, when he'd probably sleep until noon if I let him.

At least I'm not alone at the airport, saying goodbye to him. Maureen is with me because Zack and Jeremy are traveling together on the same flight to Ontario, and though they won't be roommates, they'll be living in the same residence at Western. Maureen and I have been consoling each other all week in anticipation of this moment.

"Do you have your wallet?" I ask Zack after we've checked his large suitcase and are walking toward security.

"Yes, Mom, I have everything. Don't worry."

"What about your toothbrush? Did you pack that?"

He stops dead in his tracks and gapes at me with horror. "Oh my God."

Fire explodes in my stomach.

"I left it in the bathroom. What am I gonna do? We have to go back." Then he smiles, and I realize he's teasing me. It's something Alan would have done.

I slap him playfully on the arm. "You're a scalawag."

"But you still love me."

"Always."

"And did you seriously just say *scalawag*?"

I laugh. "I think I might have."

We reach the entrance to security before departures, and Maureen and I stop. Zack and Jeremy dig out their IDs and boarding passes to show the guard. Then they turn to hug us one last time.

"I'm going to miss you so much," I say to Zack as I squeeze him tight and wish I didn't have to let go, ever.

"I'll miss you too," he replies, "but don't worry, Mom. We're gonna be fine. You and me both."

I step back and run my fingers over the collar of his jean jacket, noticing how tall he's become. "I know. But I can't promise I won't worry about you. It's my job as a mother."

He begins to back away, and my breath catches in my throat. I feel like he's slipping from my grasp. I want to dash forward, pull him into my arms again, and keep him close. Forever. But I know I can't.

Then suddenly, I remember that I'd wanted to give him something special today.

"Wait!" I reach into my purse. "I meant to give this to you before we left the house." I wrap my hand around Alan's gold watch and hold it out to Zack. "This is for you. You should have it."

He returns to me and takes hold of it, stares at the face. "This was Dad's."

"Yes. I gave it to him on our tenth wedding anniversary."

Zack's eyes lift. "He wore it every day. This means a lot to me, Mom. Thank you. I'll wear it every day too." He kisses me on the cheek one more time, then starts to back away. "I'll text you when we board."

"Okay. Safe travels. And text me when you land as well."

Jeremy turns to enter the queue, but Zack doesn't move. He stands for a few more seconds, his eyes fixed on mine. He looks at me with affection, and I know he doesn't want to leave me. At the same time, he can't wait to start this new adventure.

"I love you," he says.

"I love you too."

"Bye." He finally turns to go but glances over his shoulder to wave at me one last time before he disappears around the corner.

As soon as he's gone, I burst into tears.

Maureen hugs me and rubs my back. "We're going to be okay."

"Yes." I pull myself together and wipe my tears. "But now what do we do?"

She takes a deep breath and exhales. "We go home, look at their bedrooms, and cry our eyes out. Then we marvel at the fact that our houses are going to be so much easier to keep clean from now on."

I laugh, but my eyes fill with fresh tears at the same time. Maureen and I hug each other again. Then we turn away and head back to her car.

When I arrive home a half hour later, I walk into my quiet house and don't care that it's going to be easier to keep clean. I would prefer the mess if it meant Zack could still be here, filling my world with laughter and conversation.

Maureen, you're lucky. At least you have a husband at home and another child still in junior high school. My house is truly an empty nest now. It's just Winston and me.

Just as I think that, Winston lumbers over to where I am standing in the kitchen, feeling lost and unsure about what to do with myself. He sits down and pants and stares at me with that intense look I know so well.

"You need to go outside, don't you?"

He snaps his mouth shut, then opens it again.

"How about a walk?"

He rises to his feet and trots to the back door, tail wagging.

I follow and grab his leash, then catch myself smiling because it's nice to know that someone very special still needs me. And it's a beautiful day for a walk.

CHAPTER THIRTY-TWO

October

It's a blissful, blue-skied Saturday. A day off. I'm wearing a long woolly sweater over a turtleneck and jeans, and I'm enjoying the autumn sunshine as I take Winston for another long walk around our neighborhood.

My medications have been a godsend, and I've had no problems staying awake in my new position at a large established family practice here in Halifax, where somehow, by word of mouth, I've become the most recommended family doctor in the city for patients with sleep disorders. I've also been working closely with the neurologists who run the sleep disorder clinic where I was initially tested for narcolepsy.

All this has led to other adventures as well. In the past four months, I've spoken about sleep disorders at Harvard, Stanford, and a few conferences, and I've appeared on three television news programs as an expert on the topic. I'm now an unofficial spokesperson for a narcolepsy organization, offering hope and inspiration to those who find themselves challenged with the affliction.

Professionally speaking, I feel as if I've found my true calling. The field of sleep medicine has become my passion, and it's very exciting because it's constantly evolving.

When it comes to my personal life, there are still moments of loneliness in that big house all alone, but I do my best to take life one day at a time. My sister, Carla, calls often, and sometimes we talk for hours about our jobs, our kids, and the world in general. Maureen and I meet regularly for coffee, and we see movies with Gwen and Kate, and I'm always socializing with people from work. As for Nathan, I've not heard from him since our last texts, and I'm glad about that. I know I did the right thing when I cut things off between us, because I was in no position to get close to anyone.

Yet I think of him still.

My cell phone rings. I adjust Winston's leash in my hand, pause on the sidewalk, and reach into my sweater pocket to answer it. The call display tells me it's Zack, and I step lightly, skipping over a patch of freshly fallen leaves.

"Hi," I say, smiling in the autumn sunshine.

"I just got your message," Zack says. "What's up with Gram?"

"Oh, it's nothing serious," I assure him as I extend the length of Winston's leash so that he can sniff the base of a telephone pole. "She has to have cataract surgery next Monday. I'm going to take a couple of weeks off and go stay with her because she won't be able to drive for a while."

"Poor Gram." He pauses. "But wait a second. That's right before Thanksgiving."

"Yes, and that's what I was calling about. I'll be there for the long weekend. Are you still planning to fly home?"

"Of course. I already have my ticket. And we usually spend Thanksgiving at Gram's house anyway." He sounds confused.

"We do, so I'll pick you up at the airport, and we'll go straight to Lunenburg, if that's okay."

"It's fine. Whatever works."

As I stand there watching Winston lift his leg to pee on the pole, I remind myself that my son is no longer the little boy I used to cuddle at night when we read bedtime stories together. He's a man now, living on his own. I'm proud of him and pleased that he's independent, even though I miss him every day.

Winston sits down on the sidewalk, waiting patiently to continue our walk.

"Mom . . . ," Zack says, hesitantly. "How are you doing? You're not too lonely, I hope."

I press my lips together and shut my eyes. "I'm great, Zack. Honestly. I've been incredibly busy with work, and I'm loving every minute of it. The change in focus has been good for me. And Winston keeps me company at home. So please don't worry. Everything's perfect."

I want to kick myself for using that word, because nothing's ever perfect. I should know that by now, but I want my son to know there's no reason to worry about me. I'm amazed, actually, at how much I've been enjoying my life over these past few months. My work has been rewarding, and some days when I think of those terrifying moments when I plummeted into the ravine, I feel happier than ever and so blessed to be alive.

"I'll see you soon," I say to Zack, ending the call as I look forward to picking him up at Thanksgiving.

Secretly, I'm thrilled to spend the rest of the month of October in Lunenburg. It's always been my favorite time of year. There's nothing that compares to the sights and sounds of the busy Lunenburg harbor—fishing boats coming and going on crisp, sunny afternoons, familiar faces everywhere you go, the aroma of fish and chips from the waterfront restaurants, and a ship's bell clanging in the distance at night.

My mother hugs me when I arrive at her door with Winston, and she helps me unpack for my three-week stay. For the first time, it feels strange to be back in my old room, knowing I'll be staying for a while.

I suppose everything is different now. I'm not here with my husband and son to enjoy a Sunday family dinner and return home before dark to tackle homework with Zack and make his lunch for the next day at school. I'm accustomed to being a widow now, just like my mother. So much of my life has come to an end. And yet, standing here, looking at my childhood bed, I feel as if I've begun a new chapter.

It's definitely preferable to feeling as if my life is over.

On the Monday before Thanksgiving weekend, my mother is at home, taking a nap after her cataract surgery. It's a gorgeous fall evening—warm like summer, without a breath of wind—so I take Winston out for a walk along the waterfront. We stroll down the boardwalk, past the red-painted Fisheries Museum and tall schooners and fishing boats moored at the docks. I breathe in the salty scents of the harbor and marvel at the beauty all around me.

Despite my condition, which still makes me sleepy sometimes, I feel more wakeful and alive than ever before. I'm enchanted by the simplest things—a dragonfly flitting by me, the wind in the treetops. I'm absolutely beguiled by the wonder of our existence.

Winston quickens his pace when he sees another golden retriever coming our way. He pulls me hard, so I start to jog. As we draw closer, I recognize the other dog's owner. It's Nathan, out for an evening stroll with his two young daughters, whom I've never had the pleasure of meeting before.

I feel a bright burst of happiness at the sight of him.

"Abbie," he says with a dazzling smile as our retrievers greet each other with swishing tails and busy noses. "This is an unexpected surprise. How have you been?"

"Really good," I reply, still marveling at the sweep of joy I'm feeling. "How about you?"

One of his daughters drops to her knees and strokes Winston's sumptuous golden coat. "My gosh! They look so much alike! They could be brother and sister. What's your dog's name?"

"This is Winston," I tell her. "He's six. How old is your dog?"

"She's twelve, and her name is Dorothy. We got her a few months ago." By now both girls are spoiling Winston with attention. He sits down to bask in it blissfully.

Nathan gestures with a hand. "These are my daughters, Jen and Marie. Girls, this is Abbie MacIntyre. Her dog, Winston, was a patient of mine last year."

"Cool," Jen says, smiling up at me. "It's nice to meet you."

"It's nice to meet you too." I glance at the younger one, Marie, who looks to be about nine or ten. She wears a sparkly purple headband, and I think it's the cutest thing ever.

Nathan pats their dog, Dorothy, who sits patiently at his side. "Dorothy is a senior dog who needed a home after her owner passed away, so we adopted her."

"She's lovely."

He nods and meets my gaze. "Are you just visiting? Here for the long weekend?"

"I'm here for three weeks, actually. Mom had cataract surgery, so I'm keeping her company for a bit. And Zack's coming home from Western on Saturday, so I'm excited about that. He'll be here for dinner on Sunday."

"Zack went to Western? I didn't know that. Good for him. How's he finding it?"

"He loves it, and I can't wait to see him."

"I'll bet. I don't know what I'm going to do when these two are ready to zip off to college. It's hard to imagine."

"All the more reason to appreciate the time you have with them now," I say.

He smiles knowingly. "Absolutely."

Another couple with two smaller dogs pass by us and say hello, and then Winston lies down and rolls onto his back for a belly rub. The girls giggle and stroke him adoringly.

"How's work going?" Nathan asks me.

I realize how long it's been since we last spoke. There have been so many changes. "I'm working at a family practice now. I've been taking a lot of sleep disorder cases, which is new territory for me, so I'm learning a lot."

"I can imagine. How do you like it?"

"I love it. Much better hours than surgery at the hospital. And I've been doing some research as well. I'll tell you about it sometime."

"I'd like that."

The girls rise to their feet, and so does Winston. They all seem eager to get moving.

"Winston and I should probably mosey along," I say, looking up at the twilight sky splashed with colorful bands of pink and blue.

"We should get a move on too," Nathan replies.

Dorothy and the girls start off, leading him away. I start walking in the opposite direction, feeling pleased to have seen him, but at the same time regretting the fact that we didn't have more time to chat, because there's so much to catch up on and I really loved rekindling our conversation. My heart sinks a little.

Then Nathan calls my name. There's a pleasant rush of heat in my belly. I stop and turn.

He hands the leash to Jen and approaches me. "Abbie. This feels weird and awkward . . . seeing you like this. I'd really like to catch up some more. No pressure, and feel free to say no, but would you like to have dinner with me while you're in town?"

I'm surprised and flattered by his invitation, and I'm glad that I took Winston for a walk this evening. "I'd love to."

"Great." His eyes light up. "When would be good for you?"

"Well . . ." I pause and think about it. "Zack's not coming until Saturday. How about tomorrow night?"

"Tomorrow's great. I can pick you up at seven, if that works?"

"I'll be ready. Do you remember where my mom lives?"

"Of course. I remember everything." He turns to go. "I'll see you tomorrow night."

"Okay. I'll look forward to it."

As I continue along the boardwalk with Winston, I can't stop smiling. Winston looks up at me happily.

"Oh, stop grinning," I say with a smirk. "It's just dinner."

He starts to trot with purpose and exuberance, and I am keen to pick up the pace as well.

CHAPTER THIRTY-THREE

I'm not sure where Nathan will take me for dinner, but I decide to gussy up a bit, just in case it's somewhere nice. As it turns out, I'm glad I wore heels, because he takes me to my favorite restaurant on the south shore, which overlooks the yacht club in the village of Chester.

By the time we're seated, I've told him all about my involvement with the narcolepsy organization and how I've been accepting speaking engagements all over the world.

"That's fantastic," he says with genuine admiration as he sits back in his chair across from me. "It sounds like you've found your true calling."

"I know, right? That's exactly how I feel about it."

I pick up my sparkling water and take a sip. Then our waiter brings our appetizers, and we admire the presentation before we dig in.

Conversation with Nathan is easy. It flows because there's lots to talk about, whether it's our dogs, our careers, or the challenges of being single parents. And there have been so many extraordinary changes in both of our lives since we last saw each other—like my work and Zack going off to college. As for Nathan, his daughters are entering a new preteen phase, and every day brings new challenges for him as a dad.

We finish our appetizers and sit back again.

"How are you, on a personal level?" Nathan asks tentatively as the waiter clears away our plates.

I know what he's referring to—the fact that it's been almost a year since I lost Alan, and the last time Nathan and I texted each other, I'd admitted to being an emotional disaster.

"Well, you were right about one thing," I say. "It has gotten easier with time. But there are still days when I struggle."

"There probably always will be. You and Alan were together for a long time."

I nod my head. "And I suspect it'll always be hard not to feel hurt by the cheating. But I want to look forward now, not back. I still have the rest of my life ahead of me."

Nathan raises his glass. "To the future."

We clink and sip. Then he carefully asks me another question. "What about Zack? Did you ever tell him what really happened?"

I shake my head. "No. I just couldn't do that to him. I didn't see what good could come of it."

Looking back on it, I'm surprised that I've managed to successfully shoulder the burden alone for so long, when there was a time I wasn't sure if I could or if I was doing the right thing by keeping the truth from him.

Wasn't that what Alan tried to do with me? Hide the truth to protect my feelings? Was there some form of humanity in that? Or did he just not want to get caught?

The waiter brings our main courses, and Nathan and I lean forward to pick up our forks.

"Thanksgiving dinner on Sunday is going to be different," I say. "This time last year, I was living in a bubble of naivety. It's going to be very quiet with just Zack, Mom, and me."

"You'd be welcome to come and join us for dinner, if you like," Nathan replies. "My mom would love to meet all of you, I'm sure."

I smile at him. "Thanks, but I think we need to get through this first Thanksgiving on our own."

And I'm still not ready to introduce a new man into Zack's life. Not officially. And this is only our first date.

Suddenly I feel a need to change the subject. I don't want to talk about my marriage anymore, and I'm sure Nathan doesn't either.

"How about you?" I ask. "What else is new in your life? Your girls are adorable, by the way."

He grins and tells me about their latest achievements and shenanigans. Then we discuss what it's like to have parents who are growing older. We talk about all sorts of other things too, and time flies by. Suddenly the restaurant is closing. We're the last guests to leave.

Later, when Nathan drives me home, he gets out and walks me to the front door, which I find very gallant.

"I had a nice time," he says as we stand under the bright porch light.

A brief moment of awkwardness ensues, because I'm not sure if he intends to kiss me good night. I suspect he wants to. It's obvious there's still an attraction between us.

Yet, I'm nervous about what it might mean if we kiss, because I have a feeling there would be no turning back after that. He's an amazing man, and I admit . . . I'm a bit infatuated.

Still . . . I'm not sure I'm ready, and I want very much to be ready. I want to be 100 percent prepared to dash out of the gate full speed ahead when the moment presents itself.

"I had a nice time too," I reply.

Nathan studies my expression. "I'm not sure if it's too soon, but I'd love to see you again while you're in town. Maybe we could go to a movie or walk our dogs or something. No pressure, though. I don't want to rush you."

He's reading my mind . . .

"I'd like that," I reply.

"Great."

There's another awkward pause, and then he leans closer and kisses me softly on the cheek—a slow, lingering kiss that sends a wave of heat into my core.

All along, my feelings for Nathan have been an exercise in denial, but now, standing before him under my mother's porch light with the sensation of his kiss still warm on my cheek, I feel the enormity of my desires and realize there can be no more denying it. I want this man, overwhelmingly.

"Good night, Abbie," Nathan says with a flirtatious glimmer in his eye.

As he walks down the steps, I feel bowled over by how unbelievably attractive he is—that fit, athletic build and confident swagger as he walks.

He stops at the bottom of my mother's stairs, looks up at me again, and smiles. My body melts, but somehow I manage to stay on my feet.

He inclines his head curiously. "Any chance you might want to join me and the girls tomorrow night to walk the dogs?" He explains himself further. "Life is short. Like I said, I don't want to rush you, but I also don't like to waste time."

"Neither do I," I reply with a laugh, and I feel a deep and soulful understanding between us. We both know what it means to love and lose someone but to somehow find the strength to keep on living. "Text me when you're heading out?"

"I will."

With that, he gets into his car and drives off.

I go inside the house to find my mother on the sofa, acting nonchalant, waiting to hear everything. It's kind of like being in high school again, and I revel in the afterglow of my first date in over twenty years.

I kick off my shoes, sit down beside her, and tell her about my evening.

"He really does seem like a wonderful man," Mom says. "And he's not hard on the eyes either."

I laugh, and we watch TV in silence for a few minutes. Then I turn to her again.

"Mom, why didn't you ever remarry after Dad died? Did you ever think about it?"

She considers my question with a sigh. "Oh, looking back on it, I think I probably worshipped your father too much. I figured that I'd already had the best. Anything else would have been a disappointment." She waves a hand through the air. "And I was far too romantic about my grief as a widow. I thought it would be disloyal if I was ever with someone else—like I was cheating on your father, because I'd vowed to love him forever." She turns her gaze back to the TV. "I still do love him, but I've been alone for more than twenty years, and sometimes I regret that I didn't find someone to spend the rest of my life with. It would have been nice to have a partner and go traveling. I always wanted to see Venice. I might have, if I'd had someone."

"I'll go to Venice with you," I tell her. "Just say the word, and we're there."

She turns to me and smiles. "That's good to know. I'll file that offer away."

We gaze back at the TV again. "Rome would be pretty amazing too," I mention.

"For sure."

"Let's think about it."

"Okay," she replies. "We'll do that."

Over the next few days, I spend time with Nathan, his girls, and the dogs. On Thursday evening, he invites me to watch Jen's basketball game at the junior high school, and then we all go out for supper. The weather is crisp and sunny on Friday, so we take the dogs for another walk along the nature trails at the Ovens Natural Park, where we gaze in awe at the breathtaking sea caves in the cliffs.

All the while, I feel comfortable around Nathan, and my physical attraction to him grows more intense with each passing hour. As we stand at the rail, peering into Cannon Cave and listening to the tremendous boom of the waves as they explode onto the rocks inside the cavern, I find myself imagining what it would feel like to kiss Nathan again—to really kiss him, and not just on the cheek. I'm dying to find out, and I'm surprised that I'm not more fearful of those emotions. Maybe I'm closer to being ready than I think I am.

I suppose my understanding that life can end in the blink of an eye and should therefore be lived to the fullest trumps my fears.

When Zack flies home from Ontario, I drive to the airport to meet him, and the moment I see him coming down the escalator with his backpack slung over one shoulder, looking grown-up and happy, I feel a motherly pride that overtakes me. He smiles, and we come together for the best hug of my life. We embrace and rock back and forth with love for the longest time. There are still tears in my eyes as we leave the airport and get into the car.

He fills me in on residence life and his classes, and I'm thrilled to hear how much he's enjoying his education at Western.

"You made the right choice," I say, reaching across the console to squeeze his hand. "I'm so happy for you."

When we arrive at my mother's place, he gets another bear hug from her, and then the food comes out. Mom offers him a chicken sandwich and cookies and anything else his heart desires.

"It feels good to be home," he says to me with a smile from across the kitchen table as he devours a coconut macaroon.

I reach for his hand again. "It's good to have you here."

Winston trots over to rest his chin on Zack's lap, and Zack feeds him the last bite of his cookie.

Thanksgiving dinner is not quite as joyful as the first day of our reunion. It's difficult with only the three of us—Zack, Mom, and me. The house feels quiet and somber compared to other years when Alan carved the turkey at the head of the table and made us laugh when the juices splattered all over the tablecloth.

Today, I find myself thinking about all our family traditions, the good times when Zack was small, and I miss the laughter. I know Zack is having similar thoughts as we eat dinner and struggle to talk about things that don't remind us of what used to be.

After dinner, he seeks me out in the kitchen, where I'm loading the dishwasher. "Mom, do you think we could go to the cemetery today?"

My stomach clenches. I turn to face him, but I can't seem to find words because I don't want to go to the cemetery. Not today. I've had such a good week, finally feeling as if I'm moving on.

Besides that, I'm not sure how easy it will be to pay my respects at Alan's grave, to show reverence when I haven't yet been able to forgive him and I'm not sure I ever will. I've kept up the pretense all year, but I'm running out of energy in that area. I'm afraid I'm just not that good of an actress and one of these days I'll accidentally let down my guard and Zack will see through me.

Zack frowns. "Come on, Mom. It's Thanksgiving. I think we should lay some flowers or something."

I turn away, close the dishwasher door, and press the start button. "That's a wonderful idea," I say, with my back to him. "We can snip some hydrangeas from the backyard."

"I'll get my jacket," Zack replies.

As soon as he's gone from the kitchen, I take a deep breath and hold it for a few seconds, steeling myself, because this has to happen. I need to go to the cemetery and grieve for my late husband. For my son's sake, if not for mine.

Twenty minutes later, Zack and I are standing at Alan's grave, looking down at the headstone in silence. Zack lays the white flowers on top and steps back.

"Mom," he says without looking at me. "I know you're mad at him."

The lining of my stomach feels like it might catch fire.

He turns to me. "You're trying to hide it from me, but I can see it, and I get it. It's Dad's fault you had the accident, and that's why you have sleep issues now, and it's why you had to give up being a surgeon. I'm mad at him too, but he never meant for any of that to happen. I mean . . . you have to give him a break, Mom. I agree that he was an idiot for getting behind the wheel that night, for sure, but he just found out he had cancer. He wasn't thinking clearly."

I shake my head. "He was more than an idiot, Zack." I'm half tempted to let it all come spilling out, but I bite my tongue and do what I always do—gloss over the real truth. "He drove drunk. He broke the law. There's never any excuse for that. I'll probably always be angry about what he did. Besides, even without that, it's complicated."

Stop, Abbie. Don't say anything more.

"No, it's not. You loved each other, but now it seems like you're forgetting all the good times we had. You never want to talk about him."

It's true. I haven't wanted to talk about Alan lately. Not with Zack.

He stares down at the gravestone. "Despite what happened, I'm glad that he was my dad, and I'll never stop loving him, no matter what he did."

I feel a bit sick because I'm not sure what to say. Part of me wants to grasp this opening, to confide in my son once and for all so that I won't feel like a pressure cooker anymore. But that would be selfish, wouldn't it? I don't want to spoil all those happy memories that are such a comfort to Zack just to let off my own steam. He's so sure of himself and his feelings right now. I don't want to destroy that.

"You guys were the best parents ever," he continues, "and I'm so lucky, because a lot of my friends never had what we had. Their parents hated each other, and they fought all the time, or they got divorced. At least we had a happy home." Zack pinches the bridge of his nose. "I know he wasn't perfect, Mom. He made a really bad mistake. But he loved us."

I stare down at the gravestone and think of Alan in his coffin under the ground, and I have to admit to myself that Zack is right, in some ways. Alan may have been cheating on me, and he committed a terrible crime by driving under the influence, but he did love us. If he didn't, he would have left me for Paula a long time ago, or he wouldn't have tried to end it with her when he found out he was dying.

For the first time in almost a year, my anger over Alan's infidelity isn't at the top of my mind, maybe because Alan has already suffered the worst possible punishment. He's dead now. He's six feet under. He'll never see his son graduate from university or get married, and he'll never hold his future grandchildren. He'll never again enjoy the fragrance of fresh spring rain or a full-bodied wine or the delicious aroma of coffee in the morning. He'll never see another sunrise.

Alan knew he was dying. I wonder if he wished he could have just one more day to make everything right when they pulled him out of the wreck. Would he have confessed his affair to me after finally putting an end to it? Or was he traveling to Lunenburg that night to be with the woman he truly wanted? Was the guilt too much to bear?

I'll never know, and that's what has been ripping at my insides since the day I found out about his affair.

Suddenly I'm on my hands and knees, weeping over my husband's grave and wishing he hadn't been taken from us. Maybe there was a chance he and I could have worked everything out and grown stronger through the hard times. I don't know.

All I know for sure is that I miss what Alan and I had—the laughter and love and constant support. That's what I want to remember. I don't want to spend the rest of my days drowning in venom when I think of him.

Zack kneels beside me and wraps his arms around my shoulders. He doesn't say a word. He just sits and holds me.

I realize that I still want to shield my son from this sordidness. I don't want him to suffer what I've had to suffer, to doubt his father's love for him or for us. That's the one thing he can still cling to.

I firmly decide that I won't tell Zack. I'll *never* tell him. I'll continue to shoulder this burden alone. I'm certain now that it's been the right decision all along. I'll do whatever's necessary to take Alan's infidelity to my own grave.

CHAPTER THIRTY-FOUR

On Monday morning, I drive Zack to the airport, and it's harder than I imagined to say goodbye. I hug him outside the entrance to security, and I miss him as soon as I turn away.

When I return to Lunenburg, Mom has lunch prepared. We sit down at the kitchen table, but we don't talk about Zack or sad things. We make light conversation and speculate about the weather over the next few days.

When we've almost finished lunch, she leans back in her chair. "You know . . . I've been thinking about our conversation the other night, after you came home from your date with Nathan."

I reach for my water and take a sip. "Oh?"

"I'd still love to go to Venice. I'd love to travel more, maybe even go south for a few months in the winter, but you know what holds me back?"

"What?"

"This house." She looks around. "All my money's tied up in it, and it's a big responsibility. There's so much to maintain. Either the driveway needs to be shoveled, or the lawn needs to be mowed, and my garden needs tending. I don't ever feel like I can leave it for more than a week or two. But I've been hanging on to it because it was my home with your father, and this is where all our memories were. Also because it's your childhood home, and I always wanted you to feel that if something terrible happened in your life, you'd always have a place to come home to."

I chuckle softly. "Was that a premonition, do you think?"

"Who knows." She rises from her chair, collects our empty plates, and carries them to the counter. After she sets them down, she faces me. "But here's the thing. My memories of your father aren't in this house. They're in here." She taps her temple with her index finger. "And here." She makes a fist over her heart. "So maybe it's time I lived a little. If I downsized to a condo in a retirement village, I'd have more freedom financially, and I could meet some new people, make new friends who might turn out to be travel companions. Freedom from taking care of this big house would be nice, I think."

I look at her and smile, because I love the idea of my mother embarking on a new adventure at her age.

I rise to my feet and cross the kitchen to pull her in for a hug. "I think that's a great idea, Mom. And I would love to help you. As soon as you're ready, we can get busy decluttering the house and figuring out what we need to do to get the best possible price for it, so you can live your dreams with that money."

Her cheeks flush red, and her eyes twinkle. "Really? I was so afraid you'd be upset. Because this is your home too."

My eyebrows fly up. "Of course I'm not upset! I want you to be happy. And I agree—this house is a heavy load. You shouldn't be carrying it all on your own. You did your bit. It's time for you to kick up your heels."

She hugs me even tighter. "Okay. Let's do it then."

We tidy the kitchen together, but I feel tired afterward and retreat to my bedroom for a power nap, because if I've learned anything over the past year, it's that sleep is a great rejuvenator. As are dreams. We always get a fresh start when we escape for a short time. Then we wake up, ready to move again—and clearly there's going to be a lot to do around here, so I'm going to need all the energy I can get.

I come around to the sensation of Winston's wet tongue on my eyelids, and I lean up on an elbow on the bed.

"Good boy," I say as I stroke his thick fur and glance at the clock. He's become very good at judging how much time has elapsed and waking me about thirty minutes after I lie down. I never trained him for this, so I can only presume it's instinct or intuition. Somehow, he knows what I need, and he keeps me on track.

My laptop chimes with an incoming email, and I wonder if it's work related. Dragging myself off the bed, I sit down at the desk and open my email program.

The subject line on the newest message says, in all caps, CAN WE MEET?

My belly does a sickening flip because the sender of this message is Paula—the last person in the world I want to hear from.

She hasn't contacted me since our conversation at Alan's apartment last year, so I wonder what this is about. My heart starts to race, and my blood boils with that familiar anger I've been trying so hard to purge from my life lately.

I click on the message.

> Hi Abbie. I've been thinking of you. Holidays are rough.
>
> I suspect you're not thrilled to hear from me, but please consider meeting me to talk. There's something I would like to tell you. Let me know when you're available.
>
> Paula

I sit back in my chair and stare at the computer screen. "Let me know when you're available"? Isn't it a bit presumptuous to assume I'll say yes? Because I'm not exactly thrilled about the idea of sitting down and chatting with the woman who was sleeping with my husband for three years. I'd rather stick needles in my eyes.

Winston lays his snout on my thigh and peers up at me. He blinks a few times. His golden brow furrows.

I don't know what it is about this dog, but sometimes I believe he can see into my soul. Today, he looks at me with sorrow because he recognizes the jealousy and bitterness I still feel toward this woman.

Or is it pity that I see in his eyes?

I gaze out the window at the gentle breeze in the treetops and realize that if I'm ever going to be truly happy, I need to focus on a far bigger picture.

I think of my son. I remember him as a baby in my arms—the sweet smell of his soft head beneath my lips when I kissed him good night before setting him down in his crib. I think of him as a young boy scoring the winning goal in a hockey game and raising his stick over his head with triumph. I think of how frightened Alan and I were when he was fourteen and fell off his skateboard and was rushed to the ER. But he was okay in the end.

I think about what a good man Zack has become.

Then I think about my walks along the seashore with Nathan, the girls, and our dogs, running and frolicking on the beach while we search for rocks with fossils in them. I can almost hear the sound of the ocean waves breaking onto the rocky beach, mixed with the girls' laughter.

I love being with Nathan and his daughters. I also love being with my mom. I love our Sunday dinners and my mother's kindness and wit. Her cooking. Her love, ever since the day I was born.

We live in a beautiful world.

I'm thankful for my life.

I give Winston a pat, lean down to kiss him tenderly on the head, and begin to type my reply to Paula.

As I get out of my car on the main street in town, I hope I'm doing the right thing. Maybe it would have been better to meet Paula in a private location rather than a public coffee shop, because I certainly don't want to cause a scene. Not that I plan to fall apart or get into a screaming match—I would never lose control like that, not now—but it's hard to know what she plans to say or do.

Yet here I am, sitting down at a table at Tim Hortons, waiting for her to arrive.

The door opens, and she walks in out of a strong wind that blows dead leaves in the street.

I forgot how beautiful she is—with long, flowing blonde hair and giant blue eyes. That alone causes heads to turn. Today, she's dressed in an ivory fisherman's sweater, faded jeans, and sneakers.

Our eyes meet, and she approaches my table. "Hi."

"Hi," I reply coolly.

We stare at each other. I have no idea what to say. I don't even know why I'm here. I hope she doesn't think there's a chance we might bury the hatchet and become friends, because as much as I want to put my anger to bed forever, I'm quite certain the only way I can do that is to leave all this behind and stop wrestling with it.

At least this isn't a dive bar, and she's not passed out after guzzling multiple glasses of wine.

She tells me she's going to get a coffee. Then she approaches the counter. I sit there, tapping my finger on the table, waiting.

A moment later, she returns and sits down. "Thanks for coming."

"I couldn't very well say no," I reply with a hint of antagonism I'm not proud of, because I hate being rude, and Lord knows I'm trying to rise above all this. "The suspense was killing me."

Paula peels the brown plastic lid off her coffee cup to let the steam escape. "Sorry. I just thought we should meet in person."

"Why?" But I believe I already know the answer. I'm guessing she's had time over the past year to reflect upon the choices she's made, and she wants to apologize for the pain she caused me and ask for my forgiveness.

If that's the case, I'm just going to give it to her, because I've already decided that the time has come to move on.

So here we are. I'm staring at the light at the end of the tunnel. I want to reach for it. I suspect Paula wants to reach for it too.

But she doesn't apologize for anything, nor does she ask my forgiveness. She reaches into her purse, withdraws a photograph, lays it on the table, and slides it toward me.

I gaze down at it and feel a burning sensation in the pit of my stomach. Why is she showing me this? Has she not trespassed enough? And how did she come upon it?

I pick up the photo of Zack as an infant, look at it closely, and frown at her. "What are you trying to do here?"

Her eyes fill with wetness. "I just want you to know."

"Know *what*?"

Then suddenly I realize that I don't remember this baby picture. I certainly never took it myself, and if Alan had, he would have shown it to me. And why would he have given it to Paula anyway?

As I look more closely, the shock of discovery hits me full force. My eyes lift, and I meet Paula's troubled gaze across the table. "Is this what I think it is?"

She slowly nods her head. "Yes. That's my son."

My heart is pounding so fast I'm afraid I might fall out of my chair. The resemblance between this child and Zack is uncanny.

It's obvious that the baby belongs to Alan. There can be no denying it.

I drop the picture onto the table as if it has just burst into flames.

Paula struggles to explain. "I'm so sorry, Abbie. I didn't know I was pregnant when I met you in the bar that day. I found out a few weeks later, and I haven't had a drink since. Michael kicked me out when I told him, but not before he lost his mind with rage. So I'm not sorry to be rid of him. I'm living with my mom now, and I'm getting a divorce."

I stare wordlessly at her. I'm still numb with shock, and anger is swirling around me again. I feel like I'm being sucked back into the vortex of my grief and bitterness.

"I'm telling you this," she continues, "because we're connected. And I'm sorry that I ruined your life, but I couldn't seem to help myself. Alan was so good to me. He was such a decent guy. He wasn't anything like my husband, and I don't think you know how lucky you were." She holds up a hand. "I'm sorry. That's not what I wanted to say to you today. What matters now is that we have these two boys who are half brothers, and I just couldn't keep that to myself."

My head is swimming, and I feel sick as images of my late husband flash before my eyes.

The first moment I laid eyes on Alan in the anatomy lab.

His battered body on the table in the ER when I first realized he was the drunk driver who hit me.

Zack's grief as he laid flowers on his father's grave just one day ago.

I reach out and push the photograph away from me. "I don't know what you want me to say."

"I don't know either," Paula replies as she slips the photo back into her purse. "I'm sure this is a shock to you. Just take some time to think about it, and if you never want to see me again, I'll understand, but if you can find it in your heart to forgive me or to set aside the bad blood between us, I would love for my son to know his older brother." She makes a move to rise. "So . . . you know where to find me. I'll be here in town, and I'll always be sorry for the pain I've caused you, Abbie, and for hurting your family. I mean that. Truly I do."

She gets up and leaves.

I go home and finally tell my mother everything.

Then I call Nathan, and we talk on the phone for hours while I struggle to sort out how I'm going to handle this.

CHAPTER THIRTY-FIVE

When I was pregnant with Zack and my belly was the size of a beach ball, Alan got down on his knees in the kitchen of our new home and felt our baby kick.

"This one's going to be a soccer player," he said with a grin, "and he's going to score lots of goals."

"Maybe he'll want to be on the debate team," I replied with a playful flicker of defiance in my eyes.

"No," Alan replied. "This boy's going to be an athlete. But he'll be book smart too. And he's going to be a good person. He'll be kind and open-minded and compassionate toward others."

I pulled my husband to his feet and took his face in my hands. "I can't wait to bring him home from the hospital."

"Neither can I. And we're going to be great parents, because the last thing I want is for our boy to grow up in a house like the one I grew up in. I want to set a better example. I don't ever want our son to feel weak for being sensitive or caring." Alan frowned and shook his head with disbelief. "I never understood why my dad thought he had to be cruel and beat somebody down in order to feel strong. That's just not right."

"We'll teach our son all that," I said to Alan as I pulled him into my arms. "Just like you said, we're going to be great parents."

Today, Zack is the best person I know. I'm proud of the man he has become. At least Alan and I got that right, and I have no regrets about the job we did and all the little decisions we made while raising our son together.

But there is still so much that Zack needs to learn about life.

He's a strong young man. Maybe I need to give him more credit. Maybe I need to recognize that he's stronger than I think.

That night, as I'm brushing my teeth before bed, in my mind I see Alan walking away from me in the hospital after Zack's head injury from the skateboard accident, when we almost lost him. I remember how I stood there with concern, watching my husband take long strides down the corridor until he was gone from sight.

That was the worst of the times I felt Alan pull away from me emotionally. It was as if something snapped inside of him and he couldn't bear the weight of what might have been if Zack hadn't pulled through.

It was early July, the start of Zack's summer vacation, just before ninth grade.

A thought comes to me—a sudden connection—and I stop brushing my teeth. Then I quickly spit out the toothpaste, rinse my mouth, and pad into my bedroom, where Winston is stretched out on the bed. I grab my laptop from the desk, carry it to the bed, and open my email.

I stare at the message Paula sent me the day before. Then I begin to type a new message.

Hi Paula,

Can you answer a question for me? When did you and Alan start seeing each other? Do you remember the exact date, specifically? I can't tell you why it matters. It just does.

Abbie

I hit "Send" and sit back against the pillows, scratching behind Winston's ears and wondering if she'll reply anytime soon. My laptop chimes five minutes later.

Hi Abbie,

It was July 7, 2014. He came into the store on a Sunday, which just happened to be my birthday. There was a cake for me and he had some. I hope that helps.

Paula

I stare at the message. Nervous knots form in my belly, because there can be no mistaking the date. That was the first Sunday after Zack's skateboard accident. He got out of the hospital on a Friday, and we went to my mother's house for dinner on Sunday.

I remember how quiet and withdrawn Alan was that day. He went down to the basement to check Mom's furnace filters and tidy up the storage room. I knew he was still shaken over Zack's accident, so I simply gave him space and didn't try to talk to him about what had happened. I left him alone to putter in the basement.

Obviously, I missed something. I didn't realize how badly he needed me that day. It could all be traced back to the fact that he had grown up with a callous father who had burst into his bedroom on the day his mother died and announced her passing like a dinner call. And then he'd forbidden his son from expressing any grief over the loss of the most important person in his life.

There'd been no one to love Alan after that tragic day.

Until I came along.

I see now that Alan's worst fear was the loss of us too. And something deep inside of him—something wounded and broken—needed to believe that there would still be love somewhere else in his life if the worst ever happened.

Not that that excuses what he did. It was still wrong. But at least now I understand a little more about why he was vulnerable to Paula's attentions that day when he walked into the hardware store and ordered the furnace filter.

The following day, I text Zack at college and ask him to call me. I explain that there's something important we need to discuss.

He lets me know he'll call as soon as he's finished classes.

I pass the hours by taking Winston for a walk and picking up a few groceries at the store. While I push the shopping cart, I practice what I plan to say to my son.

Briefly, I consider making up some silly story about going on a trip down south for spring break or something. *Anything* other than what I know I must tell him. I flip-flop like a flounder on a wharf, tempted to throw myself back into the sea of hidden truths where I've been living for the past year. But I know I can't do that. Everything is different now. Yesterday, I learned something that will affect the rest of Zack's life, so I can't pretend that it's in his best interest to keep him in the dark any longer. I also know that I can't protect him from pain. Pain is part of life, and we have to deal with it when it comes.

But sometimes, a flicker of light can emerge from the darkest, most unexpected tragedies.

My cell phone rings just before dinner. My mother gives me a sympathetic look because she knows what I'm about to tell my son, and she understands how difficult it is for me to destroy the memory of his perfect, fairy-tale life.

But it wasn't perfect. Life never is. Alan and I did our best, but occasionally we messed up. We made mistakes. It's time I have enough faith in my son to admit that to him.

I get up from the table to answer the phone. Winston follows me upstairs into my bedroom, where I close the door. He jumps up on the bed and lies down next to me. As he watches me with those glistening brown eyes, I know there can be no more lies.

I take a deep breath and tell Zack everything—that his father was unfaithful to me in the last few years of our marriage and that he was having an affair with a woman from Lunenburg. I reveal how I found out—that Paula called Alan's cell phone in the hospital, and I eventually connected the dots.

Zack remains silent, and my heart pounds with dread.

When he finally speaks, there's a mixture of anger and hurt in his voice. "Mom. How could you have kept this from me?"

My insides tremble and quake, and part of me regrets that I didn't tell him right away. Maybe I should have trusted that he was strong enough to handle it.

Another part of me knows that I wasn't ready for that until now. I needed to come to terms with everything myself. The situation needed time to unfold, and I needed to understand that maybe sometimes we go through life seeing only what we want to see. With Alan, I saw a perfect husband, a gifted doctor, and a loving father. That's what Zack saw too. But there was so much more to Alan than that. Deep down he was still that young, wounded boy who had lost his mother and all the love she once gave. He harbored deep, painful fears. He was terribly afraid of losing the people he loved most. He wasn't perfect.

"I'm so sorry," I say to Zack, "but I didn't really understand why your father did what he did, and maybe I still don't—not completely. Either way, I had no answers for you, no explanations to offer. And I wanted to protect you. I didn't want to cause you pain or confuse you, and the last thing I wanted was for you to grow up hating your dad. That would have been wrong because he loved you more than anything."

"I loved him too," Zack shakily replies. "I thought he was the best father in the world, which is why I can't believe he could have done that."

"I can't believe it either," I say. "Even after a year, but here we are." Winston rolls to his side, and I stroke his belly. "Please, just remember that he was a good father, and for that I'll always love him. I hope you can still love him too."

Zack is silent for a moment. "I don't know how you're able to forgive him."

"I'm not sure that I have," I explain. "Not completely, because sometimes I still feel angry, but then I remember that he gave me you, and I'm glad I married him. I have no regrets about that."

It's a monstrous statement, and it feels good to say it. To truly believe it.

Zack says nothing, so I find myself quoting Nathan as I attempt to explain how I've managed to get through the past year. "Time helps, Zack. I promise it will get easier. The anger fades. So does the pain."

I hear Zack sniffing. "What made you decide to tell me this now, after all this time? Why not just keep it secret forever? Part of me wishes you had."

"Believe me, I have struggled with that over the past year. I didn't like hiding something from you. It felt dishonest." I clear my throat. "But things change. And now, there's a very important reason why you need to know. I just learned about it yesterday."

"What is it?"

As Winston lies beside me, I stroke his silky coat and gather my resolve. "The woman your father was seeing . . . she . . ." My heart races, but I force myself to continue. "She had a baby. A son. Which means you have a half brother."

There is nothing but silence on the other end of the line, and my chest feels like it's going to explode.

"I have a brother?" Zack finally asks. "A baby brother?"

"Yes," I reply. "I saw a picture of him, and he looks exactly like you when you were a baby."

Zack pauses, and I'm not sure what he's going to say. When he finally speaks, it's in a breathless, husky voice. "I can't believe it. I have a brother. It's unbelievable."

"A miracle, really."

Zack laughs softly. "A miracle." I listen to the sound of him breathing. "Can I meet him?"

I close my eyes and feel a tremendous wave of relief to have shared the truth with him at last. Somehow, I know that he's going to be okay. We both are. There are no more secrets between us.

And I feel absolutely certain—without a doubt—that I did the right thing today. I feel as if I've finally emerged from the darkness into the light.

After I end the call with Zack, I sit for a moment, basking in a welcome sense of calm. I relish it for a little while. Then I pick up my phone again and call Nathan.

"Hi," I say. "I don't suppose you're free right now."

"I can be," he replies. "I'm all done in the clinic for the day, just tidying up a few files, and my parents are making supper for the girls. What's up?"

"Would you like to meet me on the wharf? I have something I'd love to share with you. It's about Zack and that impossible conversation I've been avoiding all year."

Nathan knows everything about it, of course. He's been my sounding board since the beginning. "Wow. I can be there in fifteen minutes."

"Great. I'll bring Winston. You can bring Dorothy and the girls if you want to."

"No, I think I'll just bring myself tonight, if it's all the same to you."

Secretly, I'm pleased to hear it because there's so much to talk about, and on top of that, I've been fantasizing about being alone with Nathan ever since that sweet, teasing kiss on my mother's porch last week.

"Okay. I'll see you on the boardwalk. I'll be waiting in front of the museum."

"I'm on my way."

I see Nathan from a distance, walking toward me in faded blue jeans, a black turtleneck sweater, and a brown leather jacket. The setting sun illuminates his face, and anticipation bubbles up inside me, because I've been imagining this moment and so many other scenarios with the two of us together. Now, here we are.

"Hi," he says as he reaches me and bends to pat Winston on the head. "Hi to you too, big guy. How's it going?"

Winston wags his tail, and Nathan straightens to meet my gaze. I feel a rush of excitement in my blood.

"Thanks for coming. Should we walk?" I gesture toward the other end of the boardwalk.

"Sure."

We start off at a leisurely pace together, side by side, while Winston trots out front.

"I hope you didn't mind my calling," I say, "but I felt so good about my conversation with Zack I couldn't keep it in."

"What happened? The suspense is killing me."

I glance up at the sky, then give Nathan a full recap of everything Zack and I talked about. It takes me a while to get through it all, and by the time I'm done, Nathan and I have taken a seat on a bench overlooking the water.

"It sounds like he took it well," Nathan says, relaxing his arm along the back of the bench. "You must feel so good about that, Abbie. It must be a huge relief."

"It is." I tilt my head to the side to rest it on his shoulder. He rubs the back of my neck and kisses the top of my head. I remain there for a moment with my eyes closed, relishing his calm, comforting presence.

I inhale deeply and sit up straight again. "I'm glad he took it well, but it's probably going to take some time for him to fully process it. He was disappointed in his dad, which makes me feel proud, actually—that he has a sense of honor and knows how important it is to be faithful in a marriage."

"He sounds like a great kid, Abbie."

"He definitely is."

Above us and around us, seagulls call out to one another as they soar over the fishing boats moored at the docks. I breathe in the salty scent of the harbor and want desperately to reach for Nathan's hand and hold it, because I feel joyful and enraptured, but something holds me back. Shyness, I suppose. It's been a long time since I've been with a man like this. Life with Alan was so comfortable for so many years. There were never any feelings of nervousness between us physically.

I realize it's been ages since I've been touched.

"So what will you do now?" Nathan asks.

I let out a deep breath. "Somehow, I'll have to figure out how to take the next step, because Zack wants to meet Paula's son, but he's back at school now. I'll have to contact her, I suppose, and arrange a time. Zack has midterms coming up, but he said he didn't want to wait until Christmas. I told him I'd be happy to fly him home on points for the long weekend in November, if he wants."

Nathan does the very thing I was tempted to do just now. He reaches for my hand, turns it over in his, and studies my open palm. "I think you're doing the right thing, Abbie."

I feel a warm glow inside me. "Yes, I think so too. It feels good to finally have everything out in the open with Zack. I feel closer to him now—like he knows the real me, not just the perfect parent I always tried to be in his eyes."

Except that I haven't shared *everything* with Zack. He knows nothing about what's happening here at this moment, between Nathan and me.

One step at a time, I tell myself.

"I'm glad you called me," Nathan says, raising my hand to his lips and kissing the back of it.

Light from the setting sun reflects in the blue of his eyes, and I feel an intense wave of happiness. I sense that he feels it too, and we lean toward each other. Our foreheads touch. We sit like that for a blissful moment, eyes closed, our hands entwined. My heart swells with yearning.

There is a tremor inside me, the beginnings of a sea change that I am more than ready to welcome into my life. I know, beyond the shadow of a doubt, that this will be an exciting and satisfying new journey.

Nathan's lips touch mine in a deep and sultry kiss, and I melt at the sensation of his hand gently cupping the rim of my jaw. All my senses begin to hum. I feel as if I've known this man forever and I've been waiting for him. For this day.

We slowly draw back. The corner of his mouth curls up in a small grin that fills me with delight.

"I've been wanting to do that for a very long time," he says.

"Me too," I reply breathlessly.

"Really? I wasn't sure."

I nod my head with exaggeration. "*Oh*, you can be sure, Nathan. *Very* sure."

He gives me that dazzling smile I love. It makes me feel like a schoolgirl again.

"Okay then," he says, still grinning.

We sit back and hold hands like a couple of teenagers, until Winston gets restless on the end of his leash.

"I think he wants to go forth and sniff something." I laugh as I allow him to pull me to my feet.

Nathan stands up as well and walks with us. The sun is just setting, and the pink-and-blue sky is spectacular over the western horizon. The air is fragrant with the saltiness of the sea mixed with the scent of fallen leaves, and I breathe it all in, every last gorgeous bit of it.

A few weeks later, I meet Zack at the airport at noon on a Saturday because he has an important dinner engagement that evening—at the home of Paula Sheridan and her mother.

I called to let Paula know that Zack was interested in meeting her son. She was overjoyed to hear it, so I paid them a visit to meet the boy myself and discuss when Zack should come.

What a surprise it was to meet Paula's son and feel such joy when I held him in my arms. He was a sweet baby, and he reminded me of Zack at that age. But why wouldn't he? They were half brothers.

And yet their lives would be so very different. Zack grew up with a father who loved him deeply from the moment he took his first breath.

Adam would never know his father.

And Alan would never get to meet this beautiful child of his.

I bounced gently at the knees and listened to Adam coo. Then it all came rushing back—the tremendous delights and challenges of motherhood—and I couldn't help but feel happy for Paula, despite everything.

Now I am with Zack, driving home from the airport along the picturesque Lighthouse Route, past countless coves and inlets and sandy beaches where the ocean plays upon the rugged coastline. Winston is riding in the back seat, and I'm listening to Zack speak passionately about his classes and potential career plans. I notice that he's wearing his father's watch, which makes me happy.

Then he brings up a girl he has just started dating. "You'd like her, Mom. She's gorgeous and smart and confident, and she loves dogs."

I glance across at him and can see how smitten he is. It's written all over his face. "I hope I'll get to meet her sometime."

Zack never had much time for girls in high school. For the most part, he thought they were silly and frivolous, but he tells me there's something different about this girl. Her name is Sarah, and his eyes light up when he talks about her.

Soon we approach Hubbards Beach, and I flick the blinker.

"Where are we going?" Zack asks, confused by this unexpected detour.

I keep my eyes focused on the turn. "There's someone I'd like you to say hello to. A friend of mine."

"Who is it?"

"Do you remember Dr. Payne? The veterinarian who took care of Winston last year?"

"Of course."

I follow the narrow road to the beach entrance and continue to explain. "Well, he's here today with his family and their new golden retriever, Dorothy. Although she's not really new. She's a senior dog they adopted. She and Winston have become great pals."

I pull to a halt in the empty parking lot, and we get out of the vehicle. Zack lets Winston out of the back seat, and I lead the way down to the sandy beach, where Nathan is picnicking on this chilly November afternoon with his parents and daughters, and Dorothy of course, who is galloping down the beach, chasing a tennis ball.

Zack and I approach their blanket, and Zack recognizes Nathan as he gets up and walks to meet us.

"Dr. Payne, it's nice to see you again," Zack says. "It's been a while. How have you been?"

They shake hands. "Good, thanks. How about you?"

"Can't complain."

Nathan nods. "Your mom tells me you're at Western this year. How has that been so far?"

"Great. Loving every minute." Zack gestures toward Dorothy, who's chasing the ball again. "Mom was just telling me about your new dog."

Nathan turns to watch her too. "Yes, her name is Dorothy. She's old but still young at heart, as you can see."

We all watch Dorothy kick up sand as she fetches the ball. Then she and Winston greet each other with gusto.

Soon, Zack, Nathan, and I are walking together to the water's edge, where Jen and Marie are making a big fuss over Winston.

"These are my two daughters," Nathan says to Zack. "Jen and Marie, say hello to Abbie's son, Zack. He just flew in from Ontario. He's going to school there."

Zack kneels down. "Hey. I love your dog. She looks just like mine."

"They could be twins, right?" Marie replies.

The three of them pat and stroke Dorothy and Winston, and they laugh as Winston flops over and rolls in the sand like a big show-off.

Without saying a word, Nathan reaches for my hand. Love courses through me as I turn my head to gaze into his eyes.

Then I glance back at Zack, and I realize he's watching us as he scratches behind Dorothy's ears.

I'm uncertain for a second, but my grown-up son smiles and nods his head at me, as if to say, *It's all good, Mom. I'm glad you're happy.*

In that moment, I believe with all my heart that everything is going to be okay for all of us. Just like the waves that keep rolling onto the beach, happiness may recede sometimes, but then it comes back. It always comes back.

BOOK CLUB DISCUSSION QUESTIONS

1. The novel opens with the following passage: "Intuition is a funny thing. Sometimes it's a gut feeling, and you look around and just know something bad is about to happen. Other times, it's elusive, and later you find yourself looking back on certain events and wondering how in the world you missed all the signals." Discuss Abbie's state of denial in the first chapter, before she is run off the road. How effective, or ineffective, was her intuition?

2. In chapter 12, do you feel that Abbie should have taken Zack's phone away from him to shield him from the news coverage about his father's accident? What would you have done in that situation? Discuss how this approach differs from her later approach, when she wants to shield him from his father's extramarital affair. Why is this different? Or is it? If you were in Abbie's shoes, would you have told your son about your husband's infidelity? Why or why not?

3. In chapter 20, Paula says, "I'm sorry I kept this from you, but Alan made me promise never to tell you, and after the

accident, I felt so guilty . . . that it was my fault he was on the road that night. And then I figured . . . what would be the point in telling you? It couldn't change anything, and you'd only be in more pain." Then Abbie thinks, *But would I have preferred to live the rest of my life in ignorance? I honestly don't know the answer to that question. Maybe I would have.* Do you believe Abbie would have been better off never knowing about Alan's affair? Where might she have been a year later, or twenty years later, if she'd never found out? How would her life have been different?

4. In chapter 23, when Zack suggests they do something special to honor Alan's memory, Abbie thinks, *Doing something special for my lying, cheating husband isn't exactly at the top of my priority list right now. I just want to figure out how to get up in the mornings without wanting to smash our framed wedding portrait against the corner of the kitchen table.* Do you feel Abbie's emotions are normal, and is she doing a good job managing them? Or do you feel she is keeping too much bottled up and needs to deal with her anger more openly? She often works very hard to keep her cool, especially in chapter 20, when she learns the truth from Paula. What does this say about her as a woman? Does she try too hard to be perfect? If so, where do you think this desire to be perfect comes from?

5. Discuss how Abbie's choice to keep Alan's infidelity a secret from Zack is the same as and/or different from Alan's choice to keep his affair secret from Abbie.

6. Based on what you know about Alan and his upbringing, did you ever feel any sympathy toward him after learning of his affair? If so, why? If not, why not?

7. In chapter 29, Abbie says, "I realize it was sheer force of will that kept me on my feet just now, because I don't want to give Alan the power to hurt me anymore. I want to live, and live happily, and in order to do that, I need to do my best to stop fixating on his betrayal and the anger I feel. I need to focus on how I'm going to manage this condition and move on with positivity and determination, not vitriol, which will only bury me in ugly emotional muck. That won't help me at all." Can you think of a time in your life when you were angry about something and had to put aside your emotions and deal with the problem objectively or force yourself to maintain a positive attitude? Have there been any situations in your life when you allowed yourself to become bogged down in emotional muck and it took you longer than it should have to emerge happily?

8. In chapter 30, Abbie says, "I watch my son for a moment, and I know exactly what he's feeling because I'm feeling it too. I know him too well, and his pain is my pain. His joy is my joy." Zack is Abbie's only child. Do you think she is too invested emotionally in her son's life? What does this say about her as a parent, and what does it mean for her as a widow? Discuss the difficulties parents face when it comes to letting go of their children as they move into adulthood. How are these difficulties compounded for Abbie, given her situation?

9. In chapter 33, in the cemetery, Zack defends his father. Is it wrong for him to be so defensive and supportive of the man who drove drunk and nearly killed his mother? Do you feel it is disloyal to Abbie for him to be critical of her anger? Is it ever okay to sympathize with a drunk driver?

10. Do you know anyone with narcolepsy? If so, how has it affected this person's life?

11. Discuss the role of Abbie's dog, Winston. How is he a mirror image of some of Abbie's experiences throughout the novel? How does he contribute to her survival, both physically and emotionally? And do you believe that animals can sense and understand what is going on in the hearts of humans? Discuss the scene where Winston reacts to the home intruder that Abbie dreams about. Have you ever had an experience with a pet in which you believed he or she displayed some psychic abilities?

12. Abbie never actually says in the novel that she has forgiven Alan for his infidelity. In the end, do you believe Abbie forgives him? Why or why not?

ACKNOWLEDGMENTS

A heartfelt thank-you to Stephen and Laura for filling my life with inspiration and joy.

Thank you also to the following people:

Michelle Killen (a.k.a. Michelle McMaster), for your loving friendship and for always being my first reader who steers me back on track if I go astray.

Julia Philip Smith, also for your loving friendship and valuable support on social media.

Pat Thomas, for edits on the early drafts of this novel.

My agent, Paige Wheeler. This year marks our twentieth anniversary together. I'm very grateful for how you've helped to keep me in the game all these years. You've been instrumental in making this the lifelong career I always dreamed of having.

Editor Danielle Marshall. Thank you for bringing me into the Lake Union family. Thanks also to my developmental editors, Alicia Clancy and Sarah Murphy, who put tremendous thought and care into this book and were always positive and constructive along the way.

Kimberly Dossett, for your unwavering support and assistance in so many ways. I can't even begin to name them all. I couldn't manage all this without you!

My friends Julie Ortolon, Wendy Lindstrom, Shelley Thacker, and Patricia Ryan, for the supportive friendship, helpful discussion, and all-around great company.

The many bloggers who have shared stories and videos about what it's like living with narcolepsy. I am grateful to have gained some insight into your challenges. Also, Julie Flygare, author of a fascinating memoir called *Wide Awake and Dreaming*. It was very helpful in my research, and I highly recommend the book to anyone interested in learning more about the condition.

Dr. Stephen MacLean, for consultation on the medical issues in this book.

Finally, thank you to my parents, Charles and Noel Doucet, for your love and support on every possible level. I love you both very much.

ABOUT THE AUTHOR

Julianne MacLean is a *USA Today* best-selling author of more than thirty novels, including the contemporary women's fiction Color of Heaven series. MacLean is a four-time Romance Writers of America RITA finalist and has won the Booksellers' Best Award, the Book Buyers Best Award, and a Reviewers' Choice Award from the *Romantic Times* for Best Regency Historical Romance of 2005. MacLean has a degree in English literature from the University of King's College in Halifax, Nova Scotia, and a degree in business administration from Acadia University in Wolfville, Nova Scotia. She loves to travel and has lived in New Zealand, Canada, and England. MacLean currently resides on the east coast of Canada in a lakeside home with her husband and daughter.

For more information about Julianne and her writing life, please visit her website at www.juliannemaclean.com. You can also follow her on Bookbub (www.bookbub.com/authors/julianne-maclean) and chat with her on Facebook (www.facebook.com/JulianneMacLeanRomanceAuthor/), Twitter (@JulianneMacLean), and Instagram (@JulianneMacLean).